Across a crowded room . . .

She felt giddy. She felt sick. She felt elated. She felt *trapped*. An impossible range of emotions crashed down on her all at once. Then, as she was inwardly staggering, Josh turned, and their eyes met.

Marta would have sworn that he flinched. But an instant later she was willing to admit that maybe the flinch had been in her imagination. Because Josh calmly diverted his gaze and returned his attention to a stunning blonde.

Marta felt a twinge of something easily diagnosed as jealousy and told herself angrily that was the very *last* emotion she should be feeling where Josh was concerned.

This man ditched you, remember? she fumed silently. *Just keep that uppermost in mind, and hang on to your pride!*

Dear Reader,

In past months I've used this page to tell you what we editors are doing to live up to the name Silhouette **Special Edition**:

We've brought you the latest releases from authors you've made into stars; we've introduced new writers we hope you'll take to your heart. We've offered classic romantic plots; we've premiered innovative angles in storytelling. We've presented miniseries, sequels and spin-offs; we've reissued timeless favorites in Silhouette *Classics*. We've even updated our covers, striving to give you editions you can be proud to read, happy to own.

All these editorial efforts are aimed at making Silhouette **Special Edition** a consistently satisfying line of sophisticated, substantial, emotion-packed novels that will touch your heart and live on in your memory long after the last page is turned.

In coming months our authors will speak out from this page as well, sharing with you what's special to them about Silhouette **Special Edition**. I'd love to hear from *you*, too. In the past your letters have helped guide us in our editorial choices. How do you think we're doing now? Some time ago I made a promise on this page— that "each and every month, Silhouette **Special Edition** is dedicated to becoming more special than ever." Are we living up to that promise? What's special to *you* about Silhouette **Special Edition**? Share your feelings with us, and, who knows—maybe some day *your* name will appear on this page!

My very best wishes,

Leslie Kazanjian, Senior Editor
Silhouette Books
300 East 42nd Street
New York, N.Y. 10017

MAGGI CHARLES
Diamond Moods

Silhouette Special Edition

Published by Silhouette Books New York

America's Publisher of Contemporary Romance

To *Spring Training*, a fantastic magazine.
May it cause a different kind of "diamond"
to make all Steve and Merle's
fondest hopes come true!

SILHOUETTE BOOKS
300 East 42nd St., New York, N.Y. 10017

ISBN: 0-373-09497-3

First Silhouette Books printing December 1988

Printed in the U.S.A.

Books by Maggi Charles

Silhouette Romance
Magic Crescendo #134

Silhouette Intimate Moments
My Enemy, My Love #90

Silhouette Special Edition

Love's Golden Shadow #23
Love's Tender Trial #45
The Mirror Image #158
That Special Sunday #258
Autumn Reckoning #269
Focus on Love #315
Yesterday's Tomorrow #336
Shadow on the Sun #362
The Star Seeker #381
Army Daughter #429
A Different Drummer #459
It Must Be Magic #479
Diamond Moods #497

MAGGI CHARLES

is a confirmed traveler who readily admits that "people and places fascinate me." A prolific author, who is also known to her romance fans as Meg Hudson, Ms. Charles states that if she hadn't become a writer she would have been a musician, having studied piano and harp. A native New Yorker, she is the mother of two sons and currently resides in Cape Cod, Massachusetts, with her husband.

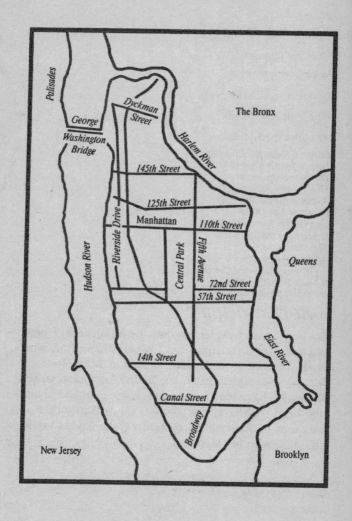

Chapter One

Dusk draped a glamorous, mauve veil over Washington. Caught in its gossamer mesh, the thousands of streetlights suddenly illuminating the city glittered like winter fireflies in the cold, clear January night.

Rush-hour traffic choked Massachusetts Avenue. With the taxi in which she was a passenger stalled, Marta Brennan sat back acutely conscious of Tony Ashford at her side.

Tea at the British Embassy with Tony had been an experience. The ambassador and his wife were charming and obviously very fond of Tony. Marta was well aware that the special treatment she had been given was because she was Tony's fiancée. Used to living on her own laurels, that had been a switch for her, though not an unpleasant one.

Regardless, the overall effect of the supposedly intimate afternoon rendezvous had been...stilted. The huge, Massachusetts Avenue embassy was formal, both in architecture and interior decor. Sir Arthur and Lady Lucinda Carrington-Smith, though delightful, were essentially "proper British" and not apt to let down their carefully cultivated guard in front of a stranger. Which, of course, was undoubtedly the way the queen's representative to the United States and his wife were supposed to be.

Marta sighed. It was occurring to her that Tony Ashford's life was far more structured than hers, and she marveled that she had never thought that through before. She glanced down at the diamond solitaire twinkling on her ring finger, and questions tumbled.

Could she tailor her life to Tony's to the extent that they could hope to have a successful marriage? Could she remain herself, maintain her own identity—and her own career—and still give an adequate performance as Mrs. Anthony Ashford? Especially since—fond though she was of Tony—she loved another man, and always would.

Tony heard her sigh and leaned toward her. "Something wrong?" he asked solicitously.

"No," she assured him.

"Then why such a deep sigh? Marta, your hands are freezing. Are you all right?"

"I'm fine, Tony," Marta told him. "Maybe just a bit tired, that's all."

Their taxi was still stalled in the eastbound traffic. "Darling, we don't have to go to the Forthingtons' cocktail party. We can find a phone booth. I can call, tell them something came up. Then we can go either to your flat or my hotel and relax for a while."

Marta shook her head. "I want to meet the Forthingtons," she insisted. She did. They were good friends of Tony's, who lived in Buckinghamshire near his mother's country place. Once she and Tony were married they would be expected to get together occasionally as a four-some on weekends, either in London or in the coun-try....

Once she and Tony were married. Thus far no date had been set for the wedding, but Marta knew Tony was cer-tain to pressure her for one before he left for London the following evening.

"Well, I do want you to meet them," Tony agreed. "Another time might be better, that's all."

Before Marta could comment, the traffic jam cleared and their taxi started up again.

The Forthingtons were living in a Connecticut Avenue apartment, sublet for the six months Guy Forthington would be in Washington on a special mission for the Brit-ish government. The apartment building was an older one, and the elevator creaked slowly upward to the fourth floor.

En route Tony glanced anxiously at Marta. "You do look tired," he observed. "I suggest we cut out as soon as possible."

"Let's see how it goes," Marta replied.

The fact was, she wanted to keep time together with Tony at a minimum for the next twenty-four hours. She still wasn't ready to make the final commitment of set-ting their wedding date.

She had been in Washington for nearly three months, on assignment photographing and getting to know high-ranking women in politics. The problem, she mused, was that her assignment was almost finished. Just a couple of more interviews to do. Then she'd either have to take an-other assignment immediately...or yield to Tony's wishes and finalize the wedding plans.

She, too, was living in a sublet, a small apartment in a Georgetown town house that belonged to a journalist friend currently working in Central America.

She suppressed another sigh, then asked herself sharply, *why this lassitude? Why this out-of-character feeling of inertia and indifference? Maybe what you need is to marry Tony as soon as possible and start putting down some roots with him in England.*

But there was no conviction to that theorizing.

She stole a glance at her fiancé. He was perhaps an inch or so taller than her, rather stocky in build, with broad shoulders and a strong physique. He'd been a star soccer player both in public school in England and later as a university student. He was also an expert skier, a good tennis player, a superb dancer.

He does everything I like to do, Marta reminded herself, *and does it well.*

And he was a gentle and considerate lover. Made few demands, was there only when she wanted him to be. She suspected that—in part, anyway—was because Tony was so terribly anxious for everything to go right between them. Forever and ever and ever. This would be a third marital go-around for him, and he was determined to make it work.

The elevator ground to a stop. Tony and Marta stepped into a wide corridor. A door at the end stood open. From it party sounds emanated.

Tony laughed. "Sheila Forthington said to follow our ears," he told Marta.

Marta managed a weak smile; then gave herself a mental kick and silently commanded herself to slip into a party mood. There was no need to be so morose. She was thirty-two years old, an award-winning photographer whose career was so well established she had chances for more plum assignments than she could possibly handle. Also, according to Tony among others, she was beautiful, with rather exotic, gypsyish looks, and the ability to wear anything well, thanks to her model-slim figure. A figure, she remembered wryly, that Josh had proclaimed "skinny" and sworn he was going to do something about.

"We need to round you out a little," he'd said, accompanying his words with that ever-so-slight smile that had the power to twist Marta inside out.

Josh. It was nearly two years since she'd last seen him. Since he had effectively dismissed her from his life. Two years, during which she had avoided any assignments that might have required her to linger in New York. Because she was afraid that in Manhattan—even with its millions of people—she might run into Josh, and that was something she still didn't think she could handle.

Later, maybe, when even more time had passed, she'd feel differently. When she was married to Tony, living in London except when on assignment and secure in her own new world, then maybe she could risk seeing Josh. Then maybe she could dare look up into his face and meet the deceptively cool gray eyes that—as she knew so well—were more than capable of becoming fired with hot passion.

At her side, Tony said, "Marta, this is Sheila Forthington."

"Marta, I'm so delighted," their hostess enthused. "Tony has talked and talked about you."

Marta mumbled something in reply, smiling in a way she hoped didn't look as forced as it felt. Sheila Forthington, she saw, was rather short, somewhat on the plump side, with curly ginger-colored hair and friendly blue eyes.

"Sorry we're a bit late," Tony apologized. "Had to make a stop for tea with Sir Arthur."

"Then," Sheila said, her eyes twinkling, "I'm sure you both need a strong drink. The bar's set up in the dining room, Tony. Guy's around somewhere...."

"We'll find him." Tony tucked Marta's arm in his, and they moved forward.

They crossed a square foyer and paused at the door of a large living room. "Now," Tony mused, "the question is, do we find the dining room—with its bar—to our left or our right?"

Marta didn't answer him. She couldn't possibly have answered him. Because she was staring across the crowded room at a man who, as far as she was concerned, towered above everyone else in the world.

She felt giddy. She felt sick. She felt elated. She felt *trapped*. An impossible range of emotions crashed down on her all at once. Then, as she was staggering inwardly, Josh turned, and their eyes met.

Marta would have sworn that he flinched. But an instant later she was willing to admit that maybe the flinch had been in her imagination. Because Josh calmly diverted his gaze and returned his attention to his companion, a stunning blonde, who, unlike a lot of film actresses, was even lovelier in person than she was on the screen.

"I say, there's Trina Cataldo," Tony murmured. And before Marta could protest, he was tugging her across the room toward the internationally famous star... and Joshua Smith.

Josh, Marta noted as she and Tony neared him, had lost none of his ability to charm. Trina Cataldo was eagerly listening to his every word as she gave him the benefit of her most brilliant smile.

Marta felt a twinge of something easily diagnosed as jealousy, and told herself angrily that was the very *last* emotion she should be feeling where Josh was concerned.

This man ditched you, remember? she hissed savagely...though silently. *Just keep that uppermost in mind, and hang on to your pride!*

"Trina, what a delightful surprise! I didn't know you were in the States," she heard Tony say.

"Tony, love," Trina Cataldo responded.

Marta watched as Trina and Tony politely embraced and kissed lightly, in greeting.

"Trina, let me introduce my fiancée, Marta Brennan," Tony said.

At that moment, Marta gazed straight into Josh Smith's eyes, and there was no masking the shock she saw in them. For once Josh was jolted. That pleased her—she'd been wanting to jolt Josh for a long time—but it puzzled her even more. Why should Josh, who had made his message so clear two years ago, care if she was going to marry someone else?

After exclaiming enthusiastically about Tony and Marta's engagement, Trina turned toward the tall man at her side to say, "Josh, darling, this is Tony Ashford of the BBC in London. And his fiancée..."

"Marta and I have met," Josh said quietly.

A shade too quietly, Marta thought.

Were there really vibes buzzing like hornets let loose? Or again, Marta asked herself, was her active imagination working overtime?

She felt Tony stiffen and heard an unexpected edge to his crisp, British voice as he said politely, "Delighted to meet you, Mr. Smith. You're with *Living, American Style*, are you not?"

Josh nodded.

"Josh is the newly appointed editor in chief for the magazine," Sheila informed them.

Marta's imaginary antennae quivered.

Two years ago Josh had been on the editorial staffs of both *Living, American Style* and its companion magazine, *Architecture, American Style*. She'd met him when he was with *Architecture* alone, later had worked for him—and with him—on assignments for both magazines.

Architecture, American Style had been an old book publishing company's first venture into the magazine field. *Living, American Style* had come later, and currently was one of the most popular magazines in the country. Marta had long thought this was largely due to Josh Smith's knack of knowing exactly what people wanted to read at any given time. Evidently the publishers had also come to that conclusion and had promoted Josh to the position he rightfully should be occupying.

She became aware that Tony was commenting to Josh on something to do with the magazine, and Josh was responding in words of scarcely more than one syllable.

Marta wriggled. Although she was trying to avoid Josh's eyes, she knew they were fixed upon her, and Josh's scrutiny had always possessed the power to make her wriggle. Trina Cataldo was filling in the conversational gaps. She and Tony were catching up on old times and old friends. Marta hoped they would continue talking. She didn't want either of them to start paying attention to her. In fact, she fervently wished someone would do something to create a diversion so she could escape from Josh's steady, gray-eyed gaze.

Someone did do something. A waiter suddenly appeared, bearing champagne. Marta switched on an automatic smile as Tony accepted a glass for her and hoped Tony didn't notice her fingers were icy as they lightly brushed his in passing.

She clutched the stem of the champagne glass and was about to sip, when Josh said evenly, "I'd say a toast is in order, wouldn't you, Trina? To the soon-to-be newlyweds?"

"Ah, yes," Trina agreed rapturously. "May the Fates smile on you forever, Tony, darling. And you, too, Marta."

Marta touched the champagne to her lips, but she couldn't possibly have swallowed. To do so would have meant risking instant choking.

The conversation shifted. Trina asked Tony when he was going back to London. Upon hearing that his departure was imminent, she followed with the next obvious query and asked Marta if she would be accompanying him.

Marta caught up with her lost voice and managed to say, "No. I'm on an assignment here in Washington."

"Marta's a photographer," Tony put in. He smiled fondly at his fiancée. "That's rather understating it," he elaborated. "She's a world-famous photographer."

"I know, darling," Trina assured him, while Josh remained mute. "One sees her marvelous work everywhere." The inevitable question came next. "Marta, when's the wedding going to be? And where are you going to be married?"

"We haven't set the date yet," Marta mumbled feebly, and didn't dare look at either Tony or Josh.

"I myself am opting for a Valentine Day wedding," Tony announced affably. "As for where we're to be married, we plan to be married in London. Marta's been living in London the better part of these past two years.

Except," Tony added, "she's forever darting off on assignments all over the globe. I'm sure I won't be able to prevent at least some of the globe-trotting. But," Tony finished with an indulgent chuckle, "I do hope to be able to persuade Marta to take a more direct photographic interest in the British Isles once we're married."

To Marta's relief, Tony finished off his champagne, set the glass down on a nearby table and changed the subject. "Have you seen Guy, by chance? I'd say it's time we caught up with our host, Marta."

Trina said she thought Guy was in the dining room, which, as it turned out, was to the left of the living room. Josh remained silent.

Tony and Marta moved off through the crowd. Marta could feel Josh's steely eyes burning holes in her back, and she shivered.

"That's supposed to mean someone's walking over your grave, you know," Tony said quietly.

"What?" she asked, startled.

"When you shiver like that. For the past fifteen minutes or so you've been looking as if someone's been trampling on your grave, Marta. Or, rather, as if you've perhaps seen a ghost."

"Please, Tony," Marta protested wearily.

"It was good to see Trina again," Tony said, again deftly changing the subject, to Marta's relief. "Stunning, isn't she?"

"Yes, she is."

"Very genuine, too, unlike so many actresses." Tony opined, and added without missing a beat, "I found it interesting to meet Joshua Smith. We have mutual friends in publishing. He's highly thought of."

"Yes," Marta murmured, wishing they didn't have to be quite so polite about circumventing the other party goers. She wanted to quickly get into the dining room and catch up with Guy Forthington, then change the present subject of discussion for once and for all.

"I didn't know you knew him," Tony continued equably. "I presume you've done some assignments for him?"

"Yes."

"When he was with *Architecture, American Style*?"

"Both for *Architecture* and *Living*."

"Ah." Tony nodded and left the next play in the conversational field up to her.

She knew she had to say something. And that the something had to involve Josh Smith. What she didn't understand was why Tony was making her feel so compelled to talk about Josh. "Josh's sister and I are close friends," she finally managed somewhat lamely.

"Oh?" Without even glancing at Tony, Marta knew he was raising a single, inquiring eyebrow.

"Jennifer is an interior decorator—an interior designer, really. We met when she was redoing an old mansion up in Watch Hill, Rhode Island, for a client. Kerry Gundersen, whom she later married.

"Josh gave me the assignment of following the entire renovation process from start to finish for a major piece in *Architecture*. The renovation took a fair bit of time and was a challenging project from a photographer's viewpoint. The result was so successful we did a companion piece for *Living*."

And in the course of all that, I saw a lot more of Josh Smith than I'd ever seen before. And I felt so deeply in love with him that—even after all that's happened—not even the best surgeon in the world could ever excise that love. I try to pretend I've gotten over Josh...but it would be more accurate to say that over the past two years I've

*been in remission, at least some of the time, where loving
him is concerned. But I only had to glimpse him to feel all
those feelings all over again....*

"Marta?" Tony asked politely.

Marta became aware Tony had said something to her,
and she had no idea was it was. "Yes?" she asked bleakly.

"I was saying...it's a pity Josh Smith is crippled,"
Tony told her. "He evidently needs to use a cane."

Marta froze. Josh was lame, yes, she conceded that.
But she'd never thought of him as "crippled." It was an
ugly word, a word she hated. A word that had nothing at
all to do with Josh.

Nevertheless...she was sure his handicap had a lot to
do with what had happened between them. Even though
Josh had gone to great lengths to convince her otherwise.
But, then, he was so damned proud, so stubborn...

"Marta?" Tony asked again.

"Yes."

"I've heard that he was a jet pilot and was injured in a
plane crash. Is that correct, do you know?"

"He graduated from the air force academy and was in
pilot training," Marta said dully. "Yes, his plane crashed.
He was severely injured. It's a miracle he wasn't killed.
Jennifer, his sister, told me it was touch and go for a
while."

"So that was the end of his military career?"

"Yes."

"Well," Tony said smoothly, "I would say the air
force's loss surely has been magazine publishing's gain."

Finally they reached the door to the dining room. Finally Tony spied Guy Forthington, talking to some people, and he and Marta made their way through the mob to
their host's side.

Guy Forthington was tall and thin, prematurely silver haired, with surprisingly dark eyes and a British accent as delightful as Tony's.

Under his spell, Marta managed to relax just a bit. Almost managed to forget that Josh was here in this same place, in the very next room. There was only a wall between them.... But there were so many kinds of walls.

As he watched Marta walk away with Tony Ashford, Josh clutched his champagne glass so tightly the stem nearly snapped.

Other people came up to converse with Sheila and him. He managed to talk to them with one section of his mind. But the part that mattered remained centered on the tall, dark-haired woman with the most expressive face he'd ever seen. Marta, he was certain, had been as badly jolted as he by this unexpected meeting.

He knew her so well. Had seen, beneath those false smiles she'd managed to glue on, that she looked tired and strained and unhappy. The unhappy part bothered him.

He wanted her happiness far more than he wanted his own.

Two years ago he'd set Marta free. That was the way he thought about it and always would. He was convinced she had no knowledge of what she was getting herself into with him. He had known one of them was going to have to make a very large sacrifice. And because he loved her so much, he was determined not to let it be Marta.

So... he'd kicked her out of his life. It had taken every steel ounce of character he possessed to do it, then live with the repercussions. For a while he had alienated his own sister, to whom he was very close. Finally Jennifer had come around to accepting his actions to an extent, but only to an extent.

He'd deliberately lost track of Marta these past two years...as much as he could. It was impossible to lose track of her totally, because people who didn't know anything about the personal side of their relationship knew they had had a professional one. So her name was frequently brought up in business conversations because her work continued to appear everywhere, more often than not in Josh's rivals' publications.

He knew she'd made London her base, was working from there. As a free-lancer by choice—a dozen different magazines including Josh's would have been happy to give her a staff position—she could work wherever she wished.

But he hadn't heard that she and Tony Ashford, whom Josh knew was one of the BBC's shining lights, had become engaged. The shock of hearing that had been stupendous...and Josh knew he hadn't entirely concealed it from Marta.

Well...it was unlikely they would meet again, certainly not for a long time to come. Her life would be centered in London, and Josh made a mental note that much as he liked London it was a city he had better plan to avoid in the foreseeable future. He was here in Washington on a short trip for *Living, American Style* and would be heading back to New York in the morning.

Josh clutched his cane more tightly, as if the smooth feel of the wood might help bolster his inner strength, and tried to pay attention to what Trina and the other people surrounding him were talking about.

Tony and Marta stood under the apartment house marquee while the doorman went to rustle up a cab for them.

"Feels like snow. The Washington climate always surprises me. I believe our embassy actually lists this as a tropical post,'' Tony said, turning up the collar of his overcoat.

Marta was cold all the way through, a condition that had nothing to do with the weather. They'd managed to weave their way through the party crowd, then finally out of the Forthingtons' apartment without encountering Trina Cataldo and Josh. But Marta had been on edge all the while, fearing that any step she took might bring her face to face with Josh again.

A cab pulled up at the curb. Tony helped Marta into it, climbed in himself. Only then did he ask, ''Do you want to come back to my hotel? We can have dinner there or go somewhere else later. Or would you rather go to your place?''

She noted that he'd said, ''Or would *you* rather go to your place?'' Not, ''Or would you rather *we* go to your place?'' And she felt an odd little warning frisson. Nevertheless she said, ''My place, if you please, Tony.''

''Right.'' And Tony gave directions to the cabdriver.

As if in answer to Tony's prediction, gentle snowflakes began to drift down as they drove, briefly touching the cab windows and then melting.

Marta thought about the intricate patterns of every snowflake that had ever fallen or ever would fall—each different, or so they said—and the fact that so much beauty was so ephemeral made her sad.

Life itself was so short-lived, and in many ways she had virtually thrown away two years of her own allotted span.

She reminded herself that many women lost the true loves of their lives for many reasons, death being the most absolute. The world was full of suffering humanity; she'd photographed tragic scenes she would never forget.

Many others cast-off more traumatically than she had been managed to pick up the pieces and go on. Or give the appearance of doing so.

That's what she had done, and she was even more successful today, career-wise, then she had been two years ago.

The cab came to a stop in front of the converted Georgetown town house where Marta was temporarily living. Tony paid the driver, then paused at the foot of the shallow steps leading up to the entrance.

A nearby street lamp spilled light over his head, making his hair a blend of gold and silver. But his features were in deep shadows, and Marta, having gone ahead and now standing at the top of the few steps, could not see his face clearly.

"Marta," he began in that mellow voice that was so famous all over England, "hold up a minute, will you?"

She'd been about to probe her handbag for the front-door key, and she paused, that odd little frisson coming back again.

"I think it's best I let you go up to your flat by yourself tonight," Tony said. "I should imagine you might prefer to be alone."

Marta snapped her handbag closed and started down the steps toward him. "But you're going back to London tomorrow," she protested.

"Not till evening," he reminded her. "We can have a late lunch. If you'll be free, that is."

"Of course I'll be free. And I plan to go out to the airport with you."

"As you like," Tony said.

"As I like? Tony, what is this?" She neared him, searching his face, bemoaning the shadows that played across it because they kept her from reading his expression. "You make me feel as if I've done something to offend you."

"Oh, no," he said quickly. "Nothing like that at all. It's only that I think you had rather a shock tonight. And so did I."

Marta frowned. "Tony, what are you talking about?"

"He's the one, isn't he?" Tony asked gently. "Joshua Smith?"

"What one?"

"The man you love."

Marta gasped inadvertently. Then before she could rally, Tony added quietly. "Darling, I've always known there was someone."

Chapter Two

A cold February wind, blasting over the Jersey Palisades and across the Hudson River, struck Marta as she started down the steep street from Upper Broadway to Riverside Drive. She let it buffet her, glad it was holding her back. She almost wished the wind would swirl her around and send her skittering back up the hill. It was going to be incredibly difficult to walk into Josh Smith's apartment, even though he was three thousand miles away.

This was her one chance, though, to see Jennifer and Kerry Gundersen and to meet their six-month-old twins for the first time.

Common sense had warned her it would be better to say no to Jennifer's invitation. But she was the one who had started this particular ball rolling. Once Tony had left for London, Marta had been totally at odds and ends with herself. She had called Jennifer from Washington because she'd desperately needed to talk to a close friend. It had been much too long since they had touched base.

When Jennifer had mentioned that she, Kerry and the twins would be in New York for a few days in early February, as Kerry had business in the city, the timing seemed just right. Especially once Marta discovered that Josh would be on the other side of the country.

"We'll be staying in Josh's apartment," Jennifer had said casually, "so why don't we have brunch there? Unfortunately we won't get to see Josh this trip. He'll be at a magazine editors' conference in California."

Marta had some unavoidable business in New York herself, or once more she would have bypassed the city that was much too reminiscent of Josh. But she needed to meet in person with an editor who was asking her to take an assignment in West Berlin, which she wasn't sure she wanted. So she had already planned to make a brief stopover in Manhattan en route from Washington to London.

She had stretched the Washington assignment as long as she possibly could. Now she simply couldn't stave off much longer getting back to London and setting the wedding date. Tony had been very patient. After that night outside her Georgetown apartment, they had not mentioned Josh again. Nor had Tony—considerate as usual, though maybe a shade too considerate—again mentioned setting their date. Marta knew he was leaving it up to her. And she owed it to him to do it soon.

Meantime she said yes to Jennifer's suggestion of a Sunday brunch. And it wasn't until after she had committed herself that the full realization of what she was getting into swept over her. She was certain to be engulfed by memories she had long been forcing herself to try to forget.

By the time she reached the corner apartment building and opened the ornately etched glass door to the marble foyer, bittersweet nostalgia was surging. As if for reassurance, Marta took off her left glove and stared down at the twinkling diamond on her fourth finger. She'd made a promise to Tony Ashford, she reminded herself. A promise she intended to keep.

So for the next couple of hours, tread carefully, she warned herself.

The hum of the elevator as it ascended to the tenth floor was a familiar sound. The equally familiar corridor that led to Josh's river-view apartment seemed a thousand miles long. By the time Marta reached this door, she felt as if she were inwardly breaking into pieces—no matter how outwardly poised she might appear.

She pushed the brass doorbell with an unsteady finger. A moment later the door opened, and she and Jennifer stood stock-still, staring at each other. Then Jennifer opened her arms and Marta went into them. And, to her horror, her dark eyes filled with tears.

Kerry Gundersen was standing just behind his wife. He moved forward to embrace Marta, and she hoped the shoulder of his tweed jacket would blot off the tears.

Jennifer stepped back to take in Marta's chic designer suit with a matching cape. Marta's nearly black hair swirled around her shoulders, and her long silver earrings glinted with every move of her head. Her black, high-heeled boots made her look even taller. And slimmer than usual, though she didn't need that. "Marta, it's so terrific to see you again!" she finally exclaimed.

"It's been too long," Kerry echoed. "Ridiculously long."

"Yes," Marta agreed, "it has been too long."

"And you've been all over the world, taking all sorts of prize pictures," Jennifer bubbled as Kerry led the way down the hall to the large living room that overlooked the river.

"Well...a few prize pictures," Marta conceded modestly, trying not to remember the last time she'd stormed down this hallway, slamming the front door behind her after that terrible, climactic fight with Josh.

A huge picture window dominated the far end of the living room. The view was ever changing with the seasons, always fascinating, and a prime reason Josh Smith had paid a high tariff for the condo. Today, there were snow clouds over the Hudson, and the water was icy gray. As her eyes focused on the window, Marta remembered the times she and Josh had shared that view together.

Then something tugged—a sudden sense, with an almost physical force. Marta turned, then caught her breath in shock. Josh sat in a corner armchair. He slowly stood. Across a distance of perhaps twenty feet, their eyes met.

Josh spoke first. "Hello, Marta," he said, his voice cool.

"Josh," she stammered, and the words tumbled out before she could suppress them. "I thought you were in California."

"I was," he stated.

While Marta was trying to digest that rather offhand remark, Kerry said briskly, "Here, Marta, let me take your cape. We were about to indulge in mimosas. Would that suit you, or would you prefer something else?"

"A mimosa would be fine," she managed, her throat suddenly dry.

"I have to check the oven," Jennifer said hastily. And to Marta's distress, both Kerry and Jennifer departed, leaving her alone with Josh.

She didn't want to look at him. And yet . . . she had to. Only to see that he looked . . . wonderful. His darkish red hair was slightly sun bleached. His skin was tanned. Certainly he had been spending time outdoors in California.

"Sit down, why don't you?" Josh suggested, and added, "I got in from the coast last night. I take it you finished your Washington assignment?"

Marta nodded, still trying to recover from the shock of seeing him.

"What are you into next?" Josh inquired politely.

Reality struck. "I'm flying back to London tomorrow," Marta told him.

Silence stretched across the room, as strained as high tension wires vibrating in a gale. Desperately searching for a safe topic to break the brittle stillness, Marta observed, "I thought Jennifer said she and Kerry were bringing the twins with them. Did they decide to leave them in Providence?"

"No," Josh said, "they're here. Asleep in the guest room." To Marta's surprise, he added, "Come on, I'll show you."

As he spoke, Josh reached for the cane propped up against the armchair. Witnessing his familiar actions, Marta suddenly wanted to cry, to wail against fate. She *hated* the damned cane because deep down inside she felt it was symbolic of her problem with Josh.

It certainly hadn't had anything to do with their physical relationship, Marta remembered, a shade too vividly. Josh had taken her to unimagined heights. Never again would she transcend the planet Earth as she had with him.

"Go on," he urged now, and she started along the hall toward the bedrooms . . . all of this, like all of his apartment, overwhelmingly familiar territory to her. Josh followed closely behind her, and it took all of Marta's willpower not to suddenly turn around and fling herself into his arms. She wanted to pillow her head against his shoulder, feel his lips nuzzling her hair. She wanted him to murmur all the soft, tender things she so yearned to hear him say. The small words of love Josh had spoken fully only once—when he'd had too much champagne. The next day he'd claimed he didn't even remember what he'd said.

But they had made love that night. It was not the first time—though it was to be the last—but it had transcended even the glorious pleasure of the previous times. Their passion blended with the champagne haze, both had been completely uninhibited. They had given freely and completely, and together they had been whisked away to the end of the rainbow, then toppled into a sea of gold. Later Marta had thought that maybe sharing that ultimate journey would bring about the needed change in their relationship. But it hadn't. Josh had preferred to pretend that their special night had never happened. His attitude had frustrated her intensely. And had led up to the terrible, final scene in which he'd done a very good job of convincing her that although it was one thing to go to bed together, sharing a life was something else entirely. And he didn't want to share his with her.

Back then Jennifer had tried so hard to play peacemaker, pleading with them both to come for a visit to the magnificent Rhode Island mansion where she and Kerry lived. But Marta had stood her ground and sidestepped a reunion, hoping Josh would apologize. When he didn't, the chance to do a long-term assignment for a top English magazine had beckoned. She'd gone to London and stayed there.

So the months had passed. She'd traveled all over Europe on subsequent assignments. She'd seen Kenya and

Morocco. Witnessed firsthand the turbulence in Cape Town and Beirut. She'd won coveted awards. But the honors had been empty without Josh to share the thrill.

She'd met Tony Ashford at a party in Mayfair. He'd asked her to lunch with him the next day, and she'd accepted. Tony was charming, attractive, witty and, above all else, considerate. At moments, he'd come close to making her forget about Josh—for almost a day once or twice. Now...it was as if the past two years had suddenly been wiped out and she was right back where she'd started from.

She preceded Josh into the guest room, saw the extra-wide crib set up against the wall. For the next few minutes it was easy to concentrate on Jennifer and Kerry's beautiful, six-month-old babies.

They were asleep, twin cherubs, a boy and a girl. Joshua, named after this man at Marta's side, and Caroline, named after Josh and Jennifer's mother.

Looking at the sleeping babies, Marta felt as if a giant had taken her heart in his hand and twisted it. She glanced at Josh and saw that the stern lines of his face had softened. His expression was tender as he smiled down at his niece and nephew, and the tenderness lingered as his eyes met Marta's.

"Great, aren't they?" he whispered.

"They're fantastic," Marta whispered back.

As beautiful as the children were, though, she found herself wanting to look at Josh. And when she finally couldn't resist raising her eyes again, she was shocked at the raw pain she saw etched on his handsome face. Pain swiftly camouflaged, of course, for Josh was an artist at hiding his true feelings.

"We'd better get out of here," he said quickly. "We're apt to wake them up, and Jenny wouldn't be exactly pleased about that."

Marta nodded, unable to trust herself to speak. Then, as she turned, her hand brushed his . . . and the effect was incredible. Desire exploded as if it had been kept under pressure all this time, and instinctively she pulled back. Feeling her face on fire, she reached up to touch her cheek. And the diamond on her finger sparkled.

Josh's eyes focused on the diamond, and he froze. He had the crazy feeling that the glittering stone was mocking him—as it well had every right to do! He'd been an idiot to cut his stay in California and rush back here just because he'd learned that Marta was coming to his apartment to have Sunday brunch with his sister and brother-in-law.

He had happened to call Jennifer in Watch Hill to remind her where she could get a spare key to his place in case she couldn't find the one he'd given her quite a while back. Jennifer had told him about speaking with Marta, about Marta's accepting her invitation. Josh suddenly had become possessed of an overwhelming urge to be at the brunch. And no sooner had he hung up the receiver after talking with his sister than he'd picked it up again and made his airline reservation.

Now, seeing the ring on Marta's finger again was more than enough to bring him to his senses. In fact, the twinkling diamond was like a cold slap in the face. But he had it coming. What had he expected? That Marta would have herself plasticized so no one else could get to her? That she would wait for him until, somehow, maybe, he eventually came to terms with his inadequacies?

Marta was young, lovely and desirable. Obviously during these two years her magnetism had drawn many men to her. She was skinnier than ever, Josh decided, frowning slightly as he appraised her. But she was still— to him, anyway—the most attractive woman in the world. Beautiful and talented, warm and wonderful, witty, sharp, incredibly moody at times, but so *giving* she could be forgiven that moodiness.

God, how he loved her!

Josh looked up and saw that Marta was staring at him, her dark eyes enormous.

He forced a smile and managed to sound casual as he asked, ''Have you set the date yet?''

She shook her head. ''No. I thought Tony and I should do that together once I'm back in London.''

''I wondered,'' Josh admitted. ''In Washington Tony said something about favoring a Valentine wedding.''

''Well, obviously it's too late for that,'' she pointed out.

''Will you be making England your permanent home, Marta?''

''London's already my base of operations,'' she said evasively.

''So you'll continue to work independently out of London?''

''I think so. Yes,'' Marta replied, adding restlessly, ''Tony and I still have to work that out. As I imagine you gathered when you met him, he's not crazy about my 'globe-trotting,' as he puts it.''

''Well, that's understandable,'' Josh said.

''I suppose so. But…it's my work. What I'm saying is, it's just not possible to confine my work geographically. Anyway…''

''Yes?''

''As I've told Tony,'' Marta said, ''we can finalize our plans while I'm in London. I think we'll probably decide on a late-spring wedding. Meantime, I'm going to need to come back to New York for a while.''

Josh felt his pulse rate racing out of control, but he said only, ''Oh?''

''There are a couple of jobs originating in New York that I've left dangling,'' Marta admitted. ''Things I'd like to do. One's a medical feature. The other involves contemporary coal mining, which would give me a chance to go to Pennsylvania and stay with my family while I work on the story.''

''You still run the whole gamut subject-wise, don't you?'' Josh murmured.

''I like variety, yes,'' she agreed.

Josh almost winced visibly upon hearing that. He was not thinking of her professional definition of variety, which he fully understood and endorsed. Rather, he was thinking of the personal variety, so much a part of Marta's life and which had been such a large factor in his decision to break up a relationship that at the time was spiraling toward a point of no return.

Now he clutched his cane more tightly, as if his need to hang on to it would reinforce his belief that there was no place in the world of a beautiful, talented woman like Marta Brennan for a guy who had to hobble his way through life and could join her in so few of the things she loved to do. Marta was quite an athlete. She enjoyed tennis, skiing, jogging and rock climbing. She also danced divinely, Josh knew, and the knowledge was bittersweet. At a company Christmas party he'd observed her dancing several times—with other men.

The memory of how much he'd wanted to dance with her himself made him ache.

He felt sure he'd always ache watching another man dance with Marta. Yet he couldn't expect her to sit on the sidelines just because he had to. And that was a problem that went beyond the obvious. Their pace was so different. True, he had been forced to adjust his tempo. But as time went by, having to give up so many physical activities had made him more and more aware of life's other aspects. He'd discovered pleasure in quiet, simple things that didn't require a lot of moving around. A good book. Listening to good jazz or a top performance of a classical work. Sometimes just observing nature, with its constant changes. Living and savoring life on a day-by-day basis, and in passing, seeing so much he'd never taken time to notice when he'd had two good legs.

Marta, on the other hand, was a study in motion. It stood to reason there was just no way two life-styles as different as his and hers could ever be blended satisfactorily.

He did have to admit there had been times when he'd been inclined to think otherwise. Times here in his apartment when he and Marta had sat together by the picture window in the living room, watching the Hudson change colors as afternoon faded into twilight. At those times they'd shared a very special mood, apart from the physical attraction that flared so easily between them. Josh remembered how, slowly, he had opened up to her and discovered they shared so many views, had so much in common. Then . . . the moment would come when a physical expression of everything they felt toward each other could no longer be denied. And they would go into . . . another dimension. Afterward, Josh would again warn himself that there was much more involved in living "daily life" than the kind of passion he and Marta shared, glorious though it was. He became convinced that if they stayed together, the moment would come when she would realize that the only time he didn't bore her or hold her back was when they were in bed together.

That thought alone had been enough to make him run scared. So scared that he'd washed Marta out of his life, even though he knew he was hurting both of them in the process.

They had two years behind them now. Two years that couldn't be bridged. Which, Josh reminded himself, no longer mattered. Come spring, Marta would be married to Tony Ashford.

Josh wouldn't have believed how much the mere idea of Marta's being married to someone else could hurt. And suddenly, as if every warning had been swept out of his mind, as if he were performing in overdrive, he heard himself saying, "Is there a chance you would have time to handle an assignment for *Living* before you settle down permanently in England?"

As he was speaking, he was mentally running through the list of topics the magazine had in its Future file, hoping to find something that would appeal so much to Marta she wouldn't be able to refuse.

Marta was dumbfounded. If anyone had asked her, "What's absolutely the last thing in the world that might happen to you?" she could easily have answered, "Ever being offered another assignment by Josh Smith."

"Well," she said, catching her breath, "did . . . uh, did you have something specific in mind?"

Josh snatched at an idea. "I've been thinking about doing a profile on 'The Politician Personality,'" he announced. "One day when I was watching a mayoral candidate speak, I began to wonder exactly what this man's motivation was. The mayor served alongside a seven-member council in the city involved, so the actual position was not that important. And the pay, I discovered, was minimal. Was his candidacy an ego trip, or the first step on a political springboard that would lead to bigger and better things?'' Josh mused aloud, off the top of his head.

"It sounds...interesting," Marta said cautiously. "But why would you need a photographer?"

Josh frowned. "To shoot photographs, of course."

"Of different politicians?"

"Not just of different politicians," Josh said, annoyed with himself for latching onto the first idea that had leaped into his mind. Although he knew that Marta's recent Washington assignment had dealt with women in politics, he reminded himself he should have remembered that political candidates, per se, weren't her thing, despite the wide range of subjects she covered. He'd kept a tab on her work these past two years. She'd done some very specialized photo essays in which that superb eye of hers was so evident. Marta "saw" life through her camera in a way that produced unique results.

Josh improvised quickly. "My thought," he said, "is to deal with four different individuals, each from a major region of the country. So...we'd have Mr. Northeast, Mr. Deep South, Mr. Midwest and Mr. West Coast. We might pick someone who's made it as far as governor, in one instance. And someone who's just starting out, a state representative, perhaps, in another. Whatever, I want to get inside their lives, into their personalities," Josh went on, warming to his topic almost in spite of himself. "So you can see the kind of photo series that would be needed for each subject. I made it clear when I took the top editor post that I still want to go out in the field now and then. I think it's essential, to maintain an up-to-date viewpoint. So I'd be working on this story personally," he added carefully.

"There'd be quite a bit of traveling involved, Josh," Marta pointed out.

"True, there would be."

Josh wouldn't let himself think about traveling with Marta on an assignment. That was something they'd never really done. Although Marta had carried out a number of other assignments for his magazines, the only story they'd ever worked on together was the Watch Hill one . . . and Marta had stayed near Watch Hill a good bit of the time, while he had commuted from New York when necessary. There hadn't been the danger of being with her on a twenty-four-hour basis. Long days in unfamiliar places . . .

Again Josh forcibly reminded himself that Marta would soon be married to someone else. And living in England.

"I don't know, Josh. I don't know if I'd have enough time," Marta said hesitantly.

To his own astonishment, Josh found himself saying, "We could hit the South next month, Marta. Then go west, say . . . to California. Then pick a state in the Midwest on our way back East."

"When you get right down to it, Josh, there are more than four sections to the United States. I mean, even in the Northeast, there's a considerable difference between Maine and Connecticut, for example."

"I haven't worked out the details yet," Josh said evasively.

They were standing in the hallway outside the guest room. Behind them they heard a definite wail.

"Uh-oh," Marta said. "Sounds like at least one of the twins has decided to wake up. I'd better get Jennifer."

The mimosas and brunch were put on hold while Jennifer attended to feeding the twins. When she invited Marta to share the experience, Marta held back for a moment. She could imagine what it would do to her heart-strings to hold one of those adorable babies. Yet it was an invitation she couldn't resist.

She held small Josh while Jennifer took care of Caroline. As she watched Josh eagerly suck milk from his bottle, she wondered if the first Josh had looked like his namesake when he was six months old.

"I nursed the twins for four months," Jennifer said. "Then my pediatrician said he thought it was time to put them on formula. They're such hungry little devils," she added, gazing down at Caroline's beautiful, little round head.

"They're adorable," Marta said huskily.

Jennifer gave Marta a long, level look, then said abruptly, "I know this is taking a plunge . . . and you can tell me to mind my own business, but though I was happy for you when you said you'd become engaged, I guess you know I've always hoped that Josh would eventually come to his senses. I've always hoped that one day you'd be my sister-in-law."

"I know," Marta said softly, her emotions swelling inside her. "I do know. But please," she pleaded, "let's not get into it now."

"It's hard not to, Marta. I mean, I care so much about you and Josh. It hurts to see you both so unhappy."

Marta laughed bitterly. "Does it show that much?"

"Actually, you do a pretty good job of hiding it, though you do have your unguarded moments. So does my stubborn brother. But . . ."

Jennifer hesitated, then said, "I have this crazy idea that Josh came back from California early because he knew you were coming for brunch today. I mentioned the brunch while I was talking to him on the phone. He didn't say anything . . . but then all of a sudden he appeared on the doorstep. Marta . . .''

Marta was trying to take in the fact there was a possibility Josh actually had come back from the West Coast to see her. She thought about the possibility, then dismissed it. Jennifer had to be wrong.

Still hesitant, Jennifer added, "Of course I shouldn't even be saying this, especially now that you've chosen someone else, but . . . my brother loves you, Marta. And I can't help but believe that you still love him. Love like that doesn't simply fade away."

Marta's mouth tightened. Then for a moment she focused her attention solely on the baby she was holding. When she looked up, the pain in her dark eyes was proof in itself that Jennifer's statement had struck home. Nevertheless she said firmly, "I doubt Josh loves me, Jen. If he loved me, really loved me, he would have stopped thinking so damned much about himself and have given a little thought to me." Marta stopped, reminding herself that she was speaking to Josh's sister. She began again, more mildly, "Anyway . . ."

"Yes?"

"It wasn't a question of my choosing someone else," Marta said with a wry smile. "I don't think I ever had a real chance with Josh. I'd say he's the quintessential bachelor and he wants to stay that way. Hasn't that fact dawned on you?"

"You know why he's like that," Jennifer put in softly.

"I'm not so sure I do. A lot of handicapped people marry very successfully. A majority, I'd say."

"Well, Josh is . . . different."

"Tell me about it," Marta agreed. "As I said, there was never any question of my choosing Josh, simply because he didn't want to be chosen." She exhaled, letting out her frustration, then said, her voice steady, "I don't want to spend the rest of my life alone, Jen. I'm sure you can understand that feeling. Certainly, being married to Kerry has taught you what it means to share your life with someone."

"Yes, it has," Jennifer acknowledged. "But," she added carefully, "Kerry and I are very much in love."

"And you're saying I'm not in love with Tony?"

"I don't know. I have no way of knowing."

"Well, I can't deny you're right, to a point," Marta conceded. "Though I wouldn't admit it to anyone but you. But the fact is, in some ways I do love Tony, Jennifer, or I would never have agreed to marry him. It's a different kind of love. There isn't the fire I felt for Josh." She paused, thinking this out, then went on. "Actually," she said, "Tony and I have a lot of great things going for us. We have so much in common. We enjoy each other's company. Tony skis well. He plays a wicked game of tennis. He's a terrific dancer."

"In other words, he can do all the things Josh can't do," Jennifer began. She was about to remind Marta how many times Marta herself had said those things didn't really matter, but she stopped short as she saw Marta gazing toward the doorway, a stricken expression on her face.

Josh was standing there, leaning on his cane. And there was little doubt that he'd heard the last part of their conversation. Those last few sentences that could only give him an entirely wrong impression.

Chapter Three

Josh, his face expressionless, sounded a shade too casual as he said, "Kerry thinks you're overfeeding his children. He's brewing up the mimosas and says the champagne will be flat if you two don't toddle along." Before they could answer him, he moved away.

Jennifer sighed deeply. "Oh, boy," she moaned.

"Don't worry about it, Jen," Marta said quickly. "He may not have overheard us."

"You know he overheard us, Marta."

"Well, then...maybe it's for the best." Perhaps it was. Still, Marta wished fervently that Josh had not appeared just then.

She tried to match his calm, cool demeanor as they sipped mimosas with the delicious brunch Jennifer had prepared, but it was hard, very hard, and she was glad when she could gracefully bow out a while later because she had another engagement.

At the door, Jennifer asked, "Any chance of your getting up to Watch Hill soon? You know how much we'd love to have you."

"I'd love to come," Marta said sincerely. "I'll call you when I get back from London."

Once in the elevator she wished she hadn't given that promise. She was beginning to feel that until she and Tony were safely married it might be better to sidestep spending any time with Jennifer. In her mind, Jennifer was too inextricably connected with Josh.

Marta had many friends in New York. She'd lived in the city for several years before taking off for London after that traumatic quarrel with Josh. Even though she was to be in town only briefly, she had been swamped with invitations.

That Sunday, besides the brunch, she was the guest of honor at a small cocktail party given by a fellow photographer and his wife. Afterward she went out to dinner with some people she'd met when she'd first come to the city as a free-lancer. She was glad she had these diversions. She was trying as hard as she could to put Josh out of her mind, and company helped.

But later, alone in her hotel room, her thoughts caught up with her. Once again Josh had misunderstood. And this time she couldn't let it go.

At brunch Kerry and Jennifer had mentioned they were going to a fairly late dinner at the home of a business associate of Kerry's. With a chuckle Jennifer had added that Josh had agreed to baby-sit. Glancing at her watch, Marta doubted that the Gundersens would be home yet, or that Josh would have gone to bed. He tended to be a night owl.

She didn't let herself think about what she was doing. She simply dialed his number. But when he answered on the third ring just the sound of his voice was enough to bring home the truth that never, for an instant, had she honestly gotten him out of her system.

She heard her voice tremble as she said, "Josh?"

There was a telltale moment of hesitation. Then he replied, "Yes."

"It's Marta," she told him.

"I know," Josh answered.

Marta's pulse began racing crazily. She stalled, suddenly shy about getting into the reason she was calling him. It was so easy to turn Josh off. On the other hand, she couldn't let him labor under yet another misconception.

"I hope I didn't wake you up," she said feebly.

"No, you didn't wake me up, Marta."

"Josh?"

"Yes."

"About today..."

"What about today?" Josh queried, sounding as if he were indulging a backward child.

"I know you overheard what Jennifer and I were saying when you came to get us for brunch," Marta managed determinedly. "But it wasn't the way it sounded."

"Oh, please," Josh protested wearily. "Not that again."

"Josh, listen to me," she pleaded, desperately wanting some honest communication with him.

"I'm listening."

"Look, just what did you hear?"

She heard Josh take a deep breath, knew he was keeping a rein on his patience with difficulty...and that at any moment he was going to withdraw completely. But he said only, "I didn't memorize your conversation with Jenny, Marta."

"Please, Josh. What did you hear?"

"Okay. You were speaking about your fiancé, saying how much you have in common. Listing all the things he's an expert at," Josh drawled. There was a pause, then he added, "That's fine. The way it should be. You should have a great marriage."

Marta took a long breath, then blurted, "You don't really mean that, do you?"

"Why the hell shouldn't I?" Josh asked, sounding honestly surprised. "You don't think I'd want you to make a bad marriage, do you?" When she didn't answer right away, he went on, "Look, Marta, it's late. You have to catch a flight to London tomorrow. I'm sure you have a lot of things to do, and you also need to get some sleep."

"Josh, what about the assignment for your magazine?"

The question lurched out of her subconscious.

After a moment of intense silence, Josh said, "I was . . . somewhat premature on that. I'm not sure I want to go with that particular story."

"Don't you mean you've changed your mind about my doing the photography? Isn't that a little closer to the truth?"

"Not at all, Marta. I simply need to review my timing, that's all. A story on politicians might be better run before a major election."

"Well, I'd like to do something for *Living*," Marta found herself saying. "It's been quite a while."

"I had the impression you'd be loaded with assignments during your final time in the States," Josh told her.

Even in the days when she was just beginning to make her way up the ladder in her profession, Marta had never been one to beg for assignments. Now, when she was so much in demand, it was odd—very odd—to be doing almost exactly that. And she wondered how she'd feel if Josh actually turned her down.

"I do have several potential assignments," she admitted. "Frankly, though, I wasn't sure which ones I wanted to take on, so I've managed to keep things open with the proviso that I'll make my decisions when I get back from London late next week. By then, I'll know how much time I'll have in the States."

"In other words, the wedding date will be set?"

"Yes, it will be."

Into the chilly silence that followed that pronouncement, Josh ventured, "I wouldn't think you'd exactly be looking for work at that point."

Marta laughed shakily and told him. "You know me, Josh. The restless type. I can't stay still too long."

"Exactly," he agreed.

His irony was not lost on her. She knew that what she'd just said had served to underline a major obstacle between them. While certainly not immobile, Josh was limited in his physical activity. She, on the other hand, was always on the go and seemed to be possessed of an unusual amount of energy. Nervous energy? Maybe. Marta knew that her inherent nature demanded fairly frequent jolts of hard physical exertion to keep both her body and mind in peak shape. But some of what she'd been putting out over the past few years could be attributed to restlessness bred of frustration.

Some of her happiest, most fulfilling moments had been spent quietly with Josh, viewing the Hudson River from his living room window and just talking. Talking about all sorts of things. Being with Josh, talking with Josh, was like turning the moon over . . . and discovering the beauty and promise of the other side no one ever sees.

Tentatively she began, "Josh..." Then she paused, sure there was no use in pursuing this. It had been foolish to call him in the first place. Josh had a stubborn streak a mile wide. She might have known he'd formed his own conclusions about what he'd overheard this morning and would only scoff at any attempt on her part to convince him he'd heard wrong. So she gave up.

After a long moment, Josh asked, "What were you going to say, Marta?"

"It doesn't really matter," she murmured.

Josh knew he should let it go at that, but he suddenly discovered he couldn't. This time his sigh was inaudible. And he felt as helpless as Marta had just sounded.

It was true that the fragment of conversation he'd overheard had served to further cement his feelings about the situation between Marta and him. Maybe if he had never skied or run or danced it would have been different. In that case he would never have fully understood how she felt about that wonderful freedom of motion. But there was a time when he'd been not only active in all those physical activities, but very good at them. Then, on a sunny afternoon in Texas, his air force jet trainer had crashed. And his way of life had been turned upside down—forever.

He'd had to learn to live so...differently. His military career had crashed with the plane. The girl he'd been engaged to, upon viewing him lying helpless in a hospital bed and learning what the future score was apt to be, had broken their engagement. Sweetly, regretfully, insisting it had nothing to do with his suddenly having become a handicapped person.

His father, a career military officer, had taken it as a personal tragedy that his only son would never follow in the family footsteps. It was a tragedy that Josh doubted

General Ashley Sanderson Smith ever had fully recovered from. At bitter moments he told himself his father probably would have accepted it better if he'd been killed in action.

As it was, emotional trauma upon emotional trauma had been piled on Josh as he was trying to recoup physically. It had been a very heavy time, but he'd worked his way through it. He'd gone on to a new career. Searched for and found new pleasures.

He'd had a few relationships with women over the past twelve years, all of which he had eventually brought to an end. He found he wanted little in his life on a permanent basis. He was honest enough with himself to admit that none of the women he'd known had been turned off by his handicap. The bad leg had not affected his sexual performance, so there were no hang-ups in that department. But when Marta had walked into his office, and thus into his life, all the doubts and uncertainties he'd had twelve years earlier had resurfaced and then had magnified. He felt as if he were constantly holding himself up to a mirror. He was overwhelmingly aware of what he considered his inadequacy where she was concerned.

Still . . . sometimes he'd wondered if it wouldn't be better to have her, even for a little while, than never to have her at all. But each time when he'd thought about that, Josh had faced up to the fact that if he had Marta and then lost her, there would be less than nothing left in his life. And he couldn't face such bleakness.

Today in his apartment, when she'd said goodbye and walked out of the living room with Jennifer, it had taken all his willpower not to go after her. He'd had no idea when, or if, he would see her again. Or if he'd ever even hear from her again.

When he'd picked up the phone and heard her softly query, "Josh?" he'd wondered if he was hallucinating. He'd half expected someone else who sounded a little bit like Marta to identify herself. Now...

The sensible thing, of course, would be to sidestep the matter of an assignment with either of his magazines—something he'd done easily on other occasions with any number of other photographers. Then he would wish Marta well, hang up the receiver and hope that both the twins would start howling at once, taking his mind away from heartbreak.

Instead, after apologizing for the long pause, he said, "Why don't you give me a call when you get back from London? I'll go over my files in the meantime, and we'll see what there is on tap that might work well."

Marta could not believe her ears. She knew she should say quickly, "That's okay, Josh. You're right. I really do have too much to handle, so it probably wouldn't be wise to take on anything for you at this point. Maybe later." And then she would see to it that later never came.

But those weren't the words she spoke. As if she were being programmed by a force beyond her control, she said, "All right, Josh. I'll call you."

"Good," he said, and added, his voice suspiciously husky, "meantime...happy flying."

It was sleeting as the jumbo jet taxied up to the terminal at Gatwick International Airport. Looking out her window, Marta grimaced. It had been cold but sunny in New York. Here everything was gray. She loved London, but sometimes the weather, especially in winter, got to her.

Once through customs, she took a cab to the small Kensington hotel where she'd booked a room. After checking in and unpacking, she began pacing the floor.

She had told Tony she would call him from New York so he could meet her flight. She hadn't called. Further, she knew that this time around Tony would be expecting her to stay at his town house near Hyde Park, not far from this hotel.

Marta had lived in a furnished apartment during most of her time in London, sublet from a photographer friend who'd decided to explore Spain for a couple of years. She'd relinquished the apartment on leaving for the Washington assignment. So it was natural for Tony to think that for these few days she would stay with him. He'd even mentioned her checking out the house to see if there were any decorative changes she'd like him to have made while she was back in the States. They'd be living in his home after a honeymoon in the Greek islands.

As she paced the room, Marta knew that Tony must be waiting to hear from her and was certain to be astonished when he learned she was already in London. She hadn't thought out an explanation for not having called from the States. Actually, she didn't have a valid explanation. In fact, it was stupid not to have called him from New York. Certainly there was no way she could hope to make Tony understand why she'd taken this room. Or why she'd called the hotel from Kennedy to book it only an hour before her flight left.

She glanced at the diamond on her finger. It seemed to wink at her in reproach. Reluctantly she reached for the phone, dialed the BBC and identified herself to Tony's secretary.

A moment later Tony was saying, "Am I imagining things, Marta? Or did Betty really tell me you're already here?"

"I'm here," Marta replied dully.

Perplexity laced Tony's crisp British voice. "Is there something wrong, darling?" he asked. "That's to say... you're all right, aren't you?"

"Oh, yes, of course. I'm all right."

"Then..." Tony paused. "I rather expected you'd be calling from New York, you know."

"I intended to, but ..."

"Yes?"

"I'm here, and I'm tired," she said, hating to deceive him.

"Did anything go wrong in New York, Marta?"

Did anything go wrong in New York? It depended on one's definition, she supposed. In a sense, everything had gone wrong—once she'd seen Josh. Having seen him again, she realized that she'd been mesmerizing herself into believing she'd gotten over him. Seeing him again had snapped her back to a reality she still wasn't ready to face.

"I was on the go all the time in New York, Tony. Now I'm tired, that's all. Part jet lag, I'm sure. I thought maybe I'd take a nap for a couple of hours. That should do the trick. I'm bound to wake up feeling... full of bounce."

"Well, darling," Tony said, "a nap for you does sound like a good idea. I have one of those demand meetings to attend in just a few minutes. But I shall escape as promptly as possible. By the time I get home I'm sure you'll be bouncing, as you put it. Meantime, tell Mrs. Hawkins if you need anything."

"Tony, I'm not at your house," Marta said heavily.

"Not at the house?" Tony echoed. "Then where the devil are you?"

"At the Bentley Arms, in West Kensington."

"Why, for God's sake?"

"No special reason, Tony. It was a hotel I knew, that's all. I stayed here when I first came to London."

"That's not what I mean. Why now? Mrs. Hawkins is expecting you. Certainly I was expecting you."

Marta couldn't blame him for sounding irritated. She said slowly, "I suppose I just wasn't thinking straight."

Tony's silence told her that he wasn't buying her explanation. He sounded especially clipped, especially British, as he said, "That doesn't sound like you, Marta. I doubt I've ever known a person who thinks any straighter than you do. So before you unpack why don't you simply check out, get a cab and go over to my place? I'll be along as soon as possible."

She had already unpacked, but she saw no point in adding fuel to the fire by telling him so. Instead she bargained for time. "Tony, I really need a nap first."

She heard someone's voice in the background, suspected Tony was being summoned to his meeting. Then, annoyance edging his words, he said, "Very well, then. Take your nap. Then get back to me, why don't you? If I'm still at the meeting leave word with Betty about what time you'd like me to pick you up."

Marta brewed herself a cup of tea—an electric teapot was one of her room's amenities—then slumped on the bed and tried to sleep. The harder she tried, the more sleep eluded her. Every time she closed her eyes she saw visions of Josh.

Finally she did drift off...to be awakened in total darkness by the sound of the phone ringing.

"I've been home for over an hour, Marta." Tony said. "I decided if you tried the office and got no answer you'd ring the house."

"Tony, I'm sorry," she murmured.

"Evidently I awakened you," he commented dryly.

"It took me a while to get to sleep, so I guess it's later than I thought . . . it was," Marta fumbled.

"It's nearly seven," Tony informed her. "Shall I come for you?"

Marta thought about moving into Tony's house, and suddenly she knew she couldn't do it . . . not even for just three or four days. The need for a little space, a little private time in which to think a few things through, became overwhelming. She found herself saying, "Tony, there's a cocktail lounge on the ground floor here, and also a small dining room where the food's quite good. Could we settle for a drink and some dinner here tonight? I'm still awfully tired."

"If that's what you want," he agreed.

His acquiescence was a relief. Marta had expected him to protest that Mrs. Hawkins, his housekeeper, had already prepared dinner and would be disappointed if she didn't come over. She felt sure he wanted her to pack up and move into the house that would soon be her home. But Tony made no demands.

"Thanks," she said gratefully. "That's exactly what I want."

Half an hour later, Marta was idling away time at the magazine stand in the hotel lobby while she waited for her fiancé. She couldn't have said why she hadn't opted to wait in her room. Heading downstairs to the lobby once she'd changed her clothes and freshened her makeup had been almost a reflex action.

From her vantage point beside a potted palm, she watched Tony enter through the revolving door and head toward the desk, evidently to check on her room number. He looked tired, preoccupied, older, and Marta felt a pang of guilt. Some of that, she was sure, was her fault.

She cared a great deal for Tony. Otherwise she would never have said yes to his proposal of marriage. But...the problem was that she was beginning to see that though caring was in itself tremendously important, loving was in a different realm. Caring had to be a part of loving, but loving wasn't necessarily a part of caring. And it was devastating for Marta to realize, irrevocably, that she didn't love Tony. That she never had loved Tony, and never would.

Knowing this, it was with tremendous effort that she walked slowly up behind him and said, "Hi, Tony."

He swung around, stared down at her. Then bent and deftly kissed her cheek.

Marta was thankful that Tony, generally speaking, was not much for public displays of emotion. At the same time, she was disconcerted by that quick, appraising glance he'd given her before bestowing the kiss. She had the uncanny feeling that he already knew what had happened to her in New York. And she wondered how he was going to handle the knowledge.

The cocktail lounge was dimly lighted. Soft music provided ambience. Tony and Marta settled into a booth and ordered drinks.

Marta had never felt so miserable. She asked Tony about his afternoon meeting, hoping to put off the personal problems she knew they would have to address. He told her about some new programming the BBC was planning. He spoke easily, so she was completely unprepared when, in midstream, he suddenly asked, "Did you see Josh Smith again in New York?"

"Are you a mind reader?" she faltered, after the shock had registered and then abated enough that she could speak.

"No," he answered. A rueful smile curved his lips as he added, "Nor would I want to be one, either. I should think it would keep one's nerves constantly twanging. However, I do know you quite well. And...I love you," he said simply.

Marta's own nerves were twanging with such force that she felt she might explode. Her misery increased as she heard his declaration. She wished desperately that she could respond by telling Tony what she knew he wanted to hear. She wished she could say she loved him, that nothing between them had changed. That seeing Josh hadn't suddenly thrust up a whole range of mental and emotional mountains between them.

"Don't try, darling," Tony cautioned softly. "You'd never make it. Your face is as transparent as a child's. That's one of the reasons why I fell in love with you, incidentally. Your honesty, your lack of subterfuge. It is refreshing in this day and age, you know. Especially in a successful career woman."

"Thank you," she managed weakly.

Tony sipped his drink before saying, "I'm in my mid-forties, Marta. I've been married and divorced twice. You already know that."

She nodded. "And I never could understand how either of your wives could bear to let you go."

"Ah," he murmured. "My ego needed that." He smiled, but it was a rather sad smile, and his blue eyes were so solemn that Marta felt a stirring of apprehension.

The apprehension was only heightened when Tony said quietly, "Tell me about New York, and Joshua Smith, darling."

Marta stared at him, miserable. This wasn't the way she'd intended their London reunion to go.

"Marta," Tony said patiently, "there's no need for you to look so guilty. You went to New York, you saw Smith..."

A small twinge of indignation flared. "You make it sound as if it were something prearranged, Tony."

"I'm sorry," Tony said, and he looked as if he was indeed sorry. "It's not my intention to make any accusations, darling, that would be the farthest thing from solving my—our—problem. I know you went to New York on business, essentially."

"Yes, and I had absolutely no intention of seeing Josh Smith while I was in the city," Marta stated firmly. "But..."

Suddenly the words began to tumble out of Marta like steam escaping from a boiler. "I...well, on the spur of the moment I called Jennifer Gundersen. Strictly spur of the moment, Tony—I want you to understand that. It had nothing to do with Josh. Though Jennifer *is* his sister, she's also one of my closest friends. I've told you about her.

"As it happened," Marta continued, "Kerry, Jennifer's husband, had a business appointment in New York, and she decided to go with him and take the twins. They planned to stay at Josh's apartment but she thought—I thought—Josh was in California. Anyway, she asked me to brunch..."

"Yes?" Tony prodded.

"I really wanted to see Jennifer and Kerry and to meet the twins, who are six months old now. So I said yes. Then Josh returned from California unexpectedly. When I reached the apartment, he was there."

Marta paused, finding this terribly difficult. She knew Tony was waiting for her to continue. She knew she had to continue. But she couldn't. Finally she met his eyes, glad that the room was dim enough to hide the tears that were threatening to overflow.

Tony interposed wryly. "I would take it that seeing Smith was . . . somewhat overwhelming."

"Yes," Marta whispered, shaken. "Oh, Tony, Tony. God, I'm so sorry."

Tony stirred his pink gin, sipped, stirred again. Then he said softly, "So am I, Marta. So am I. But to be truthful with you, I'm not completely surprised. I saw the expression on your face that night at the Forthingtons' when you looked at him. I saw what seeing him did to you, and a lot of things I'd wondered about came clear. As I told you in Washington, I'd always known there had been someone in your life you hadn't completely gotten over. There's been that . . . certain reserve about you that I never could fully get through, tender though you've been to me at times."

Tony smiled wryly. "Love can't be forced," he said simply.

"Tony. . ." Marta began, then halted, at a total loss for words.

Tony held up a restraining hand. "Don't blame yourself, Marta," he cautioned. "Some of this is my fault. I've . . . pressured you, I admit it. Sometimes you looked so lost and vulnerable, and I took advantage of that, even though I knew in my heart what it signified. I'd come to care so damned much about you. I *had* to try, as hard as I could. But now . . ."

"Yes?"

It hurt Marta to see Tony look so very sad. It hurt her to hear him remind her, "As I said a few moments ago . . . I've been married twice, darling. I think you can appreciate that, to put it very bluntly, I don't want a third marital failure on my record. People who move into the fourth-time-married class don't tend to carry around exemplary images, at least not in my opinion.

"This may sound strange, coming from me, but marriage means a great deal to me. My marriage to you would mean even more than the first or second time around. Marta, I'd want my marriage to you to have every possible chance to succeed."

Marta could barely form the words. "And you don't think it would?"

Tony beckoned the cocktail waitress to bring him a second pink gin before he answered her question. Then he asked levelly, "Do you?"

Marta closed her eyes tightly, feeling as if she'd reached the bottom of a deep, dark pit. She was hurting a man she cared a great deal about, one of the last persons in the world she'd want to hurt. Tautly she said, "Tony, I don't know. I'd give our marriage everything I possibly could..."

"Enough?"

Her lips twisted. "I don't know," she admitted bleakly. "Oh, God, I just don't know!"

"Thank you," Tony said, "for being honest. The only chance we have of making it at all is for both of us to be totally honest with each other."

"I've never lied to you, Tony." The fact was, Marta knew, she'd never lied to anyone. She hated liars.

"I know that," Tony said. "And I'm not asking you tell me anything but the truth now, regardless of my feelings." He hesitated, then stated rather than asked, "You do love him, don't you?"

"Yes," Marta admitted unhappily. "Yes, I love him. And I suppose I always will. But...there's no place in his life for me. He made that clear to me two years ago. And believe me, nothing has changed."

"Is he aware you love him?"

She shook her head. "No. Sometimes I doubt Josh believes in love. I don't know." She added helplessly, "There's so much I don't know, Tony. I'm only beginning to realize how much. And I feel so lost."

Tony reached a reassuring hand across the table, covered her hand with it. "Marta," he said with a faint smile, "there's no need for either of us to panic . . . or to do anything in a hurry."

"What do you mean?"

"I mean that we get along extremely well, darling. We have so much in common. I wanted to think that we shared the same kind of love. I now know . . . well, I know that we don't. In fact, I've known it ever since that night in Washington. But I'm old enough to appreciate that very good marriages can be based on caring and consideration."

The words were forced out of Marta. "I . . . I couldn't possibly marry you, Tony," she told him. "Not after this. You'd always know that you'd never have all of me. It would be so terribly unfair . . ."

"Perhaps," Tony said calmly. "Perhaps not. As I've said, there's no need for either of us to be impulsive, to make a spur of the moment decision we might both regret."

Marta had relinquished his hand and was twisting his ring around and around on her finger. Tony touched the ring gently, then said, "If you're thinking of returning it to me, please don't, Marta. Keep wearing it . . . at least awhile longer."

His smile was whimsical. "Put it down to my vanity, if you like, but please don't give the ring back until you've thought things through very carefully. You and I have mutual friends on both sides of the Atlantic. I shudder to think of the gossip that would circulate among them, and certainly all over the BBC, were the impression to be given that you'd flown back to London specifically to break our engagement."

"But I didn't," Marta protested.

"I know, darling, but that's the way it would appear. So for the moment, keep wearing my ring, will you, Marta? Meantime, when you go back to New York, I want you to see Smith."

"What?"

"Only if you put your reawakened feeling for him to a test will you ever know whether there's truly something still there or not, Marta. Old loves can seem so potent when they flare up...but often when one stirs the embers one finds there are only ashes left. So...give it a chance, Marta. Give us both a chance. Will you do that?"

Marta looked down at the diamond on her finger and felt surfeited by a mixture of sorrow, confusion...and relief. And she suddenly knew she was not ready to face up to friends and relatives, either, without that protective ring on her finger. Certainly she could not face up to Josh without it.

Though she couldn't have spelled out exactly why, she felt that there was safety to the diamond just now. False safety, maybe. But even so...

"Will you keep the ring on your finger till spring, Marta?" Tony asked gently. "Till we have time to reassess?"

Marta wiped a tear from the corner of her eyes. The diamond sparkled. "Yes, Tony," she promised.

Chapter Four

"Miss Brennan is on the phone."

Josh was reading an unsolicited article that had come in to *Living, American Style* "over the transom." It was good; he was seriously thinking about buying it, and had been making a few notes for possible revision.

He put his pen aside and stared at the intercom through which his secretary had just spoken. Then he focused on the telephone as if he were seeing a ghost, before he slowly picked up the receiver.

"Marta?"

"Hello, Josh."

Puzzled, he asked, "Where are you calling from?" He couldn't think of any reason she'd be calling him from London—she'd been gone only three days. It seemed a short length of time in which to see her fiancé, make wedding plans . . .

"I'm back in New York," Marta said.

"That was fast!"

"Yes, well . . . you said to call when I got back."

That was true enough. But Josh had expected her to be away longer. He'd thought he would have time to get his personal act together, including putting a strict rein on his emotions where Marta was concerned. Now . . . he wasn't ready for her.

Before he could formulate a sentence, Marta asked, "I was wondering if you might be free for lunch."

"Today?"

"Yes."

"Hold on a sec," Josh hedged, hastily glancing at his desk calendar. It was customarily blank until a three o'clock editorial conference.

"I could stop by your office and we could talk there, if you'd rather," Marta offered.

"No, lunch would be fine," he answered, then wished he'd taken her up on the latter suggestion. His office was an exceedingly functional place. No distracting bric-a-brac, no photographs, only a modest collection of reference books, a personal computer he rarely used. It reflected absolutely nothing of his personality, which was exactly the way he preferred it.

"How about L'Auberge?" he suggested. "I'll call and reserve a table."

"Fine, Josh. What time?"

"One o'clock?"

"I'll be there."

Their receivers clicked simultaneously. Josh pushed his chair away from his desk, sat back, and found himself studying the blotter, which was coffee stained and covered with pen and pencil marks. He told himself it was time to get a new blotter. Also, he needed a haircut. Also, he should stop by F.A.O. Schwarz and pick up something for the twins to take with him the next time he went to Watch Hill. Not that they didn't have enough toys, and six-month-old babies weren't that toy-receptive, anyway.

He thought about everything irrelevant he could think of, but it was impossible to avoid the current issue for very long. He reached for the phone again, dialed L'Auberge's number, asked for a table for two on the second floor, in the room with the fireplace.

Two hours later, Josh Smith was following a host to his table and wondering why he'd chosen this restaurant, this room. It was a delightful, high-ceilinged dining room with charming Victorian decor. Real logs—somewhat of a rarity for Manhattan—blazed in the marble-manteled fireplace. The setting was much too romantic.

Marta was already at their reserved table. She was staring at the hearth, so wistful and lovely in profile that Josh was staggered by the sight of her. Only the host's cheerful "This way, Monsieur Smith" motivated him to move forward again.

Marta had seldom looked so forlorn. Lost in thoughts Josh wished he could tune in on. When she became aware of his presence and turned to greet him, there was still a lingering sadness in her beautiful dark eyes.

What could Marta possibly have to be sad about? She was in love; she was engaged—Josh verified that the diamond still twinkled on her ring finger—she was soon to be married. She was a vibrant, exciting woman who'd always been innately comfortable with herself. That was one of the things he admired about her. And professionally she was right at the top, with no danger of falling off fame's fickle ladder, simply because she was too good at what she did.

Puzzled again, but conceding that Marta tended to puzzle him more than anyone he'd ever known, Josh sat down opposite her, and immediately came to the conclusion that she was exhausted. Her eyelids drooped, heavy with fatigue. And Marta never drooped.

"When did you get back?" he asked without preamble.

"Yesterday afternoon."

"Short stay, wasn't it?"

"I didn't intend it to be a long stay, Josh."

He wanted to ask if she'd finalized her wedding plans. He wanted to know if she really loved Tony Ashford, and if she would be happy living in London. He reminded himself sharply that none of that was any of his business, and instead asked her if she would care for a drink.

"Maybe Cinzano on the rocks," Marta said wearily.

Josh usually didn't drink at lunchtime. Alcohol taken at midday made him sleepy. Since he almost always had afternoon meetings scheduled, he needed to stay alert. But now, to his surprise, he found himself ordering a martini straight up.

Noting the smudges under Marta's dark eyes, he asked, "What's the problem? Jet lag?"

She smiled wryly. "Is it that obvious?"

"You look tired, that's all."

Marta managed a weak laugh. "Well, I guess I could use a few hours' sleep and a little system adjustment," she allowed. "Anyway..."

"Yes?"

Marta had noted Josh's covert glances at the diamond winking on her finger. He'd remained inscrutable as he'd done his looking, yet she was getting the impression the sight of the ring disturbed him.

That, from Josh, was an encouraging sign. Marta had seldom in her life wanted to do anything as much as she wanted right now to tell him her engagement to Tony was over. But she'd *promised* Tony to wear the ring till spring. She'd promised to give them both a chance, to see Josh again and make sure of her feelings. She'd been with Josh less than five minutes now, and the truth was already shouting silently deep within her. She loved him. There *was* no chance for Tony and her. And she felt sick about it.

Josh was eyeing her curiously, and she sought for a subject that might divert him before he asked a question she didn't want to answer. "Josh, are you going to do the politician story?" she queried.

Josh wasn't ready for the abrupt transition. He reminded himself that he would have to be especially sharp with Marta around. She had a way of tossing the ball *at* you, rather than to you, and you had to be ready to catch it—always.

"No," he said, shaking his head. "I've decided to shelve that particular story for the present. It would mean spending more travel time than I can work into my schedule." When she didn't comment, he continued, "Actually, I believe you yourself said we'd have to depict more than four demographic areas to represent the national scene accurately."

"Something like that, yes."

"Anyway, I have a dozen projects here in New York to deal with first. I mean, there's no way I could spend that much time away right now," Josh said, and wondered why he felt the need to be so apologetic. "It's not something I could take shortcuts with," he added.

"No, it isn't."

"Maybe in another year, I'll get around to doing it right. Plan it out more carefully, take the time..."

There was a small, silent interval. Then Marta said bluntly, "You don't have to invent excuses, Josh."

Josh was focusing on his martini glass, on the silverware, on the pristine white tablecloth—anywhere except on Marta's face. Now her tone and her statement forced him to look at her.

As he did so, he realized with a jolt that Marta, usually so in control of herself, was having a hard time keeping her own act together. Her lower lip was trembling ever so slightly. And was that a glint of moisture in her eyes? Marta Brennan was not the crying type.

Solicitude for her made Josh sound a shade too gentle as he said, "I'm not inventing excuses, Marta. I think if you really think about this, you'll agree with my rationale."

"No, Josh, I don't agree with your rationale," she informed him unsteadily. "Frankly, I wish you would just come out and say that you'd rather not have me do anything more for your magazine!"

Josh's surprise was genuine. "For one thing," he protested, "*Living* isn't *my* magazine. For another..."

He hesitated, recognizing that there was too much personal involvement clouding his thinking. He'd suggested the politician story in the first place, in a very off moment following his shock at seeing Marta's ring. It had been a ploy based on desperation. For even though logic told him the best thing that could happen for both of them would be for Marta to move to another country and marry someone else, his emotions had raised havoc at the mere idea. Almost immediately he'd recognized the folly of embarking on a traveling assignment with Marta. It would only mean further heartbreak.

In the end he'd evaluated the article idea from a professional point of view, and had concluded that this wasn't the right time to get into it. He'd been absolutely honest in what he'd told Marta. At the same time, again thinking strictly as an editor, he knew he would be doing his magazine a real disservice by refusing Marta Brennan an assignment. He didn't want to do that.

Josh was also painfully aware that his trump card, in maintaining professional and *personal* contact with Marta, was through the magazines. And though he despised himself for his weakness, that trump card was something he couldn't give up.

He broke the silence, trying for a light touch. "Hey, lady, you've got it all wrong," he said, accompanying his unlike-Josh protest with a rather silly smile that was also completely out of character. Then he added, "You've become famous, remember? Your name on a cover assures an automatic sellout. And like all editors, I am circulation-conscious."

For a moment he thought she was going to throw her vermouth at him. Instead she snapped, "Come off it, Josh! At least you used to level about things."

"I'm levelling now," he began sincerely, then stopped.

To his horror he saw he hadn't been wrong about that hint of moisture in Marta's eyes. Only now there were genuine tears spilling over and trickling down her pale cheeks. She reached for a handkerchief, daubed furiously at her eyes and got to her feet, nearly overturning her chair in her haste.

"Excuse me," she sputtered, and headed for the rest room.

Staring after her, Josh was dumbfounded.

Marta spent the next five minutes splashing cold water on her face and swearing under her breath as she berated herself for behaving like such an absolute fool in front of Josh.

The fact was . . . she was more than tired. She was exhausted. London and the scene with Tony had taken a terrific emotional toll.

Marta glanced down at the ring on her finger and was glad that she'd gone along with Tony's request to wear it for a while longer. It was protection, plain and simple. If Josh thought she was still engaged, her mounting determination to make a last-ditch stand aimed at getting him to come to his senses wouldn't be so obvious. If only he would toss aside his stubbornness and face up to the fact that they belonged together.

Marta picked up her handbag, knowing she still wasn't nearly as composed as she would like to be. But she couldn't spend the rest of the afternoon hiding from Josh.

He stood as she approached their table. "Are you okay?" he asked anxiously, his handsome face full of concern.

"Yes," she fibbed.

"Look, would you rather we cut out of here?"

And go where? she wondered, but did not pose the question. "No," she said, and resumed her seat.

The waiter was hovering. Josh asked, "Are you ready to order?"

"Yes."

She was aware of his worried eyes caressing her face. Right at that moment, she would have sworn that Josh loved her. But the moment passed quickly, and he again became as impenetrable as the Rock of Gibraltar, the Sphinx and Fort Knox put together.

Thinking that, Marta muttered something short and succinct under her breath.

Josh heard and glanced up, startled. "What was that all about?"

"Nothing," she said hastily. "I'll have the consommé madrilene, please."

"Anything else, mademoiselle?" the waiter asked.

"Nothing right now, thank you." She didn't want to say that she was too churned up emotionally to eat anything solid. "Maybe some dessert later."

Josh shot a speculative glance in her direction as he gave his order—a mushroom omelet. That was all.

Usually, Marta knew, Josh had a very healthy appetite. In fact, she sometimes wondered how he kept his trim physique, because he had a terrific sweet tooth, which he freely indulged. But he exercised regularly, despite his handicap. Or, perhaps more correctly, because of it. Worked out on Nautilus equipment and swam every other day at an athletic club he belonged to.

The fact that he'd settle for just an omelet clued her to the possibility that he, too, was on an uneven emotional keel. Even more surprising was his order for a second martini.

He fished out the olive and ate it. Then he said slowly, "While you were in the rest room, I thought of a story idea that might interest you."

"You don't have to conjure up assignments to appease me."

His mouth tightened. "Must you be so touchy?"

"That's funny, Josh, coming from you. You're the touchiest person I've ever known!"

Normally that would have caused him to glare at her. But now he said, almost mildly, "We're not here to discuss me. At least, I didn't think that's what you wanted to see me about."

He looked at her, and attempted another smile. It was again a rather poor excuse for a smile, and not at all like Josh. He wasn't a person who turned smiles off and on. His smiles were relatively infrequent. But when he did smile, it was like a day full of sunshine, dazzling and wonderful.

Oh, God! Marta thought helplessly. *Why do I have to love him so much?*

Her fingers trembled as she picked up her tumbler and drained the last of the vermouth.

Noting the gesture, Josh promptly asked, "Want another?"

"No, thanks. I'd go under the table." She paused, then admitted, "I guess I'm more tired than I realized, Josh. I guess it wasn't such a smart idea trying to get into business before I've gotten the jet lag out of my system."

Josh yearned to dispense with the table that separated them and to take Marta in his arms. Then he would get her out of this place and spirit her off to his apartment, where he would tuck her into his king-size bed and let her sleep until she was thoroughly rested. After which he would make love to her . . . again and again and again.

The concept was so powerful that Josh found himself suddenly swamped by a desire that threatened to rage out of control. It was already out of control in one very telltale way that made him glad the table he'd wanted to obliterate a moment ago was still in place. He needed its camouflage.

Josh yanked on his willpower. He had a considerable amount of it, but it still took all his effort to force his attention away from the physical and back toward the professional. In the process, he began to feel like a monk who'd been meditating on a lonely mountaintop for months.

It occurred to him that he'd been virtually living as a monk for much too long. Nothing wrong with that, if you were cut out to be a monk. But despite the wall of privacy he'd carefully built around himself starting twelve years ago, he'd never been one for the monastic life.

He cleared his throat, reached for his martini, reminded himself that he was in danger of getting blitzed. On the other hand, his adrenaline was flowing full force through his bloodstream. He both hoped and suspected that it was a lot stronger than the alcohol content in a couple of drinks.

Very carefully he said, "Marta, when we've finished lunch, I'm going to take you home."

"I don't have a home in New York."

Stubborn! The woman was stubborn. Josh had a sudden vision of Marta having a home in London. He gritted his teeth, then said as patiently as possible, "Okay, I'm going to take you back to your hotel and tuck you in."

"Am I losing my mind?" Marta pondered aloud. "Did you just say you're going to tuck me into bed?"

Josh ignored the edge to her voice, which he could easily have taken as sarcasm. "Yes, that's what I said," he told her gently. "You've had it. You need to sleep the clock around."

"Right now I don't think I could go to sleep. I'm too tired. And I . . ."

"Yes?"

It was devastating having Josh look at her the way he was right now. He had the most gorgeous gray eyes she'd ever seen, light and clear as London rain. Too often they were ice cold. But right now they were as warm and soft as a kitten's fur.

Emotionally she was feeling like a mound of spun sugar. Brittle, so easily shattered, so easily dissolved.

"Oh, God, Josh," she said, briefly releasing some of the tightness. "I just won't want to be alone in my damned hotel room, that's all. I guess I need a cocoon to crawl into. Are Jennifer and Kerry still at your place?"

"No," Josh said levelly. "They drove back to Watch Hill yesterday."

Marta saw Josh beckon the waiter, heard him ask for the check. He was only partway through his omelet, she'd barely touched her consommé. She started to protest that he should finish his lunch, but he wouldn't hear of it. She was glad to let him guide her toward a discreet back elevator—stairs were difficult for him—and a couple of minutes later they were side by side in a taxi.

Marta, slumped in a corner of the seat, couldn't figure out what was happening to her. She was in such a funny state. She thought of the old childhood query, "Funny ha-ha or funny peculiar?" This state she was in was definitely "funny peculiar." Nothing to laugh about. She'd never felt less like laughing.

She'd traveled extensively around the world during the past couple of years. She'd handled jet lag time and time again. Generally it didn't bother her much. Certainly not on the relatively short flight from London to New York.

It wasn't until the taxi whizzed past the hotel she was staying at that she realized she hadn't even heard the instructions Josh had given the driver. Then they were heading up Riverside Drive, and she knew—incredible though it was—that Josh was taking her to his apartment.

She preceded him into the marble foyer; they remained silent as the elevator ascended. She stood uncertainly at his door, watching him use his key.

"Come along," he said once inside. Then he led her down the hall into the living room and made the left turn that led to the master bedroom. His bedroom. At the threshold he gazed down at her and actually grinned.

"Stop looking like a lamb being led to slaughter," he teased.

Marta couldn't believe either the grin or the teasing...they were out of perspective. She felt as if she were peering through the wrong end of binoculars. But before she could speculate any more on Josh's unusual mood, it changed.

"Look, Marta...I know a lot's gone down between us," he said seriously. "But that's all in the past. Right now, I think what you need most is a friend. And I'd like to volunteer. Even at the worst of our times, I've always considered myself your friend."

Friend? At the airport in London where he'd seen her off, Tony had told her solemnly that no matter what happened between them he always wanted to be her friend. Now Josh was telling her the same thing. Only, Marta thought dizzily, it was one thing with Tony and something entirely different with Josh. She'd never thought of herself as Josh's friend. Though she was, of course, in the sense that she would do anything, anytime, to help him if he ever needed her.

So often, so very often, she'd actually prayed that Josh would suddenly realize he needed her and issue a summons. If that had ever happened, she would literally have dropped her camera where she stood and taken off....

She looked up at him helplessly. There was no way on earth or in heaven that she could ever negate her love for him—or the sexuality that had flowed between Josh and herself almost from the first moment they'd met.

She remembered that meeting vividly. She'd queried *Architecture, American Style* about doing a photo feature on a fabulous house she'd come across while vacationing in Florida. The architect, she thought, was exceptional, combining the best of several worlds in his concepts. Interested in her idea, Josh had arranged for his secretary to set up an appointment.

He had stood as she'd walked into his office. She'd noticed first how tall he was . . . and what a terrific physique he had. Broad shoulders, slim waist, a nice tautness about the way he was built. Then she'd noticed that special air he had about him—she called it a quiet gravity. A way he had of listening, as if what she was saying to him was the most important thing in the world.

As she sat across his desk from him, their eyes had met—and Marta had never felt the same since. A mythical Swiss carillon had started playing. Bells began to ring inside her head. As for her heart . . . her heart had been swamped by a tidal wave of pure joy. An exhilarating high had taken possession of her, making her feel as if her psyche were soaring to an altitude of at least fifty thousand feet.

By the time she'd realized that Josh had to use a cane to get around it had seemed . . . intriguing. Just one more unusual thing about a very unusual man.

"Marta?" he queried softly, breaking into her memory.

"Yes?"

She watched him move over to his closet and tug out a thick white terry robe. "Go take a good hot, soaking bath, then put this on," he ordered. "I'll turn on the electric blanket and draw the curtains. Crawl into bed and sleep till midnight, okay? Sleep all night if you can."

"But . . ."

"I have to go back to the office for a meeting that can't be cancelled at this late hour. But I won't be long. The answering machine is on, so ignore the phone if it rings.

Just go to sleep. When I get back, I'll be working in my study if you need anything," he continued. "I have several articles that need going over, and this'll give me the chance to catch up."

"Josh . . ."

He went on as if she hadn't spoken his name, "I'll order a pizza once you're awake again. But there's no hurry about that. I know a place that'll deliver until the small hours." He handed her the robe. "Okay?" he asked.

"Okay," she replied.

In the doorway he paused. Turning, he added hesitantly, "One thing, Marta."

"Yes?"

"Well, I wish Jennifer were here, because then . . . well, nobody could misunderstand any of this."

"What do you mean by that?"

Josh shifted his weight, leaned on his cane. Rather stiffly he said, "I suppose it might seem a bit odd to your fiancé, that's all. But then there's really no need for anyone but you and me to know about this particular little interlude, right?"

Marta smiled faintly. "So you're protecting my reputation. Is that it, Josh?"

"I was thinking about Tony Ashford," he said. "If I were engaged to you and I found out you'd spent a number of hours sleeping away your jet lag in another man's apartment, I might be a bit . . . upset."

Again Marta was terribly tempted to tell him that she and Tony were no longer engaged. But this was not the time for revelations. If Josh learned that she wasn't betrothed to another man, he might very well hustle her into a taxi and speed her back to her hotel!

As it was, he was lingering. And there was a sad sweetness on his face as he said, "Get some sleep."

Marta very nearly bridged the gap between them. If she hadn't been so tired, maybe she would have taken a chance, tried, at least. As it was, she mumbled only, "Thanks."

A half hour later, wrapped in Josh's terry robe, she was filling his prescription. She crawled into his bed and turned her face into his pillow, which smelled ever so slightly of him. Had she not been completely exhausted, the scent would have served as an aphrodisiac. It would have evoked a stirring, sensuous response.

Instead she quickly fell asleep.

Chapter Five

Josh's bed was positioned to take full advantage of the apartment's window view. Marta stirred, opened her eyes and saw the Palisades across on the Jersey shore twinkling with lights. For a moment she lay still, memories rushing over her in a warm wave. The last time she'd seen that view from this angle Josh's arm had been around her. They'd both gone to sleep as the sunset was lavishing molten gold over the Hudson. They'd awakened to a rhinestone-studded darkness, turned to each other and made love again.

Reviving the memories made Marta ache for Josh. And she was so used to having him far away that for a moment she forgot he actually was within hailing distance.

Unless, that is, he'd changed his mind about coming back to the apartment with her in it and had stayed at the office.

She stood, went to the window, and the ache for him grew within her. The lopsided moon hung over the Hudson; the stars and the planets were all in place. The lights, both celestial and man-made, shimmered across the river's black water. Everything seemed in sync in the world and its environs. Why was it all so wrong for her?

"Marta?" She felt as if she were hearing a ghost whisper her name through the darkness.

She stiffened, took a step back—and collided with Josh.

Josh's bedroom was carpeted with a wonderfully thick and soft material. Marta remembered vividly how luxurious it had felt to her bare feet when she would come to stand at this window after they had made love. She'd never tired of looking out at Josh's view. Now she discovered that the sensuous carpet was a soundproofer. Josh, literally, had sneaked up on her...though she was sure that "sneaking" was not what he'd had in mind as he'd come across to the window. Sneaking was not Josh's style.

Tilted slightly off balance, she felt his steadying arm. And suddenly it was as if she'd been a glacier and his touch was beginning to melt snow long trapped in hidden crevices. The warmth went through her in a wash of exquisite pain. She, who never cried, was suddenly blinded by tears, for the second time in one day. Inadvertently she sobbed, and Josh's hand tugged at her, urging her to turn around. When at first she resisted, the hand became considerably more insistent. Yielding, because she had no choice, she faced him in the moonlit dimness, and heard the sharp intake of his breath.

"My God!" he muttered disbelievingly. "You're crying again."

Marta closed her eyes, but the treacherous tears kept escaping. She heard Josh swear softly...then she felt both his arms close around her, and she was as lost as she'd ever been. She clung to him, letting the fabric of his shirt dry her cheeks, letting the warmth of his body and the clean, woodsy scent of him assuage her.

She heard him urge, "Look at me." Slowly she opened her eyes, and knew at once that she'd made a mistake. The moonlight made Josh's gray eyes appear silver and emphasized his fine features. Every facet of those features was beloved to her. And it was as right as rain to lift her face to his, and to meet his lips with hers. It was second nature to abandon herself to his touch, his kiss....

Josh broke off with a short expletive he didn't pull out of his everyday vocabulary.

He released her as if she'd burned him. She saw him grope for something on the bed, saw him retrieve the cane he must have tossed there. "I came to see if you were all right, that's all," he said stiffly.

"I...I know," Marta assured him shakily. And she did know. There had been nothing prearranged about Josh's seeking her out. He'd had no intention of initiating any lovemaking, no intention of even going so far as a kiss. She would have banked her life on that. She knew him so well.

"You've been out of it for hours," he said, his tone slightly milder.

Marta ran her fingers through her tousled hair, her gesture an unconsciously nervous one. "I must have been more tired than I realized," she admitted.

"I'd call it exhausted," Josh informed her briefly. He hesitated. "Look..."

"Yes?"

Marta didn't know what he'd been about to say, but she was sure he'd changed his thoughts in midstream when he stated, "I think we both need something to eat. I'll order up some pizza. Relax for a while longer, okay?"

She nodded without comment and turned back to the window. Josh hadn't said in so many words that he didn't want her to join him until the food came. Nevertheless he'd conveyed that message, and she could understand why. Dealing with food and drink would keep their hands and their mouths busy. Relieve some of the tension between them, maybe. Make it easier to get on a more casual course—not that she and Josh could ever follow a casual course for very long.

Frustrated, Marta clenched her hands... and felt something sharp dig her palm. She looked down at the twinkling diamond, and silently echoed the word Josh had spoken aloud just a few minutes before.

She was going to have to talk to Tony. She was going to have to tell him time wasn't going to do anything for the two of them. She was going to tell him that she'd stirred the ashes of her love for Josh... and found them only a light cover over a bank of glowing embers that could so easily burst into flames. It was unfair—unfair to Tony, even more than to herself, to go on with this sham engagement of theirs. She must make him see this. Nor did it matter how people might talk about them. The talk would soon die down.

Ending her engagement publicly would probably have very little to do with Josh and her, she conceded. She could be freer than air, and Josh, with careful deliberation, would undoubtedly still see to it that she was kept out of his life. But whether or not it mattered to him, he would at least know she didn't belong to someone else.

Whether or not it mattered to him? It *had* to matter to him, Marta thought savagely. That kiss a few moments ago had carried an emotional wallop that in no way could stem from indifference. Josh had been as aroused as she had.

Marta sank back on the bed, propped pillows under her head and, staring into the silver-tinted darkness, reminded herself that arousal didn't necessarily mean carving out a place in one's life for someone else. There were no permanent niches in Josh's life left to be filled. He'd made that so clear two years ago that she was not apt ever to forget even one crystal shard of the lesson he'd taught her.

Yet, she thought with a small, almost mischievous sense of satisfaction, she still did have *some* power over him, after all. Power enough to nudge him into doing something he'd had no intention of doing...such as kissing her with all that fire, all that pent-up passion. Josh was probably chastising the hell out of himself for that involuntary gesture. That kiss could have been quite an opening wedge in the shut door of their relationship if he wasn't possessed of an absolutely iron willpower.

After a time, Marta heard a doorbell ring and the voice of the pizza delivery boy. She got up and fussed with her face and hair so that she, too, would have more of a mask to hide behind when she rejoined Josh. She only hoped her façade would be some match for his.

Josh was, indeed, chastising the hell out of himself. He'd gone to the kitchen after leaving Marta, had poured himself a shot of straight Scotch and had downed it without even bothering with a chaser.

Then he sat down at the round kitchen table and yielded to the impulse of burying his head in his hands.

He couldn't *believe* he'd taken Marta in his arms and kissed her like that. But when he saw her tears shimmering in the moonlight, all his mental armor plating suddenly slid away.

The touch of her, the feel of her, the soft, musky scent of her, had driven him nearly crazy. And their kiss had plunged him so close to the edge he still wasn't sure how he'd managed to pull back in time. Reflex action, he supposed grimly. Habit. He'd conditioned himself so long, so hard, to resist Marta that—fortunately for both of them—he'd retrieved enough of his armor plates, though certainly not all of them, to put a stop to things.

Josh straightened, shook his head like a man coming out of a daze and absently rubbed his left thigh. The leg was hurting the way it did when he was very tired, or had really overdone it, or had become wrung out emotionally, which was the diagnosis in this instance. He'd learned long since—a lesson Marta had unwittingly but thoroughly taught him—that emotional tension and frustration had a direct link to physical pain. Probably a result of unconscious muscle tensing, he supposed.

He'd dug a bottle of burgundy out of his small wine closet, opened it so it could breathe a bit and had put two long-stemmed glasses on the kitchen table next to the wine bottle, when the doorbell rang. As he paid the delivery boy and then carried the pizza into the kitchen, he was hoping that Marta had heard the bell, too. He didn't want to have to go in search of her—the moonlit bedroom just now was as dangerous as a field full of unexploded mines.

It was a relief when Marta appeared, and they sat down at the table together. As he served up a couple of slices of pizza, Josh took a quick but all-appraising survey of her. He discovered that despite the long sleep she looked as exhausted as she had when he'd met her for lunch. Fatigue shadows bruised that soft area under her eyes he loved to kiss—*had* loved to kiss, he amended quickly—and those eyes were lackluster, whereas the eyes he was accustomed to almost always sparkled, either with delight, with fury, with indignation, with some very definite mood, to be sure. Which, after all, was Marta. The way she was. The way he loved her to be.

He saw her lift her wineglass, and the damnable diamond sparkled on her ring finger. He tensed, felt a resulting bolt of pain knife through his bad leg, and silently cursed. He was going to have to do better than this!

He plunged into the first thing he could think of, the need for some dialogue between them urgent since his thoughts were impossible to deal with right now. "How long are you going to be in town?" he asked her.

Marta seemed to be staring into space as she sipped her wine. Or else she was gazing fixedly at a spot a couple of feet above Josh's head. And he happened to know there was nothing but blank wall there.

"I suppose," he persisted, "you have a full schedule lined up."

"Mmm," Marta said, taking another sip of wine before continuing. "Relatively so. I've been holding a couple of ideas in abeyance for quite a while, and I should either get on with them or abandon them."

"Only you could keep editors waiting like that," Josh observed without the acidity he might have expressed had someone else followed a professional behavior pattern similar to Marta's. As it happened, her work was well worth waiting for.

"There was never a deadline involved in these things," Marta returned noncommittally.

"Well, then," Josh began. He paused to wonder, briefly, why he didn't shut up right now. Why was he persisting in wading into deeper waters in a situation where there was no chance of ever emerging? He was certain to plunge in over his head yet again, he thought. But he couldn't seem to stop himself.

"Well," he began, "I have something I thought I'd put to you ... for *Living, American Style*, that is."

"Oh?" Marta said, and even a psychic couldn't have judged whether she was in the least interested in hearing what Josh had to say.

"The story I have in mind involves what I'm calling 'Transitional Life-styles,'" he went on doggedly. "I've been noticing the pattern to contemporary moving habits..."

"Moving habits?"

At least she was listening to him, Josh decided. "Yes. Young couples tend to start out in the city, maybe in small apartments. Then they move to the suburbs, maybe once a kid is on the way. Then, as the family grows and the couple prosper, to the exurbs. Even the country, relatively speaking. The father makes a long commute..."

"What about the mother?" Marta queried.

Josh got the message. "Okay, so the mother makes a long commute, too. Essentially, though, these people are living rural types of lives, compared to the way they started out. You'll find the husbands and wives, though their jobs are in the city, begin to take active interests in local community affairs, small-town politics, school boards and so forth. In short, they trade the bright lights for quite a different kind of existence."

"Mmm." Marta nodded.

"The kids grow up, of course, go off. Retirement comes..."

"Aren't you thinking of awfully stereotyped people?" Marta questioned.

"Marta, most people retire."

"I can't imagine ever retiring."

"Most people *want* to retire," Josh informed her patiently. "It's like the pot of gold at the end of the rainbow. The rainbow's been great, but once they get into the pot of gold they can sit back and do all the things they've wanted to do and never had time for...."

She looked at him skeptically. "That sounds great. But judging from the people I've interviewed, it isn't always what comes to pass, Josh, my love."

There'd been a time when she'd often called him "Josh, my love," uttering the three words as if they were one. For Josh, hearing the trio again was like encountering a sudden emotional roadblock. He very nearly ran into it, but stopped and got hold of himself just in time. "Marta, just go with me in this, okay?" he continued.

"Okay."

"I admit there are a lot of variations on this theme. For the sake of a story, though, I need to tie this down to a premise. Right?"

"If you say so."

"Well, if you're so damned indifferent about it maybe I'd better stop boring you," Josh gritted out, this whole scene suddenly getting to him. Even an iceberg could only hold up so long.

"You're not boring me, Josh," Marta told him, sounding faintly surprised. "Go on, will you."

"Generally speaking," Josh went on after a rather taut moment when he almost decided not to continue, "for either personal or economic reasons the dream house becomes too big. Maybe the novelty of small-town or suburban life and politics wears off. The city begins to appeal again. Basically cities are easier to live in—at least that's my reasoning. Let's say you live in a condo, everything's done for you. You don't have to worry about heat and hot water and all that kind of thing...."

"Maybe you don't," Marta stated, "but I've done my share of worrying about heat and hot water and a lot of other things when I was living right here in Manhattan."

"When you were sharing that loft down in Soho with that other photographer, I suppose," Josh said darkly. "What was his name?"

"What *was* his name, Josh?" Marta couldn't suppress the urge to tease.

"Okay, his name was Stan," Josh said, the beautiful, mobile mouth Marta loved so much becoming set in what she could only describe as an extremely stubborn line.

She nearly chuckled aloud. It was ridiculous to feel this sense of victory because Josh was still jealous of her old housemate, Stan. Stan was a big, amiable photographer-artist who'd needed the skylight of the Soho loft for his painting. They'd both needed the space for their photographic work, and there'd even been an old double laundry tub—how it had ever gotten there Marta never did find out—she'd used, with implementation, for her developing. In fact, with those primitive contrivances she'd turned out some of the best black-and-white pictures she'd ever taken, Marta thought nostalgically.

Probably nothing in the history of the world had ever been more platonic than her relationship with Stan, she remembered now. Stan had only been attracted to her on those occasions when she'd cooked something and offered to share it with him. He'd had an insatiable appetite and not much money with which to appease it. They'd both been mainly concerned with coughing up their shares of the rent.

She had been "living" with Stan when she first met Josh, and she could remember Josh's reaction when he'd learned she had a male roommate. She would have sworn she'd seen flashes of emerald in those cool, gray eyes, and she'd loved it. She took a long look at Josh now, and maybe it was a trick of light, but it was easy to imagine a few green flares.

She said, keeping her enjoyment under wraps, "We did have a few heating and plumbing problems down in Soho, yes. Other places I've lived, too, I..."

"It's where you've lived," Josh said abruptly.

For a moment, Marta thought he was going to add "and with whom," and she nearly chuckled aloud.

"Anyway," Josh went on, "in 'Transitions' my people opt to go back to the city for its conveniences, the proximity to all the facilities they may need and want, the cultural advantages, the whole gamut. Which completes the circle."

"Doesn't it sometimes work in reverse?" Marta asked him.

"What do you mean?"

"Well, how about people who start out on farms, or in the country, and their big aim is to move into the city while they're young. They even raise their kids in the city. People do raise kids in the city, you know. They become affluent enough, maybe, to have a summer place somewhere, like up on Cape Cod or down on the Jersey coast...or wherever. But later in life, with the kids grown, they yearn to get back to the wide-open spaces. Or maybe the small town, where they'll be more intimately involved in things. Though in my opinion, Josh, cities are merely series of small towns strung together. You might think that concept over. There could be a story idea there."

"Thank you," Josh said rather coldly, "and I'll put the thought in my mental file, Marta. About cities being a series of small towns strung together, that is. It's not a bad idea. However..."

"First things first?"

"Yes, if you want to put it that way," he agreed stiffly.

"Matter of fact," he added when she didn't answer him at once, "I'd rather like to see 'Transitional Life-styles' in a fall issue of *Living*. My thought is to feature six different couples... different backgrounds and economic statuses. Some professional, some nonprofessional. Some with kids, some childless."

"Would all this be wrapped into a single story, or are you considering six separate stories?"

"Six separate stories with a central piece that would wrap up the whole theme. The six separate stories would be on the short side...each featuring an applicable photo layout. The central story would use photos highlighting the six couples... maybe emphasizing common denominators. I haven't thought that through yet."

"There'd be quite a lot of picture taking involved," Marta pointed out.

"Yes."

"You're going to write this one yourself?"

"Certainly the central piece, at least. But even if I farm out the individual pieces, I'm going to keep close tabs on them."

That meant they would be together a lot if she elected to take on the assignment. Marta thought about that and nearly went overboard with enthusiasm personally. Then she bumped into the professional side of her nature and had to say honestly, "I'm not sure this one's for me, Josh."

"Oh?"

"I can see the merit of the idea, and I'm sure that done the way you'd handle it, the result would be excellent—" Marta began.

But Josh cut her short. "Spare the flattery, Marta," he advised her roughly. "If you think it's a lousy idea, just come out and say so."

"It's not a lousy idea, Josh. I'm just not sure it's for me," she said honestly.

Josh poured himself another glass of wine, noted Marta's glass and poured one for her, too. That was enough to give him away, as far as Marta was concerned. He was innately polite; when in full control it would never have occurred to him to pour his own wine before checking on hers. Guests always received his full measure of courteous attention. And that's what she was, wasn't she? A guest?

"I suppose I should thank you for being so frank," he said. "In fact...I do thank you, though I disagree with you. I think you could do a great job with this. Focusing on people is very much your thing. I don't think I need to tell you that."

"I'm not sure I would find the people you plan to deal with sufficiently...stimulating," Marta hedged.

Josh shot her a quick look, his eloquent eyebrows slightly raised. "That sounds pretty snobbish," he informed her.

"I don't mean it to be. These past couple of years, Josh, I've worked in all sorts of places under all sorts of conditions."

"I know that."

Did that mean he followed her work as closely as she liked to think he might? That he cared about what she was doing, perhaps not just professionally but personally, as well?

Of course he cares about what's happening with you, idiot, the small silent voice came from out of nowhere. *Just as you care about what's happening with him. But that still doesn't build a bridge across this chasm between the two of you.*

"I've found that maybe I do best where there's been a certain amount of suffering involved," she said carefully.

"You like to follow in the wake of revolutions, catastrophes and other such happenings, is that it?"

It was Marta's turn to stiffen. "I don't like the way you say that, Josh," she warned. "I don't envision myself as some kind of Calamity Jane."

"Okay, okay. Are you saying, though, that the kind of people I'm talking about have experienced no suffering in their lives, Marta?"

"Not the same kind of suffering," she allowed cautiously.

Josh scowled at her. "The hell they haven't," he stated crisply. "Marta, I don't think there's ever been a person on earth who hasn't gone through a hell of a lot in one way or another on the way from birth to death. When you go into a war-stricken village or a town that's just been hit by an earthquake, you're seeing something overwhelming, to be sure. Raw, human misery...and yes, you capture that magnificently in your camera lens. And I'm not negating the agony, the horror of what you're talking about. But sometimes quiet suffering can be even more profound. Sometimes emotional and mental suffering can be even more overwhelming than physical suffering. What you're talking about is drama, the distillation of an experience. Like what happens in an accident..."

Marta saw the expression on Josh's face and knew that whether it was his intention or not, he was being personal

right now, very personal. Never once had he talked to her
about the jet trainer crash in which he'd been so severely
injured. In minutes the whole course of his life had been
completely changed. Once or twice she'd tried to steer toward the subject. But even when they'd been the most intimate he'd always turned the conversation around so
she'd never gotten even close. It had been his private ta-
boo.

She saw him lean back, saw the spasm of pain that
passed over his face very quickly, saw him close his eyes,
and knew this was physical pain she was witnessing, which
daunted her. The result of that awful crash, his damaged
leg, was something Josh never talked about, either. That
she'd learned early on. And if he still suffered from it at
all, it was something he'd camouflaged completely—until now.

Disturbed, she stirred restlessly, then couldn't suppress
the question. "What is it, Josh?"

He opened his eyes. "What is what?"

She dared. "Just then," she said, "you looked as if you
were hurting."

"I'm fine, thank you," Josh informed her coolly. "I
was trying to make a point, but there's no reason to build
up a case if the assignment idea doesn't appeal to you,
Marta. In fact, I suggest we drop it."

There was a finality to the way he spoke, and Marta's
heart sank when she heard it. On a personal level, she'd
been written off by Josh before. Now she felt he was
about to write her off professionally, as well.

She couldn't let that happen. On the other hand, she
couldn't in all fairness embark on the project he was suggesting with unqualified enthusiasm.

She had to come up with an idea of her own, and
quickly, Marta thought feverishly. And suddenly the

conversation she'd had with Jennifer that recent Sunday here in Josh's apartment came back to her.

They'd talked about Josh and the way his handicap affected him. About the way he'd shut her out. Jennifer knew more about that than anyone else, and had always stuck by Marta. Now Marta remembered remarking that many handicapped people achieved highly successful marriages. She'd admitted at the time that it wasn't a fact apt to make much difference in her relationship with Josh, who resolutely steered his own course. But still...there was a potential for a heartwarming series in the idea itself.

Did she dare suggest it?

Josh said, "I recognize that expression on your face, Marta. You're brimming over with something. What is it?"

"Just a...thought," Marta temporized, already beginning to see the risks of suggesting this idea.

"About something for *Living*?"

"Yes."

"So, what is it?"

"Please hear me out before you leap to any conclusions, Josh," Marta urged him.

"Why should I leap to any conclusions?"

"What I'm saying is...just hear me out, all right? As you know, for the past few years there's been a decided increase in concern about the rights of the handicapped and in putting across concepts designed to improve the life-styles of people with physical problems."

Marta didn't dare look at him.

"Mainly the physical improvements have been emphasized—special parking places, ramps, adequate rest room facilities, doors wide enough to admit wheelchairs, and all the rest of it—and that's fine. But I think there's a lot to be dealt with on the other side of the coin."

"What other side of the coin?"

There was nothing to be read at all in the tone of Josh's voice...and, knowing him as she did, that did nothing to reassure Marta.

"Well," she said, "the personal side. Emotional side. I think this could be a very upbeat series, Josh. Dealing with people who, though handicapped, have done marvelous things with their lives and achieved highly successful relationships. Marriage. Parenthood. Becoming forces in their communities."

"I don't really see the parallel you seem to between the concept I discussed with you, and an article on how the handicapped cope," Josh stated politely.

Marta could hear the warning bells, but she went on, "Not just 'cope,' Josh. There's so much more than that...."

"Forget it," Josh advised her icily. "I'm sure there are magazines for the handicapped that would be happy to consider such a piece, especially with you as the photographer," he added, his words small, glacial chips. "I certainly do not feel that it would be material for *Living*, nor would I personally be interested in delving into such a subject."

Marta could feel the frigid air creeping between them, and it engulfed her as he finished, "It's enough to deal with a handicap on an individual basis, Marta. The thought of wallowing in a mass attack of the subject doesn't thrill me in the least."

Chapter Six

Marta was determined not to cry again in front of Josh. She couldn't understand what was happening to her. She was reaching the edge of tears frequently, and that was very unlike her. She'd gone through all sorts of experiences absolutely dry-eyed. Even on that terrible night when Josh had cast her out of his life she'd stalked from his apartment blazing with anger, resentment, frustration, but there had been no tears.

Now it was as though she were going through a major chemical change. As if her body—as well as her heart—were urging to her to let go, to let it all out. She could imagine flooding the Hudson were she able to funnel all the tears she wanted to shed through Josh's windows and into the river.

Josh broke the silence between them. "Your pizza must be freezing. Want me to zap it in the micro?"

Marta shook her head. She'd barely touched the pizza, but even the thought of swallowing another morsel made her want to choke. "No, thanks," she said. "I'm not hungry."

"I've hurt your feelings," Josh decided.

Few things he could have said would have surprised Marta more. She could remember past occasions when he'd definitely bruised her feelings, must have known it, but certainly had never been moved to acknowledge it. His last statement was almost . . . well, close to . . . an apology.

"Look, Marta," he continued, "I didn't mean to come on so strong. I admit, you hit on a touchy subject with me."

That was quite an admission, coming from Josh. Marta eyed him narrowly. Was he, too, suffering a few chemical changes?

"I think," Josh said slowly, "maybe we'd better try for something else."

So . . . he wasn't writing her off. Marta instantly felt better and gathered up her lost gumption. "Josh," she said, "let me do some further thinking before you toss out any more ideas to me. What I'm saying is, I'm having second thoughts about your 'Transitional Life-styles' concept."

"Oh?" Josh queried, and she couldn't blame him for sounding suspicious.

"You're right," Marta conceded, and actually he was. "I may be off base in my attitude, because, as you've pointed out, I've concentrated on catastrophe so much these past couple of years."

That, she had to admit, was true. For the past two years, she had angled for any assignment that would take her to places where there were major happenings, major chaos. She had needed to be lost in areas that took her completely outside herself, where there was constant tension, danger, tragedy, dramas beyond belief being enacted on a minute-by-minute basis. Having a full load of such harrowing work on her agenda had somehow lessened her own personal sorrow. It had kept her going, kept her—for stretches of time, anyway—from thinking about Josh.

Then, in the in-between times in London, there had been Tony. Always there when she wanted him and needed him. Lavishing attention and affection on her. Gracious and urbane and charming and witty, Tony—for small stretches of time—had enabled her to go to bed without falling asleep thinking of Josh, dreaming about him and waking up thinking about him all over again.

"You don't have to mollify me, Marta." Josh softly interrupted her thoughts. "It's I who hurt your feelings, not the other way around."

"Josh, I'm used to rejection," Marta said quickly. She was speaking about professional rejection, but somehow what she was saying became hung up on a personal tree, and her cheeks flushed. She added, to clarify, "At least I was—and for a long time, too, when I was starting out."

Josh let the implication, and her flushed face, pass. "I imagine few editors would even think about rejecting a Marta Brennan idea," he said smoothly. "In fact, I've probably just given you a first, in that respect, in quite a while."

He had, but she wasn't about to say so. Just *thinking* about the story idea she'd suggested to him was becoming so embarrassing she felt herself beginning to flush all over again. How could she ever have thought of suggesting a series about success among the handicapped to Josh of all people? It had been inexpressibly gauche of her...even though she had only wanted to make Josh aware of his real worth. She should have known better. Much better.

Still painfully conscious of her gaffe, she forced herself to return to Josh's story idea. "I'm not trying to mollify you," she told him. "There'd be no point to that." Which was true enough. "It would show in my work if I approached an assignment tongue-in-cheek. I won't say I'll do 'Transitions' with you unless I'm sure it's right."

"Fair enough," Josh agreed, more easily than she'd expected him to. He rose slowly. "I guess I'd better see about getting you back to your hotel," he suggested.

How could she possibly have forgotten that she had a spacious, beautifully appointed room in an exclusive, midtown hotel? Though they'd never "lived" together, it was so *natural* to be here with Josh. In another era she'd have stayed through the night on an occasion like this.

Hastily she said, "If you'll call a cab, that will be fine."

When the doorman rang up to say the taxi was at the front door, Josh insisted on going downstairs with Marta. The night was icy cold, and as he followed her outside she remonstrated, "At least you could have put a topcoat on."

"I'm going right back in," he said. He held the cab door for her; she had to brush close to him to get in. Crazy, how even the slightest contact with him could make her feel warm on a frigid February night, she thought, and was annoyed at herself because she reacted so instantly and so intensely to Josh.

"Try to get some sleep," he said. "Sleep late as you can, in fact, and order up some breakfast. And then eat it, okay?"

He was talking to her as a brother. Marta recognized the tone of voice. All her life, her brothers had been trying to tell her what to do whenever they had the chance. Which, more's the pity, wasn't often. These days she didn't get back to her hometown in Pennsylvania nearly as frequently as she wished she could.

But then Josh leaned over and kissed her swiftly, and light though the kiss was, there was nothing brotherly about it. "I'll call you at your hotel in the morning," he told her, an odd huskiness to his voice. "Meantime, do some thinking about 'Transitions,'" he added, "and we'll see what we come up with."

With that last statement, Josh seemed very much an editor, and this helped put Marta back on an even keel. Even so, by the time she reached her hotel room, she felt shaky. Tonight's experience was catching up with her.

The message light was blinking on the phone. She checked the desk and found that Tony had called from London three different times. A glance at the clock told her it was much too early in the morning in England to return his call, which was just as well. Right now she wasn't up to dealing with what she needed to tell Tony. In fact, it was going to be difficult at any time to say what she had to over the phone. Much as she dreaded the thought of it, they needed to meet in person. She would return his ring and hope that he wouldn't be too angry at her, so that they could remain friends.

That night Marta didn't dream of Josh, but of diamonds. Mines full of diamonds, with grimy-faced laborers working to unearth the gems that, once dug out, were fully cut and sparkled brilliantly. Finally the whole world was full of sparkling diamonds, whirling around and around and around. And Marta was frantically trying to catch a fistful of them, because she needed to give them to Josh. But when her fingers at last clutched a stone, it turned to dust at her touch.

* * *

As if Josh had her room wired for video so that he could keep tabs on her every move, Marta obediently ordered up a breakfast the next morning and forced herself to eat it. She was on the second cup of coffee, when the phone rang.

"I hope I didn't wake you up," Josh said.

"No, I've been up for ages."

"You shouldn't have been. Look, Marta, I have an idea."

"Yes?"

"It might be easier for both of us to come to a conclusion about 'Transitions' if we visit one of the couples I have on my list of candidates."

"You already have a candidate list?"

"Yes," he admitted. "I've had some staff members looking around. So I have a fair-size dossier at this point. I've been trying to weed it down to a manageable number from which we can extract six finalists—if we both feel there should be a green light on this project, that is. I know this is a decision we'll have to make without too much delay because of your own schedule."

"My schedule?"

"You do need to get back to London for your wedding, don't you?"

Trapped, Marta said reluctantly, "Tony and I don't plan to be married until late spring at the earliest." This was not the moment, definitely not the moment, to reveal her sham engagement.

"Well, say that's two—even two and a half—months from now," Josh tabulated. "That doesn't give us an overabundance of time, especially since I know you have a couple of other stories you want to do out of New York."

"About visiting one of the couples," Marta reminded him. "Who and where?"

"The wife in question is a successful architect," Josh told her. "One of the staffers ran across her in the course of doing a story for our companion magazine. Her husband is an inventor. Toys and games, I gather. What happened in this instance is that when these people moved from the city to the relatively rural area, she was the one who had to face the daily commute, while he could work primarily out of a studio in his own home.

"Now she wants to semi-retire and work at home herself. They both feel a need for a change of living place. They had three kids, who are now grown, married, and have moved away. They admit that without the stimulus of the kids, life gets flat for them at moments. They think getting back to the city, where they'll be more in the mainstream of action, will resolve that."

"How are they going to find a place in the city big enough for both of them to work in?" Marta asked.

"That's something you can ask them when you meet them," Josh told her. "I phoned them before I called you to find out if they might be available to talk to us today. The husband's recovering from some minor surgery and the wife took a short leave of absence from her firm to be with him. They'd be happy to see us. If you're free, of course."

"Where do they live?"

"Upstate, about eighty miles from here."

"Would we take the train?"

"We'll drive," Josh stated. "The roads are clear—I checked—and there's no snow forecast. Upstate, it should be a regular winter wonderland."

* * *

It was every bit the winter wonderland Josh had promised. The small towns were Christmas card material, while the open country vistas, with snow-frosted farmhouses and barns and fields covered with white blankets, brought to mind winter paintings by master artists. Josh had a comfortable Mercedes, and he was an excellent driver. As the miles slipped by, Marta felt herself relaxing, and made a quick decision.

Nothing, nobody, could take this day with Josh away from her. And so she was going to enjoy every minute of it.

At Josh's suggestion, they paused for a sandwich and coffee before they made their call on Arnold and Lucille Grant, the couple to be interviewed.

After showing Marta and Josh around their beautiful, fifteen-room house—with an adjacent studio for Arnie—the Grants proffered homemade pound cake and an excellent port wine. By the time Marta finished that repast, she felt so tension-free she could have curled up and taken a nap.

She and Josh stayed with the Grants for nearly three hours, and found them charming, interesting, vital people who—though in their late fifties—were entirely contemporary in their outlook and opinions. They'd had their share of personal tragedy—their eldest son had been killed in Vietnam—and their share of professional frustration.

After they'd been talking for a while, Marta produced the camera she always carried with her and she took a few photographs. Glancing at Josh, she saw a gleam of pleasure in his gray eyes as he watched her at work.

Until then it hadn't really hit her how much he wanted her to work on this story with him. *This* story? Or simply, *a* story? It could be because he wanted her work in

Living again, she conceded. That made more sense than assuming he wanted to work with her because he wanted to be with her.

Yet she couldn't help but wonder. . . .

She was still wondering as they started the drive back to the city. The days were short this time of year. Dusk was already brushing the countryside, creating interesting effects on the snowy fields, barns and houses. Marta was distracted temporarily by the scenes unfolding before her. She was tempted to ask Josh to pull over and let her out of the car for a while so that she could take a few shots. But she didn't want her work to intrude just now. There would be other times to photograph snow scenes.

Josh, who'd been much absorbed in his own thoughts, suddenly suggested, "How about stopping along the way for a drink and a few appetizers? Then we can have dinner after we get back to Manhattan."

Marta chuckled. "I don't believe you," she told him. "You pigged out on three pieces of cake at the Grants', and you had lunch just a short time before that." She surveyed him. "You should be fatter than five pigs."

"You should be one-hundredth as fat as a pig!"

"Josh, I'm just naturally slim."

"Slim? Is that what you call it?"

Exasperated, she sputtered, "Damn it, Josh, why are you always poking fun at the way I look?"

Genuine surprise laced his voice. "I wasn't aware that I ever poked fun at the way you look," he said seriously. "I worry because you really are too thin, though believe me, I know half the women in the world would give those proverbial eyeteeth to have a figure like yours. I guess I'm just afraid that if you ever got sick or anything you'd have very little resistance. . . ."

Josh's words trailed off, and he became very busy concentrating on the road ahead—even though right now his was the only car on it.

Josh was worried about her? Josh was afraid for her? Dazed, Marta tried to remember exactly what he'd just said. Had he put it in the past tense? No...she was almost certain Josh had been speaking in the present.

She tried to concentrate on what she, at least, considered a mundane topic of conversation. "I never try to diet, Josh," she said. "I guess sometimes I get so busy I go without eating, but I catch up sooner or later."

"I doubt that."

"I'm healthy as ten horses, though," she promised him. "Anyway, I guess we're both lucky we don't have to try to keep slim."

"I definitely have to try to keep slim," Josh confessed, to her surprise. "Because, as you may have noticed, I tend to eat as much as ten horses, and my job is mostly sedentary—except when I go off on an occasional excursion like this one."

He didn't add that his handicap prevented him from getting the kind of exercise he'd once enjoyed. Marta felt a twinge of pity for Josh because he was so limited in the physical activities he could pursue, but then she squashed the twinge fiercely. Josh neither wanted nor needed her pity, or anyone else's.

Lightly she said, "You follow a pretty rugged exercise program, though, don't you?" And when he nodded, she admitted, "I don't know if I'd have the self-discipline to do that sort of exercise on a regular basis."

"Well, you have a wider range of choices," Josh said with surprising calmness, and again Marta couldn't believe what she was hearing. It was one of the closest references he'd ever made to his handicap. And as Josh spotted the welcoming lights of an inn off to one side of the road and drove into the parking lot, she wondered if this could possibly be a sign of recent progress. Was Josh maybe, just maybe, going to knock a few stones out of the wall he'd so carefully constructed around himself?

It was too much to hope for, she decided as she sat down opposite him in a booth padded in soft blue leather. She watched the way the waitress responded to his smile...par for the course when it came to the way all women responded to Josh Smith's charisma. He ordered a Scotch and soda for himself and, at Marta's request, Perrier with a slice of lime for her, plus an assortment of appetizers to share.

The inn was charming, with dark beams across the ceiling, whitewashed walls, maple furniture, hanging copper pots and a huge blaze roaring in the big fireplace. Again that surprising feeling of relaxation crept over Marta. She felt the tension ebbing out of her bones. In another minute she'd be purring, she told herself, and smiled at the thought.

Josh caught the smile and asked, "What's so amusing?"

"Nothing's amusing, really. Nothing specific, that is. This has been such a...very nice day, that's all," Marta said, and hoped that Josh wouldn't make some remark to spoil her mood. At times he had a talent for doing exactly that.

He didn't. Rather he said softly, "Yes, it has been." Then his tone became brisker. "I like the Grants. Didn't you?"

"Yes, I did. But I think they should stay where they are and not move back to the city."

"They feel they're lost in space in that big house, Marta."

"Only because Mrs. Grant hasn't started working at home. Once she does, she'll need her elbow room just as her husband does. That house is perfect for them. He already has his studio exactly as he wants it. She can set up her working quarters on the opposite side. There's an ell that would be perfect for an architect's studio—good light and plenty of space for drawing boards."

"Well, you did take it all in, didn't you?" Josh commented.

"Yes. I liked them. I thought about what they're planning to do. Wondered if they've really considered all the options."

"They're intelligent people, Marta. I would say they have."

"Even intelligent people make mistakes in life, Josh. Maybe that's especially true of intelligent people."

Josh smiled. "Maybe I'm choosing the wrong approach with this series."

"No, you're choosing the right approach. It's just that I think the Grants might make the wrong move, that's all. But...it is their decision, after all, and we should get some good pictures to go along with your story about them."

"I think I *will* do the Grant piece myself," Josh said. "Marta...does what you just said mean you're giving me an affirmative on 'Transitions'?"

She nodded. "Yes. I think you must have realized I was hooked fifteen minutes after we stepped into the Grants' house."

"I hoped you were hooked," Josh said, without looking at her. "I'll start mapping out a plan of action tomorrow. I'm going to try to narrow down the list to the six finalists. You might glance over the material I have and give me your thoughts."

"I'd be glad to do that, if you'd like me to."

"I'd like you to. Then as quickly as possible we can arrange other appointments. You might prefer to go with the writer, at least on an initial visit. After that, it might be best if you went on your own. Whichever way, I don't want to hold you up. I know you have only so much time to give this project."

"I'll allow all the time needed," Marta said, but she felt a sharp pang of disappointment as she uttered the words. That was foolish of her, she acknowledged, because Josh had made it plain from the beginning that he was going to assign writers to most of the separate stories. Still, he'd be involved himself in writing the central one, and now the story on the Grants, as well.

It occurred to her that he was the one who lacked extra time. She knew from past experience how busy he was in his job. She could imagine how things must have piled up on his desk in his absence today.

Two years ago he'd been *an* editor at *Living*. Now he was *the* editor. Which meant that he had that much more responsibility—and undoubtedly that much more paperwork, as well.

Nevertheless...she wished that Josh had decided to take a busman's holiday and do the entire "Transitions" story himself.

Though Josh invited her to have dinner with him later that evening, Marta declined. Her common sense told her that the two of them had been together enough, over the past twenty-four hours or so. Any more shared time right now would only put them both on edge.

Maybe it was her imagination, but it did seem to her that Josh had glanced more and more at the diamond sparkling on her left hand once they were in the inn and then later on the drive home. And once in the city itself, every time he stopped for a red light she felt as though his eyes were boring a whole in her ring finger.

Perhaps she was unduly conscious of the ring, she admitted as she showered, put on a vivid-yellow satin lounging robe and then started brushing her hair. Sometimes just brushing and brushing with slow, steady strokes helped when she was tense. She felt tense now, and was beginning to be glad Josh *hadn't* decided to do the whole "Transitions" story himself.

Make up your mind, she advised herself. *Just a while ago you were deploring the fact that he was going to turn most of the segments over to other writers. What do you want, Marta?*

What did she want?

She mused over the question. Now she simply wanted Josh . . . forever and ever and ever. She wanted him here in this room with her; she wanted him in her bed with her; she wanted him wherever she was and wherever she went. And that's where things began to get sticky.

Josh had his own life, and a career that was just as important to him as hers was to her. As far as the other aspects of his life were concerned, Josh had done very well for himself after weathering adverse circumstances that might have thrown a weaker person forever. She admired him for that, gave him real credit for it.

Josh was secure, self-confident, had all the money he needed, striking good looks, scads of charm. Men liked him. And too many women tended to fall in love with him, Marta allowed mournfully. There was no doubt in her mind that whenever he wanted female company, all he had to do was reach for the telephone.

Josh was not frustrated, not starving for affection, not a hermit—he led as active a social life as he wished to. If, in the process of learning to cope with some considerable physical difficulties, he'd become something of a loner, he was in no way misanthropic. He liked people, liked being with them—look how the Grants had responded to him this afternoon. On the other hand, he was one of those fortunate individuals who could be content with his own company. Marta had no doubt that the hours he spent sitting by his living-room window, looking out over the Hudson, reading a good book or maybe listening to a symphony on his excellent stereo, were very good and complete times for him.

In lots of ways, she thought ruefully, he'd adjusted better to his life than she had to hers.

And the conclusion tolled. What he said two years ago was true. *Despite this overwhelming attraction we have for each other, he has no space for me.*

Dispirited, Marta sank back on the bed, propping pillows behind her head. The telephone rang.

Her pulse rate jumped. Her intuition told her this was Josh calling. And she was ready for the sound of his voice as she lifted the receiver. But it wasn't Josh. It was Tony.

"I was beginning to wonder..." he began.

Marta instantly glanced at the clock, calculated the time difference and asked, "Is something wrong?"

"No," Tony informed her. "Except that I've been phoning you with monotonous regularity, and you're never there. I finally stopped leaving messages."

"Tony, I'm sorry," Marta said quickly. And she was. "It was late when I got in last night. I didn't want to wake you. That's why I didn't call you. And I was gadding around a lot of today."

"Down to business again already, Marta?"

"Yes," she acknowledged, without elaborating.

"Well, I admit I was beginning to worry about you," he said with a slight, self-deprecating chuckle. "Incidentally, by any chance did your ears burn rather late this afternoon, British time?"

"What?"

"Isn't that what one's ears are supposed to do when one is being talked about?"

"Who was talking about me, Tony?"

"Trina Cataldo's in town," Tony said. "We met for a drink at the Ritz. I think she's going to sign a contract to do a couple of pictures in England. Frankly, her last American film didn't fare too well, and there's a producer-director here she thinks might bring her out of the slump. She was asking me about our wedding plans."

"What did you tell her?"

"Naturally, I hedged. I rather think Trina might like to make a few wedding plans of her own, however."

"Oh?" Instinctively Marta's senses went on red alert. "With whom?"

"Your friend Josh Smith, I'd say. She appears to be tremendously smitten with him...though that doesn't necessarily indicate a permanent condition with Trina. I've known her for years, and she tends to be...mercurial, shall we say, in her romantic involvements. But she's as serious about Smith as she's ever been about anyone."

Marta's grip on the receiver tightened while she fought a stab of pain that might as well have been physical. She chided herself for being ridiculous—jealousy was out of style, to begin with, and she had no claim on Josh, anyway.

"I'm sorry, darling," Tony said suddenly.

"Sorry about what?" Marta had to force herself to speak.

"I shouldn't have told you that. It was...childish of me. Oh, it's true enough—Trina's present feelings, I mean. But that doesn't mean Smith returns them. I was trying to advance my own cause by weakening his," Tony admitted.

"There's no question of a cause where Josh is concerned," Marta said, a shade too sharply. "But, Tony, you and I need to talk."

"I know we do," he agreed. "Which brings me to the real reason I've been trying to get hold of you, aside from my concern for you. You remember Sheila and Guy Forthington? We went to their cocktail party in Washington."

"Of course I remember them, Tony," Marta told him impatiently. "It was only last month."

"It seems ever so much longer," Tony reflected. "Anyway...they've rented a chalet up in New Hampshire in the White Mountains. Guy phoned earlier this evening, and he says the skiing's excellent. He's invited you and me to join Sheila and him up there next weekend. How about it?"

The thought of skiing was tremendously appealing. The clear icy air guaranteed to clear out mental cobwebs. Nature would be at her winter best. And Marta knew from having skied the White Mountains on several occasions, that there would be slopes challenging enough to make her work to prove her skill.

A skiing holiday would provide the chance to relax, and thus she would be able to talk to Tony calmly and tell him this sham engagement must end.

"I'm for it," she said.

"Excellent," he told her approvingly. "I'll call Guy in the morning and then set about making my plane reservation."

Chapter Seven

The snow-covered White Mountains were magnificent. The skiing was exactly what she had needed, Marta told herself as she set out with Tony for a second day on the slopes. The previous day they'd skied down Cannon. Today they were trying some of the trails at Loon. And the glorious, blue-sky, gold-sun winter weather couldn't have been more cooperative.

Last night they'd lingered beside the fireplace in the lodge. They'd drunk something called a "broken leg," made out of bourbon and apple juice and a couple of other things, Marta recalled hazily. Served warm, the liquor had been a perfect nightcap for her. She'd fallen asleep as soon as her head touched the pillow, relieved that the Forthingtons—evidently still a bit more conventional than a lot of people—had assigned Tony and her to separate rooms.

Tony had strolled in this morning, though, with a cup of hot coffee for her, a cheery greeting and a swift, affectionate kiss. He'd sat on the side of the bed while she sipped the coffee, but he'd had the wisdom—bless Tony, he had an inherent sense of timing about so many things—not to speak about anything except their surroundings and the sheer pleasure of skiing in mountains such as these.

For Marta, the skiing went beyond pleasure. As she showered after they returned from Loon Mountain late in the afternoon, she accepted the fact that needing the stimulation of strenuous exercise was a basic part of her nature. She was naturally well coordinated, sports were a challenge to her, and thus far she'd never had any trouble learning any of them. During a brief assignment in the Yucatán the previous winter, she'd snatched the opportunity to take a few scuba lessons and within a very short time was diving off Cancun with some of the experts. In addition to snow skiing, she loved to water-ski. Tennis, Ping Pong, for that matter, the participation in almost any game, set her adrenaline flowing. And yes, she liked to win, Marta conceded, although she was not a poor loser.

The participation in sports was something she could always share with Tony, as she'd told Jennifer that day at brunch in Josh's apartment. But one couldn't spend all the hours of one's life on a ski slope or a tennis court. And she'd begun to wonder how she and Tony would handle the day-to-day activities...even before she'd met Josh again.

But you didn't really need to meet Josh again to know the real answer to that and a lot of questions, an inner voice reminded her. *Deep down in your heart, you knew. You've always known. You could fill the quiet patches forever with Josh...with total contentment. In fact, there would no longer need to be so many of the frenzied times....*

Marta stepped out of the shower, wrapped herself in an oversize towel and sighed. She was beginning to sound like a broken record to herself. She needed to stop thinking of Josh right now and consider her priorities. First on the list was dealing with her engagement to Tony.

Tonight, Marta promised herself. Since they were going back to New York tomorrow, and Tony planned to return to London on Tuesday, tonight was the time.

But it wasn't that easy.

The Forthingtons, it developed, were celebrating their twelfth wedding anniversary—hence the special ski holiday. They revealed the occasion to Tony and Marta at dinner that night in the lodge's dining room.

The secret was given away when a waiter appeared with a silver bucket containing an iced bottle of champagne. Then Guy explained the reason for the celebration and Sheila giggled conspiratorially. "This was a date we wanted to share with you," she told Marta and Tony, "and we want to make a date right now to celebrate again in a dozen years. That will be your twelfth anniversary and our twenty-fourth."

"May you be as happy during every day of those first dozen years of married life as Sheila and I have been," Guy added, holding his glass out to clink it with everyone else's.

Marta felt as if she'd been turned to stone. A fraud made out of stone! She was thankful that Tony was able to rise to the occasion and propose a civilized return toast to Sheila and Guy. She couldn't have voiced a word, and even a sip of champagne stuck in her throat.

There was a small combo playing, and she was thankful when Tony asked politely, "Shall we?" But once they were on the dance floor she knew she was like a wooden stick in his arms.

In a voice meant for her ears only, Tony said, "Darling, I'm sorry that happened, but please try not to take it so seriously. Sheila and Guy mean well, and the two of them really are veritable turtledoves. If, remarkably, they still see everything in a romantic haze after a dozen years of marriage, they're not to be blamed. Commended, rather, I should think. So you must realize they were only trying to share their happiness."

"Spare me, Tony," Marta said, her throat still so tight it hurt to talk. "Anyway, how could I possibly blame Sheila and Guy for their good intentions? I'm wearing your larger-than-life ring on my finger. They don't know we're not really engaged."

To her astonishment, Tony said, "But we *are* really engaged, Marta."

She leaned back slightly so she could look at him and, in doing so, missed a step. "What are you talking about?" she asked.

"Us," Tony answered easily. "And yes, I remember our conversation in London and precisely what we said to each other. But it's my recollection that we both agreed to keep our relationship going awhile longer. And you know what my hopes are . . ."

"Tony, we did not both agree to remain engaged." Marta informed him, temporarily evading the issue of his hopes. "I agreed to keep wearing your ring . . ."

"Which amounts to rather the same thing, wouldn't you say?"

"No, and you know it doesn't."

"Perhaps not between *us*," Tony conceded. "But to the world at large it does. Marta . . ."

The music stopped abruptly, silencing Tony. And suddenly Marta felt a bone-penetrating weariness. It was as if all the benefits she thought she'd derived from two days of skiing had suddenly evaporated. Half under her breath she muttered, "I'm not up to this."

The music started again and Tony asked, "Would you rather sit this one out?"

She shook her head. "No. I can't face up to the Forthingtons right now."

The music had a slow, easy tempo. Tony glided into it with his usual expertise. He was one of the best dancers Marta had ever known and usually a perfect partner for her. But tonight she felt as if her toes had become all thumbs. She came close to stumbling over her own feet.

Keeping his voice low, Tony said urgently, "Marta, I had no intention of upsetting you like this. Obviously I've misread things."

It wasn't that he'd misread things, Marta thought miserably. It was that he was reading what he wanted to read, hearing what he wanted to hear. She couldn't blame him; in fact, she understood that kind of block. It was something she'd indulged in herself with Josh, until their denouement two years ago. Josh had given her indication enough that theirs was not to be a forever relationship. She could see that now, but she'd been blind to the signs then. He'd warned her outright. She just hadn't been listening.

She suddenly knew she couldn't do to Tony what Josh had done to her. She couldn't just . . . cut him off. On the other hand, she certainly couldn't marry him. Nor could she talk to him about any of their problems during their stay in New Hampshire. There wasn't going to be time, for one thing. Also, the atmosphere was all wrong. Unwittingly Guy and Sheila had given the whole occasion a

Valentine twist. Nothing could have been more inappropriate, as far as Marta was concerned. But she could see how Tony might have wished she'd succumb, even a little, to the Forthingtons' mood. Call it wishful thinking, call it anything, but when a person was in love he was not always as rational as he might be.

The music stopped again, and this time Tony led her back to their table. The evening passed. The night passed. At breakfast together the next morning, Marta learned the Forthingtons were going to travel with Tony and her to New York, where they planned to spend a couple of days before returning to Washington. She'd intended to take advantage of the trip back to New York to talk to Tony; now there was no chance to do that and by the time they reached Manhattan she was thoroughly frustrated.

To make matters worse, Tony suggested that the four of them dine together that evening at a small French restaurant in the East Fifties that was a favorite of his. Sheila and Guy were delighted to accept his invitation, and Marta could only hope her dismay wasn't showing.

She sidestepped letting Tony come up to her room once he'd taken her back to the hotel by claiming that she had a headache. It was a claim she'd never before made in her life, and she couldn't blame him for looking skeptical, but actually, it was no ruse. She did have a staggering headache, and she couldn't wait to blacken her room, then lie flat on the bed.

Alone in the darkness, Marta reminded herself that a major reason for her being in New York was to wrap up some loose career ends before moving to London permanently. At least...that had been a major reason. Now London, where Tony lived, was beginning to seem just as treacherous a place for her as New York, where Josh was.

Regardless of where she decided to go next, though, she did need to deal with her career. And one idea she'd nearly developed before leaving New York two years ago was on her immediate agenda. In fact, she thought with a groan, she'd made an appointment for ten o'clock tomorrow morning with Dr. Gerald Baskin, a leading orthopedic surgeon who'd been making tremendous strides in his field two years ago and, from what she'd learned, had progressed in quantum leaps since then. People who couldn't walk at all, she'd heard, could now walk tall and straight and without even a trace of a limp, thanks to his surgical skill.

The thought of facing anyone at ten o'clock tomorrow morning was anathema at the moment. But she had no intention of postponing her appointment with Dr. Baskin. A photo essay on his work was something she'd wanted to do two years ago and, if anything, wanted to do more than ever now.

Marta admitted in the darkness what she wouldn't have admitted in broad daylight. From the first moment she'd heard of Gerald Baskin, she'd wondered if there might be a chance—even the slightest, most minute of chances—that he could help Josh.

If Josh could walk sans cane, without even a trace of a limp, would it make the major difference their relationship needed? Would it bridge the gap?

Josh's attitude had gone a long way toward convincing her that his handicap had nothing to do with his determination to avoid serious commitments. Rather, his decision was in keeping with a life-style he'd chosen voluntarily. But she still wasn't entirely sure about that. And regardless, there was no negating what it would mean to Josh to be able to move freely again...and to ski, dance, do all the other physical activities he'd once enjoyed as much as she did.

Naturally she was not going to rush pell-mell into a discussion with Dr. Baskin about Josh. First she'd delve into his work even more deeply than she did into most subjects she was photographing—and that was very deep, indeed.

In a sense she'd be working backward, a process that was not unusual with Marta. When she discovered a subject that struck her so intensely she couldn't bear not to photograph it, she often mapped out her own plan, then teamed up with a writer to do the text later.

She wondered if there might be even the slightest possibility Josh would consent to work with her on this project. Then, remembering his reaction when she'd suggested doing a story on handicapped people who'd achieved highly successful relationships, she decided that was a thought she'd better forget, and quickly.

Finally Marta requested a wake-up call for eight in the morning, ordered coffee and rolls to be sent to her room and then went to sleep to dream of Josh skiing down Alpine slopes, and climbing to the top of Everest, and doing all sorts of impossible things, while she watched him from the sidelines.

Marta was sipping her morning coffee when she realized that her ten o'clock appointment with Dr. Baskin meant she couldn't go to the airport with Tony to see him off.

She'd intended to do that, thinking that maybe they could arrive early and, protected by the anonymity of an airport waiting lounge, have a decent chance to talk.

Chagrined, and feeling more than slightly guilty, she called the hotel where Tony was staying. It had surprised her slightly when he'd automatically booked a room at a different hotel from hers in New York. She had thought— feared?—that he might want a bit more proximity.

Most of the time Tony didn't try to push her. The choice of a separate hotel indicated that. On the other hand, on the dance floor last night he'd been strangely adamant that they were still engaged.

I've been honest about Josh, Marta thought, and this reflection brought with it a fair bit of resentment. *Tony knew in London—he had to know—that I agreed to keep wearing his ring for a time primarily for the sake of saving face.*

That wasn't entirely fair, she conceded. Tony had made it clear he also hoped the situation between them could change. Though he hadn't said it in so many words, the implication was that once she'd been in contact with Josh again, spent some time with him, the truth would suddenly triumph. She'd know that there was no future for Josh and her. She'd turn back to Tony....

And in some ways that would be so easy to do.

There was no answer the first time she tried to call him. She drank two cups of coffee, ate half a roll and called again. Still no answer. She wasn't sure of his flight time, didn't even know which airline he was booked on. Frustrated, Marta dressed, tried Tony's number one more time, then went off to keep her appointment with Dr. Gerald Baskin.

For the next two hours she forgot about everything except what the eminent orthopedic specialist was showing her and telling her.

Eminent? Well, he certainly was that, highly distinguished in his field. Yet Gerald Baskin somehow managed to look like a boy who had never grown up. He was short, rather plump, had freckles, an engaging grin and tousled light-brown hair. By the time she'd talked to him for ten minutes, Marta felt as if she'd known him for years.

They spent that initial interview in his office. Gerald Baskin had many photographs of his own to produce—nothing reflecting the kind of technique that made Marta's work famous, yet those before and after pictures told their own eloquent stories.

"There's another side to the coin, however," he told her as they sipped coffee together toward the end of the interview. "Not all of my cases are success stories. I'm not a miracle worker, Marta." They had easily slipped into a first-name basis. "So much depends on timing. If I'm in on things from the beginning, often there's a great deal I can do. Later...the chances dim. Bones, muscles can be ornery things. Sometimes I'm lucky enough to be able to undo old damage—or at least to alleviate a situation. Often what has been done is done, and any repair is beyond my skill." He smiled ruefully. "I guess my problem is I want a miracle for everyone," he confessed.

Marta nearly started to tell him the story of Josh Smith then and there. Could there be a miracle for Josh? Could this man help him at all? Maybe she was afraid to know the answer, she admitted to herself as she was leaving Dr. Baskin's office. For whatever reason, she hadn't posed the question. But there would be more than enough time later. Gerry Baskin had suggested that she accompany him on his hospital rounds Wednesday morning. Then he wanted her to sit in on a variety of conferences with patients. His patients ran the gamut in age from toddlers to the elderly. The photographic possibilities, she thought enthusiastically, should be fantastic.

Gerry Baskin was also going to let her photograph one of his operations. All these future photo sessions, of course, hinged on the agreement of the patients involved. "But I doubt they'll refuse us," he said with a smile, and Marta could easily imagine that his rapport with his patients must be excellent.

Further, he'd given permission for her to tape the various sessions. The dialogue and information gleaned in this manner would be invaluable to whoever wrote the story.

When Marta returned to her hotel room the message light on the phone was blinking again, and a square white envelope had been thrust under her door.

She opened the envelope first and saw Tony's distinctive handwriting. "Did we get our signals crossed?" he had written. "I thought we were to meet down in your lobby for breakfast at ten, and then you were going out to Kennedy with me. Anyway, I'll call you from London . . . and I love you."

Had she told Tony she'd meet him for breakfast at ten? Marta's headache the night before had been so overpowering she supposed it was possible she'd temporarily forgotten all about her appointment with Dr. Baskin and had agreed to have breakfast with Tony. She simply couldn't remember.

You'll really be losing it if you don't watch out, she told herself darkly then checked her phone messages.

Josh had called at 10:00 and again at 11:30. Marta glanced at her watch, saw that it was 12:35 and promptly dialed Josh's office number. But a secretary told her that Mr. Smith was at lunch with some visiting editors and probably wouldn't be back until late in the afternoon.

To be certain that Tony really had left town, she phoned the hotel where he'd been staying and learned that he'd checked out a couple of hours earlier.

Frustrated, Marta sought the only cure for mounting restlessness she knew. Exertion. She left the hotel and walked across town to Fifth Avenue, then turned north, striking a brisk pace along the wall rimming Central Park. She walked faster and faster, but the rapid movement wasn't having the relaxing effect on her it usually did. Usually if she moved vigorously—whether walking, playing tennis, or whatever—she calmed down emotionally. Now, as finally she reversed direction and started back to the hotel, she felt just as pent-up as ever. And she began to tell herself bitterly that she shouldn't have come back to New York, regardless of photo assignments hanging fire, regardless of anything. Even this towering city, where millions of people lived and worked, was too small to contain both Josh and her.

Josh tried to pay attention to what the editor of a leading French magazine was telling him in fluent but heavily accented English, but he lost the gist. He nodded in agreement when the French editor paused and hoped the man had said something he was supposed to agree with.

The luncheon stretched on interminably, at least for Josh. His guests were enjoying themselves thoroughly, indulging now and then in a round of flattering toasts accompanied by broad smiles and the clinking of glasses.

Josh kept trying to rise valiantly to this series of small occasions, and evidently he was doing a good job in the eyes of the others, because they seemed to approve of him thoroughly.

Remarkable, he thought wryly, how you can put on a convincing front when inside you feel as though you're made up of broken drumsticks still trying to keep tempo on a dozen different drums.

Where had Marta been this morning? She hadn't said anything about an immediate assignment. Wouldn't she have told him if she was starting to work on something? Since, after all, she'd already started to work on the "Transitions" piece with him.

It wasn't that there wouldn't be time enough for her to carry out her assignment with him and do one, even a couple, of other assignments simultaneously, Josh thought. He had the right to know, that's all. Any editor would have the right to know under similar circumstances, he assured himself, then recognized his defensiveness and was annoyed.

He had to admit he hadn't thought too much about Marta's not answering her room phone at shortly after 9:30 in the morning until he'd had occasion to speak with a friend at NBC an hour or so later. The friend mentioned in passing that he'd been talking a few minutes earlier to Tony Ashford of the BBC. Apparently Ashford had been in the States for the weekend on a skiing jaunt with his fiancée, but was heading back to London, or he would have suggested the three of them have lunch together.

"Ashford's a great guy," the NBC man had commented. "I think the two of you would get along."

"I've met him," Josh had replied rather shortly, and let it go at that.

At that point, though, his morning had been shot. Logic reminded him that Tony Ashford had every right to fly over to New York for the weekend to take his fiancée skiing. But logic had a very weak voice, and Josh discovered he was fighting a green monster.

It was a relief when the luncheon finally broke up. Then goodbyes were said and the men went their separate ways.

Back in his office, Josh faced a stack of priority mail and a stack of messages. He pushed the mail aside, tackled the messages, looking to see if Marta had returned his call. When he found she had, he let out his breath, feeling as though he'd been holding it in for hours. He promptly dialed her hotel, and was told Ms. Brennan wasn't in her room.

Josh left another message and, ignoring the many important matters on his desk vying for his attention, sat back and waited for Marta to call him back again.

Chapter Eight

Did you have a pleasant weekend?" Josh asked politely.

He and Marta were in the Algonquin bar. He'd suggested they meet there for a drink at 5:30, then had deliberately arrived half an hour early and was on his second Scotch when she walked in.

He gazed at the amber liquid in his glass and wondered about his own behavior. Way back, years back, an inner voice of caution had warned him it would be folly ever to try to escape problems through alcohol. In fact, it would be dangerous, could even become disastrous. Josh had always heeded that voice, and he didn't care that much for drinking, anyway...under ordinary circumstances. Now he reminded himself that belting down a swift Scotch in preparation for a meeting with Marta shouldn't be necessary.

He waited for Marta's reply, fought back the green monster again and told himself not be so damned suspicious. What did he have to be suspicious of, after all, where Marta was concerned? Or jealous about?

Before long, she'll be someone else's wife, Josh reminded himself. He felt slightly sick.

Marta was toying with the stemmed cherry in her whiskey sour. Josh saw her lips tighten and immediately wanted to kiss them back to their usual fullness. Savagely he warned himself he'd better change the focus both of his eyes and his errant thoughts.

He shifted, hoping this would help ease his aching leg. The leg had been kicking up too much of late. He felt certain that was due to tension, frustration, the complete inability to relax. Lately his sleep had been dream plagued, which was unusual for him. Each morning he woke up feeling rigid, stiff as a board.

"Well," he asked again, unable to keep a slight bit of acid from dropping on top of his words, "*Did* you have a pleasant weekend?"

"Hmm?" Marta asked absently. She looked at Josh, her lovely face bemused. "Oh," she said, "the weekend. Yes, the weekend was fine."

Josh had his glass raised to his lips. He nearly bit the edge of it. "Do anything special?" he managed.

"Tony came over, and we went skiing up in the White Mountains with some friends of his," Marta reported.

"Good skiing?" he asked, forcing the question to sound casual.

"Yes, excellent. Great snow," Marta told him.

"I imagine Ashford's a pretty good skier?"

"Yes. Tony's an excellent skier."

"Better than you are?" Josh asked.

"Yes."

Josh sensed her reluctance to talk about skiing with him, and it annoyed him. He wanted to tell her that if she thought she was making things easier for him by avoiding conversation about things he'd once loved to do but could do no longer, she was all wrong.

He couldn't imagine Marta being a magazine editor, but that certainly wouldn't preclude his discussing his work at *Living* with her. He couldn't think of any subject he'd avoid talking to her about. Which made it rankle all the more that she evidently felt she needed to pick and choose what she said to him as if half of what she might say was automatically forbidden ground.

Honesty compelled him to recognize that Marta's reasoning was motivated by kindness. Kindness mixed with pity?

It was his fear of her mixing up what was love and what was pity that had led him to enact that terrible scene two years ago when he'd told her he wanted her to get out of his life for once and for all. He had wanted *all* love from her and no pity, but he didn't think it was possible. He was as convinced as ever that his analysis of their situation and his subsequent decision had been the right one— even though it had torn him apart to do what he'd done to her.

Nevertheless . . . he was damned if they were going to sweep the subject of skiing under the rug.

"I used to get in a lot of skiing when I was at the air force academy," he said as calmly as if this were something he talked about every day. "A bunch of us used to hit Aspen and some of the other resorts whenever we could get weekend passes, which you don't much until you're an upperclassman."

Josh wasn't looking at Marta as he spoke, so he was unaware that her jaw literally dropped.

She couldn't remember him ever even mentioning his years at the air force academy before. She knew he'd been an expert skier, but that had been information garnered solely from Jennifer. In fact, once Jennifer had shown her a snapshot of Josh on skis—a very young-looking Josh, who, though very good-looking, was not as handsome in Marta's opinion as the man sitting by her side. Josh had been maybe twenty or so when the snapshot was taken. Years had mixed character with his looks. His suffering, she felt, had only enhanced that character. He was strong as steel, and it showed.

Marta averted her gaze from his face, afraid that if he looked at her directly he'd see more than she wanted him to see—her heart in her eyes.

"Jenny never did care much about skiing," Josh went on, referring to his sister. "I was the one who always hoped Dad would be stationed someplace where there were mountains. Were you up around Franconia this weekend?"

"Yes," Marta said rather shakily.

"I went up there one time on a Christmas holiday," Josh informed her. "Beautiful country."

"Yes, it is."

Marta suddenly felt herself being pinned down by Josh's gray gaze. Before she could wriggle away from it, he said, "Marta, you don't have to censor everything you say to me."

"What . . . do you mean?" Marta stammered.

"If you were a ballet dancer, I wouldn't expect to be your partner. I never would have been a Baryshnikov, not even when I had two good legs. I know you're trying to spare me, if that's the way to put it, but just the reverse happens. I feel as though you're patronizing me, and I hate like hell to be patronized."

Marta's head snapped back as if he'd struck her. "The last thing I'd ever try to do is...patronize you," she managed after a moment of shock in which she couldn't say anything.

"Okay, then, from now on come out with things, will you?" Josh suggested irritably, and, to Marta's astonishment, ordered another drink.

She couldn't refrain from observing. "I hope you don't plan to drive home from here."

"I keep my car garaged when I'm in Manhattan. You know that," he told her.

"No," she contradicted him. "I didn't know it."

"It's the only thing that makes sense," he said. "Otherwise, if you have a halfway decent car it's either apt to get ripped off or you have a constant hassle trying to find a parking space. So when I leave here, I'll entrust myself to a nice, big yellow cab. Okay?"

Josh, for perverse reasons he couldn't understand, was annoyed with Marta and even more annoyed with himself. He couldn't help but wonder if the green monster had shown through his sharp retort.

He had to laugh at himself. If anyone had ever asked, he would have sworn he didn't have a jealous bone in his body.

He became aware that Marta had a very un-Marta-like expression on her face. She resembled a child who's just been spanked. Guiltily Josh said, "Marta, I didn't mean to snap at you."

"It's okay," Marta said, staring down at the whiskey sour she'd scarcely touched.

"Look, it's just that I...just that I wish you'd treat me the same way you do everyone else," Josh blurted, to his own intense surprise. God, he wasn't even in control of his own words these days!

"It would be very difficult for me to treat you the same way I do everyone else," Marta said, her voice muffled. "Because..."

"Yes?"

"Because, that's all."

"Why don't you come out and say it?" Josh suggested, his voice steel edged.

"No."

"Then I'll say it for you. Because I'm crippled, right, and so you feel the need to protect my tender sensibilities. That's it, isn't it?"

Marta looked at him, outraged. "No," she stormed, heedless of the other people in the bar. "That's not *it* at all. You're reading me all wrong. You've always read me all wrong, damn it!"

Marta grabbed her handbag and slid out of the banquette in one swift motion. She tossed her head as she moved, and her dark hair swirled around her shoulders. Her eyes were snapping, her chin held high, as she moved across the small room. She was wearing a bright blue, full-skirted coat with a huge, black, fake-fur collar, and she made quite an exit.

Somewhat staggered, Josh tossed a bill down on the table, reached for his cane and started after her. Though he knew how fast Marta could walk, he was determined to catch up with her. As it happened, he didn't have to go very far. She was standing under the Algonquin marquee, and the doorman was trying to hustle up a cab for her.

Without a word, Josh joined her, took her by the arm and held tight when she tried to wrench away from him. His grip was strong; there was no chance Marta could break it.

A cab pulled up at the curb and Marta hissed, "Let me go, damn it, Josh."

"No way," Josh informed her. "You're getting in that cab and I'm getting in with you."

"And then what do you think we're going to do?" she challenged.

"I'll tell you that once we're both in the cab," Josh retorted.

He was edging Marta toward the curb as he spoke. The doorman held the cab door open. Marta got in, and for a minute Josh was afraid she'd tell the driver to start up before he had a chance to get in himself. Normally he moved pretty smoothly, but when he had to hurry or when he was uptight, he tended to be clumsy, and he'd never felt clumsier than he did right now.

He gave the cabdriver his Riverside Drive address, then slumped back and waited to hear what Marta had to say to that.

She didn't say anything.

After a moment Josh stole a glance at her. She was looking at him defiantly, her eyes still sparking, her lips slightly parted, and Josh's heart flipped over at the sight of her. She had never looked more beautiful, and it was with considerable effort that he kept both hands at his sides.

He began tentatively, "Marta . . . ?"

Her response was immediate, her voice taut. "I don't know what you think this is going to accomplish, Josh."

"Look, we got off on the wrong foot back at the Algonquin." He grimaced. The expression was a shade too appropriate. "Anyway . . . we need to talk about the 'Transitions' project."

"Yes," Marta said rather snidely. "I'd imagined that was why you'd asked me to meet you for a drink."

It hadn't been why he'd asked her to meet him for a drink. He'd wanted to see her so damned much that when he returned her call he hadn't been able to suppress the urge. A bar seemed to him the safest place for an encounter. A place full of people, many of them having just come there from work, lots of chattering and the clinking of glasses.

How wrong he'd been. There were no safe places where Marta was involved.

"I've done a general outline for 'Transitions,'" he said, and this fortunately was true. "If you're not tied up for dinner, I thought maybe we could go over it."

"I'm not tied up for dinner," Marta said, and the minute the words left her mouth, she wished she could retract them.

With the moods she and Josh were in right now, she couldn't imagine their agreeing about an article outline or much of anything else. Also, she was still reeling from Josh's astonishing conversation about skiing, and then his coming out and asking her to treat him as she did everyone else.

She'd started to tell him that wasn't possible because she loved him too much. You couldn't treat someone you loved as much as she loved him the same way you treated everyone else in the world.

She'd nearly said the dangerous words aloud, then at the very last second had realized what she was doing and so had to backtrack. And Josh, of course, had gotten another entirely wrong impression.

Marta asked herself how many times that had happened since she'd known him. More than she liked to think about. Because Josh was damned sensitive about his limp, though he concealed that sensitivity so well she

imagined few people—even people very close to him—
ever realized it.

Marta suddenly thought of Dr. Gerald Baskin. And
knew that as soon as she got to know the orthopedic surgeon a bit better she was going to tell him all about Josh.
In the meantime, she would pray and pray and pray that
there was something Gerry Baskin could do to solve
Josh's problem.

Once at the apartment, Josh made a pot of coffee. They
took their cups into the living room, and Josh drew the
drapes across the picture window, blocking out the view.

Marta looked at him curiously. She couldn't remember
his ever having drawn the drapes before. Did the shimmering Hudson and the lights on the Jersey shore evoke
too many memories of some intensely romantic moments
the two of them had shared with that same view as a
background?

Seated, he got down to business with an efficient
promptness that was in itself almost suspicious. Usually
Josh was considerably more casual in initiating story discussions, leading in gradually.

She scanned the outline he produced, trying not to be
so intensely conscious of Josh himself that she couldn't
assimilate what he'd written. He was sitting in an armchair opposite her, making rapid notes on a legal-size pad
of yellow paper. The light from a lamp on the table at his
side spilled over his dark-red hair, bringing out rich, coppery tones. Evidently he was intent on what he was
doing—at least, he certainly seemed to be. Marta let her
eyes feast on his beloved face in profile for just a minute.
She began to ache with pure yearning for him; desire
stirred with a twisting pain, reminding her of another kind
of need. A need no man had ever satisfied as Josh had.

She forced herself to concentrate on the outline. It was excellent, which came as no surprise to her. Josh had outlined six stories, each focusing on a specific couple. He'd selected a diversified group of couples, of different ages, different backgrounds, with different rationales for the moves they were contemplating making.

The Grants, she saw, were first on the list. And Josh definitely had assigned that story to himself, which meant he'd be working on it with her. Thinking about that, Marta's pulse began to beat a little faster. She'd known he'd originally intended to write the Grant story, but she'd been afraid he might have decided it would be wiser to step back and assign the writing to someone else. There would have to be a great deal of personal contact between the writer and photographer in producing "Transitions."

She finished reading, and looked up to find Josh's eyes upon her. Rather, upon the sparkling ring on her finger. And there was an expression in his silver-gray eyes that tore at her heartstrings. She would have given anything, *anything*, to have been able to read his mind.

She wished she felt free to tell him that the ring was a prop and the engagement a sham. But she couldn't. Sometimes Marta thought her strong sense of loyalty was more of a curse than a blessing. But she'd made a pact with Tony, and she felt she owed it to him to remain mum on the subject of their engagement until they'd talked things through.

If only they'd been able to do that in New Hampshire last weekend! She should have grabbed an opportunity, Marta chastised herself. Regardless of the Forthingtons and their anniversary celebration, she should have taken Tony off someplace where they could have had the chance to straighten things out.

Where? she asked herself logically. The temperature had hovered around zero; everything had been snow covered. The setting had hardly been conducive to taking a stroll around the grounds seeking a place where they could have some privacy. And there'd be no spot in the lodge to get away from the Forthingtons—the whole place was predicated on Americanized *gemütlichkeit*, with everyone in a convivial mood, enjoying every one else's company. Nor had she been about to suggest that she and Tony hole up in either her room or his for their discussion. That kind of proximity would have been terribly unfair to Tony. He said he loved her, and there was no doubt at all about Tony wanting her physically. And satisfying that want was out of the question.

She saw Josh wrest his gaze away from the ring, but before she could avert her eyes, he looked at her directly. For just a moment his expression was incredibly revealing. So revealing that it was all Marta could do to stay where she was. She wanted to go to him, throw her arms around him, toss aside pride, resolution and everything else and simply implore him to make love to her.

She fought back her instincts, but she had to move away. She rose quickly, too quickly, intent on refilling her coffee cup from the pot Josh had left on a side table. Her toe caught the leg of her chair, and she went sprawling, her cup and saucer sailing on ahead of her and crashing to the floor.

For a moment she lay still, totally strung out. She heard Josh swear softly, heard him get to his feet. She looked up to see him anxiously standing over her. "Are you hurt?" he demanded.

"No." Slowly Marta struggled to her feet. She glanced in dismay at the shattered cup and saucer. She felt sure they were family heirlooms, and she stammered, "Josh, I'm sorry."

His eyes followed her gaze. "For God's sake, don't worry about the china," he advised her sharply. His right hand shot out to touch her shoulder, tentatively at first, then more firmly. "Answer me, Marta," he pleaded. "Are you hurt?"

She said weakly, "I don't know."

"What do you mean you don't know? Where do you hurt?"

"Nowhere . . . physically," Marta told him.

"What?"

"I'm okay, Josh. That's to say, the fall didn't hurt me," she elaborated, "but inside I'm so messed up about so many other things . . ."

It was the last thing she'd intended to say to him. His eyes swept her face, lingered, darkened. He tossed his cane onto the chair he'd been sitting in and reached for her. She went into his arms as if she were walking in her sleep and couldn't do anything else. Josh brushed her hair away from her forehead with a hand that wasn't entirely steady and surveyed her face. Marta, meeting his steady gaze, swallowed hard. And there was no way she could have resisted what happened next. His lips descended, and she melted into his kiss.

There was no wrenching away this time. Slowly, slowly, they parted, but only for Marta to move her head the fraction it took to lean against his shoulder. Then he drew her even closer, stroking her back with an easy rhythm. He mumbled something softly against her hair, broken words she couldn't make out. She didn't need to. She knew the message they were conveying.

Maybe Josh would never, ever admit it to her, but this moment and those broken words convinced her that he needed her as much as she needed him. Marta's emotions were as fragmented as his words.

She couldn't wait for the following day and her meeting with Dr. Gerald Baskin.

The order of business for Marta the next morning was making rounds with Gerald Baskin at the large hospital where he was presently chief of surgery.

If she had been impressed with the man at their first meeting, she was doubly so when they returned to his office after rounds. They discussed the patients Gerry Baskin had just introduced her to and he went over the surgery he had scheduled the following day. They decided to postpone Marta's operating room visit until she'd taken a few preliminary pictures around the hospital, his office and while following him on rounds a second time.

It was only when all their business had been taken care of that Marta said, "Gerry, I know the schedule you're handling, but if you could spare just a few minutes, there's a personal matter I'd like to bring up with you."

Gerry Baskin grinned engagingly. "I'd like to suggest lunch," he told her, "but today I'm going to have to settle for intermittent bites of a cheeseburger my secretary will be bringing in. Perhaps tomorrow..."

"Right now would be fine," Marta said with a slight smile. "I don't plan to take up *that* much of your time."

"Okay." He smiled. "I'll ask my secretary to get two cheeseburgers if you'll take a rain check for a bona fide luncheon some other time." He spoke to his secretary on the desk intercom, then sat down in his swivel chair and said, "All right, Marta. What do you want to know?"

"I'm wondering if you might be able to help someone very close to me," Marta said honestly, and began telling him about Josh.

By the time the secretary brought in two cheeseburgers and two chocolate milk shakes, Marta had told the orthopedic surgeon everything she knew about Josh's accident and its aftermath, and had described for him exactly how Josh appeared to be today.

"He's made a very good life for himself, Gerry," she concluded. "And he's a terrific person. But, though he'd be the first to deny it, I feel in my heart that his limp is a real stumbling block to him in some areas. I know you said you're not a miracle worker, but I also know the miraculous things you've done for people. They seem miraculous to me, anyhow. If you could do even a fraction as much for Josh..."

Gerry Baskin put his cheeseburger aside, sat back and surveyed her thoughtfully. "This man means a lot to you, doesn't he, Marta?" he asked.

"Yes," she admitted frankly.

"Well, I guess you could say that's all the more reason I would be the last to hold out false hope," he said. "I think I told you when we first met that the more time that has elapsed since an injury occurred the less chance there is of my doing anything significant for the afflicted person."

Marta nodded. "I know you said that."

"Twelve years is a long time, Marta."

"I know, I know," she said quickly. "But Josh was so young when his plane crashed. He was only twenty-two."

"Do you have reason to think that the care he had at the time wasn't as good as it might have been?"

"No," she said hastily. "On the contrary, his sister, Jennifer, told me that Josh had the very best of care. His father was a high-ranking army officer, and his mother is independently wealthy. I'd say that some of the best specialists at the time attended him, and I recall Jennifer's mentioning that he had several operations before they decided nothing further could be done for him. But," she went on, "that was a dozen years ago, Gerry. Surgery has advanced so tremendously over those years." She paused. "I don't have to tell *you* that," she reminded him.

"No, you don't," he agreed. "And you're right. Surgery—my branch and most of the others, as well—has made terrific strides since the time of your friend's accident. But I'm going to say the same thing to you now that I said at our first meeting. I'm not a miracle worker. On the other hand," he went on, "I don't give up easily. I'd like to see your friend, talk to him, go over his medical history with him and check him out, if he'd be willing."

Marta knew the answer to that one. "He wouldn't be," she said flatly.

"There's no other way I could evaluate him properly, Marta," Gerry Baskin pointed out.

"I know," she said. "But I also know Josh would never make an appointment with you voluntarily. On the other hand, if he could get to know you first I think he could be lured into it."

As she spoke, the wheels in Marta's mind were turning rapidly.

Chapter Nine

Once again the message light was blinking on Marta's phone when she returned to her hotel after her session with Gerald Baskin. And there were again messages from both Tony and Josh.

She hesitated before returning either man's call, wishing there were first time to think a number of things all the way through. But that would take more than a few minutes, she realized.

She'd spoken to Tony briefly right after his return to London. He'd called her from his BBC office and had been within minutes of taping a program. So of necessity they'd had to keep their talk short. Marta was thankful; she hadn't been ready to get into any depth with Tony.

Now, because of the time difference between New York and London, she called him back first.

It was nearly seven o'clock in London, but he was still at his office. He sounded weary and, in response to her solicitous inquiry, admitted he thought he was coming down with a touch of flu.

Marta sympathized, cautioned him to take care of himself, and then—because she just couldn't put it off any longer—started to talk about their engagement. At once Tony interrupted her. "Frankly, darling," he said, "I'm not up to getting into all that right now. Anyway, I think it's something we must discuss face to face. Why don't I fly over on the weekend?"

"That's fine...provided you don't make plans with the Forthingtons or anyone else," Marta told him rather tartly.

"I won't. Matter of fact, why don't you ring up my favorite hotel in New York and book a room for me for Saturday and Sunday. That should give us time to straighten out everything."

Marta agreed, and made Tony's hotel reservation before dialing Josh.

Josh was in a conference, but his secretary knew he'd been trying to get in touch with Marta, so pledged she'd see to it that he called her back the minute he was free.

In the meantime Marta literally paced the floor. Last night she and Josh had both put their brakes on...she would have sworn she could almost hear those brakes squeal as they meshed into position. Josh applied his just a fraction sooner than she did hers. And she also would have sworn that it was the twinkling diamond on her finger that had motivated him. She'd very nearly cast her promise to Tony to the winds at that point and blurted out that she was free.

Instead she'd swept up the broken cup and saucer and left a few minutes later. Josh had walked her to his door after phoning the doorman to get a cab for her, but he hadn't gone down in the elevator with her, nor had he kissed her good-night. He'd looked tired and strained, and she'd worried about him all the way back to her hotel.

When the phone finally rang, she answered it on the first ring to hear Josh say politely, "Sorry I couldn't get back to you sooner, Marta. I want to set up a schedule with you that will jibe with the times the Grants have told me they'll be free."

Marta got her appointment book, and they worked out three sessions with the Grants, the first one on Friday.

That was the day after tomorrow, Marta noted with anticipation. And she wondered how she could stand not seeing Josh for all those hours in between, when the two of them were right in the same city.

She had promised the editors of a couple of other magazines she'd worked for in the past that she'd touch base with them while in New York. So that afternoon she set up appointments for the following day, then went down to the hotel swimming pool and swam vigorously for an hour, then spent some time in the sauna. But like most of the prescriptions for relaxation she'd been trying lately, this one didn't work.

Back in her room, she put on a lounging robe, then tried to decide what she wanted to do next. Liberated woman though she felt herself to be, she didn't like going into bars alone. Yet right now she would have enjoyed a glass of wine.

She could have some wine sent up from room service, she reminded herself...but that didn't appeal to her. Nor did the thought of going out for a solitary dinner.

Finally Marta faced the fact that she didn't want to be alone. She reminded herself that she had plenty of friends in New York. She could call up a number of people and be certain of prompt invitations. But that wasn't what she really wanted, either.

She wanted to be with Josh.

More than that...she wanted Josh. She yearned for his touch, his kiss, his lovemaking. In the wake of the lovemaking, she wanted to sit by his river-view window with him and talk about all sorts of things. The variety of subjects one could talk about with Josh was virtually endless.

She missed him so much! Suddenly angry, she spit the words "And there's no need for it!" into an empty room.

So Josh had made a highly satisfactory life for himself in which he'd alleged there was no room for her. That's the position he'd taken two years ago, anyway, and Marta suspected he would take it again now. She was not about to thrust herself into Josh's life only to face rejection again.

But I can worm my way into his life, damn it, she told the unresponsive walls. *And by the time he realizes what I've done it'll be too late for him to push me out again.*

She walked to the window, which looked out on a busy city street. Far below people were hurrying along, all of them giving the impression that they had some important place to go.

And where am I going? Marta asked herself. *What am I going to do? Sit here all night and feel sorry for myself?*

The answer was a firm shake of her head. A second later she started to dress. Twenty minutes later she was stepping into a taxi in front of the hotel and giving the driver the address of Josh's Riverside Drive apartment.

That February evening, Josh stayed late at his office because he dreaded going back to his empty apartment.

There was always paperwork to catch up with at *Living*. But finally he gave up on it, in part because thoughts of Marta kept interfering with his concentration, in part because his leg was giving him considerable trouble. He knew the best remedy for the pain was to stretch out in a horizontal position for a while.

At his apartment he poured a stiff drink for himself—which precluded taking any painkillers, but, then, he disliked taking medication unless it was absolutely necessary. During the first years after the crash he'd had enough injections and pills to last him more than a lifetime.

He carried the drink into the bathroom with him when he went to take a long hot shower. Afterward he put on a thick terry robe and stretched out on his bed.

Still nursing the Scotch, he tried to force relaxation by using all the tricks he'd learned during long-ago therapy sessions. The technique worked. He was at the edge of dozing off, when the doorbell rang.

Josh swore softly and wished that whoever it was would go away. But the caller was persistent. The bell pealed and pealed and pealed, and finally Josh gave up trying to ignore it.

He'd been told years ago that he should use crutches when in the throes of an occasional bout of pain, because his weight would then be more evenly distributed and there would be less strain on his bad leg. Now he reached for the crutches and started toward the long corridor that led to his front door.

The bell ringing stopped, and Josh nearly turned around and started back to bed again, assuming his caller had given up. But then the strident sound resumed. Josh reminded himself to have the present bell replaced as soon as possible with chimes, or something a little easier on the ears.

He was not in the best of moods as he opened the door... and found Marta on his threshold.

Marta looked up into icy gray eyes, but having Josh appraise her coldly was hardly a new experience. She was more concerned with the weariness stamped on his face, echoed in the dark shadows under those eyes.

Then she saw the crutches, and a bolt of fear shot through her.

"What's happened?" she demanded.

"Nothing. Why?" Josh asked.

Marta suddenly remembered that when she'd first known Josh he'd used a single crutch even more frequently than he did a cane. But then he'd evidently "graduated" to the cane alone, and she'd taken that as a sign of progress, even thought that maybe one day he'd no longer need the cane.

Impatiently, Josh repeated, "Why?"

"I... just wondered," Marta managed.

She waited for him to step aside so she could enter his apartment, but for a long moment he didn't. He merely stood there, stone faced, and Marta fought back the instinct to streak for the elevator and get away.

Finally he said, "Excuse me," and moved to one side. "Come in, won't you?" he asked her.

Marta had never received a cooler invitation. Nevertheless she went past him, down the hall and into the living room. Josh had turned on a single light on his way to answer the doorbell. As a result the room was full of shadows, and Marta shivered slightly.

Too much darkness, she thought. *Too much darkness all over everything. Josh needs so much more light in his life.*

Behind her Josh said rather tersely, "You'd better take your coat off...so you don't freeze when you go out again."

He might as well have come out and said that he didn't want her to stay around very long, Marta thought wryly. But she shrugged out of her coat and tossed it over a chair back. Then she sat down on the nearest chair because her knees were shaking so badly she was afraid they were about to give out on her.

She stared bleakly at a painting on the wall across from her. She was aware that Josh, still standing, was not only watching her closely, but waiting for her to tell him why she'd come and what she wanted.

Well, neither of those questions could be easily answered. On the other hand, she was going to have to offer him some sort of explanation.

She tried to think of something she might mention about the "Transitions" story they were working on...but there was nothing that couldn't wait until tomorrow or the day after.

She wasn't sure whether she imagined that Josh muttered something under his breath or whether he really did mutter something. But after a moment he said rather wearily, "Would you like coffee, Marta?"

"No," she told him. "But I'd like a glass of wine."

"Okay," he said, and started for the kitchen.

Marta had sprained her ankle severely once while playing basketball in high school. She remembered now how having to go around on crutches for a couple of weeks had been. When you used crutches you couldn't carry anything.

At once she was on her feet, heading for the kitchen after Josh. He was just taking a bottle of wine and a glass out of a cabinet.

He turned to her and raised a quizzical eyebrow. "Change your mind?" he asked. "Would you prefer something stronger?"

Marta shook her head. "No," she said. "I just wanted to help, that's all."

Josh scowled at her. "Why?"

"Because I thought..." she began, aware of a gaze she could only call disapproving. "Because I thought I could carry the glasses," she finished, and told herself it was ridiculous to feel such desperation over stating something so simple.

"I have a tray table on wheels for moments like this," Josh informed her. "It works very well. I just push it along in front of me. I presume that was what you were wondering about."

Marta faced him, wanting to screech. But she managed to control her voice as she said levelly, "I don't really give a damn anymore, Josh. From past experience, I know it's not easy to lug stuff when you're using crutches, that's all. If that offends your pride, I'm sorry." With that she turned on her heel and started out of the kitchen.

To her surprise, she heard Josh chuckle. She turned to see his lips twisted in a self-deprecating smile. "You're right," he admitted. "Okay, why don't you find a tray in the dining room so you can take the wine, bottle and all, plus some Scotch for me?"

Marta couldn't remember when she had felt quite so uncomfortable as she did walking down the corridor of Josh's apartment, carrying the drinks.

She set the tray down on the coffee table in front of a long, dark-green upholstered couch, sat down on the couch and poured herself a glass of wine with trembling fingers. Glancing surreptitiously at Josh, she saw him set the crutches aside and lower himself carefully into an armchair, then reach for the drink she'd placed on the table at his side.

"So," Josh said, leaning back and surveying her through slightly narrowed eyes, "what brings you here tonight, Marta?"

Marta had no ready answer for him, and she was too emotionally weary to come up with a spur-of-the-moment invention.

She settled for the simple, unvarnished truth. "I was lonely," she confessed.

Josh's expression was the definition of skepticism. Marta readied herself for a caustic comment. She knew very well that Josh—basically kind and wonderful though he was—could be caustic, especially when he'd been put on the defensive.

He surprised her by saying mildly, "I wouldn't have supposed you were ever lonely."

It was her turn to feel defensive. "What makes you say that?" she demanded.

"Oh, I don't know." He surveyed her as if looking at her might give him the answer to her question. "It's difficult to picture a person who's always on the move as lonely."

When she made no response, Josh continued, "I guess what I'm saying is that I wouldn't think you'd have time for loneliness. You always seem to be going somewhere or coming from somewhere or about to do something, usually something exciting, glamorous, fascinating, sometimes even dangerous, for that matter. I guess it's my feeling that you thrive on activity and change and so willingly never stay still long enough to acquire firm attachments."

His observation was not meant to be derogatory. There was no reason it should hurt. But it did. Stung, Marta said, "You could be wrong, you know."

"About you?"

"Yes, about me."

Josh spoke softly... and his voice sounded incredibly seductive. "Am I wrong, Marta?" he asked.

"I'm not some kind of... whirling dervish," she told him, the hurt lingering.

Josh laughed. "A dervish happens to be a Muslim ascetic, technically speaking," he informed her. "Historically dervishes do whirling dances to achieve their kind of ecstasy."

"Is that what you think I'm doing?" The hurt deepened.

She saw Josh frown. Then he said gently, "Marta, don't take me so seriously. You're looking at me as if I'd just hit you."

Marta's lips trembled. Her eyes stung. "I suppose I should thank you for the definition," she managed.

"Hey," Josh protested, "I was only *teasing* you. Sweetheart, I..."

Sweetheart. Marta latched onto the term of endearment as if it had been coined especially for her. Yet paradoxically it made her want to cry. *What's happening to me?* she asked herself, exasperated. *I'm becoming a regular tear bucket....*

Josh stared at her and said, "I don't believe this."

Before she realized what he was about to do, he fished in his robe pocket, withdrew a large white handkerchief neatly folded in thirds and tossed it to her.

"I don't believe this," he said again. "And I don't like it. You're a bundle of nerves, Marta. If someone so much as looks at you in what you think is the wrong way, you bristle. If someone says a word you can take the wrong way you take it and start to cry. You *never* used to cry."

"Don't worry," Marta advised him, fighting a small battle for self-control. "I am not about to cry."

"Well, you could have fooled me," Josh told her. "Look, I know how hard you work, how you drive yourself when you're on assignment. But you must have been beating yourself to death these past couple of years. You've lost weight you couldn't afford to lose—I seem to have said that before, haven't I?—and you're strung up like a high-tension wire. That's not good, Marta. You know it's not good. You've got to unwind."

Marta was tempted to tell him he should go take a peek in the mirror. He looked exhausted, and he hadn't exactly been Mr. Calm himself during their few encounters. But before she could say anything Josh asked abruptly, "When are you and Tony Ashford going to get married?"

Marta stiffened. One of the reasons she'd yielded to her impulse to visit Josh tonight was that she'd come close to the end of her rope. She had decided that although she would keep her pact with Tony as far as the rest of the world was concerned, she had to tell Josh the truth about her engagement.

Maybe Josh would thrust her out of his life again, anyway. Regardless, she had to let him know that she was not about to marry Tony Ashford or anyone else.

Still she hesitated, and couldn't have said why. Except that Josh's sudden question was completely unexpected, and she didn't know what to say by way of answer.

She'd wanted to tell Josh about the engagement in her own way, leading into the subject gradually. Now he'd put her on the spot, because she couldn't bring herself to say

"We're not going to get married," without some prior explanations.

Before she could say anything at all, Josh muttered, "Frankly, Marta, I think the sooner you get the wedding bells ringing the better it's going to be for you."

She stared at him incredulously. Did Josh *want* her to marry Tony?

"You need some stability in your life," Josh went on. "I know you don't intend to stop working once you're married, but—what was it Ashford said there in Washington? Something to the effect that he hoped once the two of you were married you'd be more interested in the British Isles as a subject for your photographs. I endorse that, Marta. I'm beginning to think the reason you race around the way you do is that you're trying to catch up with something. And so far you don't know yourself what that something is...."

Marta sat back and poured herself a second glass of wine as the truth of Josh's words washed over her. The truth of some of his words, anyway. The reason she kept going and going as she did was that she was indeed trying to catch up with something. In reality, two years ago she'd lost her chance ever to reach the point where she wanted to be. With Josh. Here in this apartment, or wherever else Josh wanted to be. Forever and ever and ever.

So she'd kept on racing, trying to mend what in an earlier age might have been called a broken heart. Her heart had still been badly cracked when she'd met Tony Ashford. He'd helped fill in a lot of the spaces with gentleness and affection and understanding. But the cracks had opened up all over again that night in Washington the previous month when she'd suddenly found herself confronting Josh. Now she knew she could never stop running. Concentrating her photo work in the British Isles, were she to marry Tony, had little to do with it.

"Marta," Josh said, "you've got to catch up with what you want out of life and stop running . . . or you're going to wear yourself out completely before you're very much older."

Josh shifted, and Marta, seeing him grimace, knew he was in pain and became so concerned about him she didn't even hear what he was saying to her. Her attention swerved back to his words only when he said sharply, "Marta!"

"Yes, I'm sorry," she murmured.

"Knowing you as I do, I'm sure you probably resent my talking to you like this," Josh said. "But I'm thinking of you and your welfare, as I'm sure Ashford must be. I admit he's a more patient man than I'd be under similar circumstances. If I were your fiancé, I'd be damned if you'd be racing around New York while I was at work in London."

"Tony's coming to New York this weekend," Marta said absently.

Josh's eyebrows shot upward. "Again? He was here last weekend."

"Yes, I know."

"Does the man intend to commute back and forth across the Atlantic until you're married?"

"It's really not that long a trip," Marta pointed out. "Some people commute, more or less, to California without thinking anything about it."

"Regardless . . . have you set the wedding date, Marta? I need to know because of the 'Transitions' series. In fact, it's something we should have cleared up before we even got started on the series."

"Believe me, I will complete my work on 'Transitions' for you," Marta said steadily.

"I believe you. But as you very well know, even with a photographer as excellent as you are, sometimes pictures have to be shot over again. Or more photographic material is needed to round things out. You know what I'm saying."

"If that becomes necessary I...I'll come back from England to finish up," Marta stated firmly. "I've never reneged on a job, Josh."

"I don't think I suggested you might renege," Josh pointed out. "But I still need to know your wedding date. And frankly, I'd rather see you settled down and happy, even if it means assigning a couple of the 'Transitions' segments to someone else."

Marta stood abruptly and walked over to the picture window. Her back to Josh, she closed her eyes tightly. *I'd rather see you settled down... you need some stability in your life... the sooner you get the wedding bells ringing the better it will be for you...*

Had Josh really said those things to her?

Playing his words back in her mind, she had the crazy impression that Josh felt as if he'd be gaining a new measure of freedom himself once she was married. At least, that's the way he was coming across to her.

Had loving her—because, damn it, there was a time when he had loved her—been such a burden to him? Did he want her out of his life so much he would truly be happy seeing her married to another man?

Staring into the night, Marta saw that it had started to snow. It was a winter world outside...matching the winter in her heart. She felt cold all the way through, past tears. Her tears were frozen.

She turned to Josh, and for the first time ever told him an outright lie.

"Tony and I plan to be married on the tenth of June," she said.

Chapter Ten

"Marta," Tony said, his blue eyes echoing the anxiety in his voice, "you look tired. Have you been doing too much, darling?"

They were in the cocktail lounge of her hotel. Marta had been reflecting that cocktail lounges were logical rendezvous choices for people who didn't have homes—people like her.

"Marta..." Tony prodded gently.

"Oh, yes," Marta said, and shook herself out of her reverie. It hadn't been that deep a reverie. She'd heard what he'd said, and she was getting sick and tired of people forever telling her how thin and weary she looked.

Especially Josh, she conceded.

"*Have* you been working too hard?" Tony persisted.

Actually, Marta had been working as hard as possible, but she didn't want to put it that way to him. She'd left herself precious few spare hours because she didn't want time to think.

Since Wednesday, she'd talked with three editors about assignments, turned down two, but had accepted the one dealing with coal miners because it would involve a trip to her hometown in Pennsylvania. In fact, while she was working she could stay with her father and those brothers still at home.

She felt a stab of sorrow at the thought. It would be the first time she'd gone home since her mother's funeral nearly a year ago. She remembered the harshness of that raw, March day. The terrible bleakness etched on her father's face. Her brothers, solemn as she'd never seen them, trying to rally later back at the house. They'd drunk a lot of beer, a lot of whiskey, everyone determined to cheer everyone else up.

"Marta, you still haven't answered my question," Tony said. "I have this ridiculous feeling that you're drifting farther and farther away from me. Something's bothering you. What is it?"

"I was thinking about an assignment I've accepted that will entail going back to my hometown in Pennsylvania, that's all," Marta said.

"Ah, yes." Tony sounded relieved. "You mentioned you were contemplating something like that."

"As for other work," she told him, "I'm working with Josh on the 'Transitions' series I told you about. We're only doing one of the segments together, and I think I've pretty well finished my part in it."

She and Josh had spent several hours with the Grants yesterday. Marta had deliberately taken twice as many pictures as could possibly be needed so there'd be no cause to go back again. She liked the Grants, felt genuinely sorry when, in parting, they'd told Josh and her they hoped they would come out for dinner one night. "Strictly social," they'd said.

She and Josh had both murmured they'd love to...but she'd known, and was sure Josh had known, too, that it was an invitation they would never accept—any more than they would ever again work on another assignment together. Taking on this project together hadn't worked. Josh had never been so aloof as on yesterday's drive out to the Grants and back. For that matter, he'd been an ice man from the moment she'd told him her invented wedding date. Yet that's what he'd wanted, wasn't it? To be sure she was getting married to someone else?

It occurred to her she was going to have to tell Tony her invented wedding date, too. And make it clear that the date was exactly that—invented. Last night, tossing restlessly on her hotel-room bed, she'd actually thought about marrying Tony. For a while, the thought had been like looking at a ship securely moored in a safe haven where no storms could get to it. She needed the haven. She and Tony could make a good life together. Not an exciting life, but a good one. And after all, she did love him.

There were all kinds of love, she'd philosophized wearily. How did she love Tony? Like a brother? No, there was really no resemblance between her affection for Tony and her feelings for her four brothers. Like a father? No, she didn't see Tony as a father figure. She supposed she loved him more as she would an uncle or a cousin of whom she was especially fond. Or a friend.

On that thought she'd drifted into a dream-plagued sleep.

This morning, sipping a cup of coffee brought up by room service, she'd thought again about marrying Tony. It was the one act that would forever sever her from Josh. Because if she married Tony, she would never be unfaithful to him. And she would probably never come to New York again, she'd thought a bit incoherently. And she would pray, pray fervently, that she never ran into Josh anywhere else.

Before she'd finished a second cup of coffee, though, Marta knew that marrying Tony was completely out of the question. Only idiots chose marriage as an escape route. And only a woman with absolutely no conscience would marry a man like Tony purely to serve her own purposes. She did love him—in her own way—too much to do that.

"There you go again," Tony said now.

Marta frowned slightly. "What?"

"I can't follow your thoughts, Marta, but I wish you'd share them."

"All right," Marta decided. When the chips were down, she almost always settled for candor. "I did a dumb thing."

Tony smiled indulgently. "Do tell. What kind of dumb thing, darling?"

"I told Josh Smith we're going to be married on the tenth of June."

When Marta saw the expression on Tony's face, she wished she'd bitten her tongue instead of speaking. He looked as though she'd created Christmas out of season. He said rather unsteadily, "Darling...I never expected this."

"Oh, Tony, Tony," Marta cried remorsefully, "it's a fake date."

"What are you saying? The tenth of June sounds like a pretty real date to me."

"I can't marry you, Tony. On the tenth of June or any other time." With Tony looking at her as he was, those were the hardest words Marta had ever needed to speak.

The joy faded from Tony's handsome features. His British accent sounding especially clipped, he said, "I've never been much for word games. And I rather think you've chosen the worst possible example of one."

"I'm not playing games, Tony," Marta told him wearily. "We spoke about all this in London. You knew..."

"That you fancied yourself still in love with Joshua Smith?" Tony finished for her. "Yes. And you wanted to break the engagement then. But you agreed—largely for my sake, I realize, largely as a face-saver for me with my colleagues—to keep wearing my ring, to pretend we were still engaged...."

"I know. And it was a mistake."

"Perhaps," Tony admitted. "I'm still not sure about that, Marta. You've been seeing Smith, working with him, and I don't think I've ever seen you look more unhappy. That rather proves my contention..."

"What contention, Tony?" Marta asked.

"All right," Tony said uncomfortably. "I think what you've felt for Smith has been far more infatuation than love. With, I admit, perhaps a very strong sexual attraction. And maybe a rather large measure of pity. I think it might be said that Smith has a rather Byronic quality. Handsome, crippled...it's easy to imagine that he inspires very tender feelings in the female breast. I should think that's Trina Cataldo's problem. Like you, no doubt, she wants to make up to him for everything he's lost. Envisions herself as a glamorous Florence Nightingale, soothing Smith's brow and bringing laughter back into his fractured life."

Marta eyed Tony coldly. "Have you finished?"

"I'm sorry, Marta," Tony said. "Truly. I got rather carried away. Let's be honest. Call it jealousy. I'm jealous as hell of Smith—have been ever since I saw you

ooking at him that night at the Forthingtons'. I told you
hat same evening I'd always known there'd been someone in your life. So imagine my feelings when I found
myself face to face with him and realized you'd never
gotten over him.

"Nevertheless," Tony went on, holding up a restraining hand as she was about to speak, "I still say that you
look miserably unhappy. I still feel, straight to my mar-
row, that I can make you happy... if you'll give me half
a chance. You may not feel for me the great passion you
apparently feel for Smith. Perhaps you never will. But you
do care for me, I know that. I think in time the caring can
grow into genuine love. Marta... I would like to hold you
to your June 10 date."

The anger that had been bristling in Marta over Tony's
first words ebbed, and she felt profoundly touched by
what he'd just said. Still, she shook her head firmly. "It
can't be, Tony," she said, not without reluctance. "Believe me, I wish it could. You don't know how much I
wish it could. And, it might interest you to know, Josh
thinks I should marry you as soon as possible."

"*What?*"

"You heard me. He thinks I need to settle down. Thinks
the best thing that could happen to me is to get over to
England and make a life with you."

Tony's blue eyes were steady. "Has it occurred to you
that maybe he's right?"

"He's not right," Marta said sadly. "It certainly *has*
occurred to me that I'm probably going to spend the rest
of my life as a single. That's not something I look forward to. On the other hand, there's only one man I could
ever possibly marry, Tony. And I assure you, he won't
have me."

Marta leaned back, feeling as if her energy had been totally sapped. "There," she said wearily, "there it is. Now the crazy thing is that I have a favor to ask of you."

"I think you know I'd grant you anything within my power," Tony told her.

"This is going to be a difficult one, in view of what I've just said. I'm going to ask that you let me wear your ring awhile longer."

Tony stared at her, perplexed. Finally he said, "I simply do not understand—"

"I don't blame you," Marta cut in. "But you see...it's my pride that's involved this time. You told me that a lot of the reason you didn't want our engagement broken in London last month had to do with your pride."

"That's true," Tony conceded, "but only partly true. My saying that was partly a subterfuge. As I think you know, my hope was that this resurgence of feeling you were having for Smith would be...transitory. Then you'd come to realize we have a great deal going for us. Then you wouldn't *want* to give my ring back. But," he finished slowly, "it's not going to happen like that, is it?"

"No," Marta admitted tightly.

"Then...if you want to wear my ring forever, it's fine with me," Tony told her. "But I would like to know why."

"To save *my* face," Marta said. "Once Josh and I have culled the pictures for the story I've been working on with him, that particular assignment will be over. However, I've contracted to work on five other segments for this particular feature. I'll be working with other writers, not with Josh, but there are certain to be story conferences, photo-editing sessions and so on at which we'll both have to be present. It would help to have your ring on my finger, Tony. Josh is extremely observant. He'd notice if it were missing and ... I just don't want to have to explain at this point. I'm not ... up to it.''

"Yes," Tony agreed gravely. "I can see that."

"Once there's nothing more to be done on the 'Transitions' story ... well, I'll fly over to London, and we can break the engagement by mutual consent. We'll figure out a way to do it with as little resulting gossip as possible. And I know this sounds terribly, terribly trite, but ... I want to be your friend forever, Tony.''

"I echo that," Tony said softly. "As for Josh Smith ... I can't help but tell you I'd like to wring his neck, Marta.''

"This sounds pretty trite, too," Marta acknowledged, "but in many ways Josh really is his own worst enemy, so don't blame him too much.''

The following Tuesday, Marta and Gerry Baskin had a late breakfast together in the cafeteria at his hospital.

She'd been at the hospital with the orthopedic surgeon since early that morning and had watched him perform a delicate operation that would bring new hope to a young woman who had been confined to a wheelchair for nearly a year after a car accident. Now there was every reason to believe the woman would walk again.

"And you say you're not a miracle worker," Marta said, half teasing, as she sipped a small glass of orange juice.

"I'm not," Dr. Baskin assured her with a smile. "Actually, though that was a rather tricky procedure, it was simple in comparison to a lot of things I'm called upon to do.''

"Mmm," Marta mused, thinking about Josh. The surgeon had already told her how difficult, if not impossible, it was to try to undo old damage. Nevertheless ...

"Gerry," she said, "I've told you about my...my friend who was so severely injured in a plane crash a dozen years ago."

Gerry Baskin nodded. "Yes."

"If I can persuade him to make an appointment with you, will you see him?"

"Of course I'll see him, Marta," he assured her. "I've already given you an indication of what the odds are apt to be, though."

"I know. But I feel that even the slightest of chances would be worth taking."

"Then give me his name and I'll alert my secretary so that she'll find a slot for him on our calendar. Under ordinary circumstances I'm booked pretty far ahead."

"I can imagine. His name is Joshua Smith. He's the editor of *Living, American Style*. You may be familiar with the magazine."

"You'll find it right on my office coffee table. Marta. Just to refresh my memory...fill me in about him, will you?"

Marta told Gerry Baskin all she knew about Josh's accident and his injury—which wasn't very much, she realized when she'd finished the telling. Most, if not all, of what she'd learned had come from Jennifer.

She concluded with, "A problem is that Josh is quite stubborn. I'm afraid if I ask him straight out to phone and make an appointment with you, he'll flatly refuse. I wish you could meet him first away from your office."

"Socially, you mean?"

"Yes. But I'm staying in a hotel while I'm in New York, so there's no way I could casually entertain."

Gerry grinned. "I have a bachelor pad in the Village and a summer shack on a lake upstate," he confessed.

"Then it will have to be an accidental encounter."

The surgeon's smile deepened. "An arranged acciden-tal encounter, huh?"

"Yes."

"Well, there's a new place on East Sixty-second I'm planning to investigate tomorrow night. It's called Les Amis. My date is Jeanne Latimer. She's a model. You'll probably recognize her. Her face keeps popping up on magazine covers, to say nothing of TV commercials. If you could get your friend Josh to take you out to din-ner..."

"I'll try," Marta promised. "It may not be easy. I don't want to arouse Josh's suspicions."

"To begin with, I'll change my reservation to a table for four," Gerry decided. "We'll be arriving at seven. Why don't you plan to arrive with your friend at 7:30? I can give the excuse that the other couple—another doctor and his wife, let's say—couldn't make it at the last minute and then invite the two of you to join us." He grinned. "From what you're telling me about Joshua Smith, you'd better say yes quickly."

"You can count on it," Marta assured him.

Josh had just finished dictating several letters, when his secretary informed him that Marta Brennan was on the phone.

He picked up the receiver and held it for a moment, his grip tightening on the smooth plastic surface. It was get-ting harder and harder to be with Marta, and even talk-ing to her over the phone required the self-control he was finding increasingly difficult to maintain. Sometimes it took every last gram of his considerable discipline not to blurt out to her how much he loved her, wanted her, needed her. If suppression could make a person go qui-etly insane, he was on his way, he told himself grimly.

"Marta?" he said, trying to give the impression by the way he spoke her name that she'd interrupted him in the middle of something important. "I haven't had a chance to go over the Grant pictures yet..." he added quickly, to further this impression.

"I haven't developed them yet," Marta informed him.

Well, that had been a slip. She knew he knew that she always did her own developing. In fact, she'd been given a small but excellently equipped photo lab of her own at the magazine. Since it was on a different floor from the editorial offices, though, she could have been at work without his knowing it, Josh reminded himself. Even so, her pictures had not yet crossed his desk.

"I plan to work on the Grant pictures tomorrow," Marta told him. "But that's not what I'm calling you about."

"Oh?"

"Josh..."

He heard the hesitation in her voice, and it both puzzled him and alerted him. With Marta one never knew what was coming next.

"I wondered," she said, "If you might be free tomorrow night."

Josh assumed that she was about to suggest they go over her pictures then, and he was agreeable to that. Except that he was going to suggest, in turn, that they do so in his office. He didn't think he had the strength to be alone with her one more time in his apartment without showing the hand he was so determined to keep hidden.

He was totally taken aback when Marta said, "How about going to dinner with me at a new place on East Sixty-second. Les Amis. Have you heard of it?"

"Yes," Josh admitted.

"Friends have recommended it highly, and I don't want to go alone," Marta told him.

Didn't she have any other friends in New York? Josh came close to asking her, then told himself he already knew the answer. Marta knew scads of people just about everywhere. There were probably at least a dozen men who'd gladly escort her tomorrow night to Les Amis or wherever else she wanted to go.

"I was thinking," she went on, "that perhaps we could meet there at 7:30. Would that be convenient?"

Josh could feel the trap closing. To attempt to spring it before it shut entirely would mean being blatantly rude. He couldn't come out and tell her he didn't want to go out to dinner with her at Les Amis or anywhere else....

Besides that would be a very large lie.

The fact was, he wanted to see Marta so much it was all he could do not to ask her to meet him right now. He shut his eyes tightly and wondered how much more of this he could stand. He'd already made up his mind that on the tenth of June he was going to go out of town, anywhere out of town. He would hole up in a hotel room and then get quietly but totally drunk.

Still, when he'd told Marta the best thing she could do was marry Tony Ashford, he'd been honest. He knew a lot of media people who knew Tony. Despite Ashford's two marital failures, they had nothing but good to say about him, blaming the failures on the women involved. From everything Josh had been able to learn about Ashford, he was a decent person, highly respected both personally and professionally. And rumor had it that he was crazy about Marta.

Well, Marta needed someone who loved her and who would—could—take care of her. Deep inside the charismatic woman there was a very vulnerable little girl....

Josh broke away from that heart-twisting fact as Marta demanded impatiently, "Josh? Are you still there?"

"Yes," he said. "Sorry. What were you saying?"

"I was asking you if it would fit in with your plans to meet me at Les Amis tomorrow night at 7:30."

"Of course," Josh said as nonchalantly as possible. He wondered what he might be letting himself in for. Knowing Marta, he couldn't help but suspect that she had something more in mind than merely trying out a new French restaurant.

Marta had not connected Les Amis with the popular Chalfonte Hotel. Now she discovered that the hotel had merged two dining rooms and a cocktail lounge into one entirely new, beautifully decorated restaurant-nightclub.

Tables were arranged on tiers, each table with its own, small, rose-shaded lamp. There was a center dance floor, large enough for floor shows, as well. Soft music was playing and there were a few couples already dancing, as Marta was led to the table Josh had reserved.

She saw that Josh was already seated at the table, but before she could reach him a familiar voice hailed, "Marta. This is great. How are you?"

She turned to see Gerry Baskin smiling at her enthusiastically. "Marta, Jeanne Latimer," he said, and Marta found herself looking at a young woman whose face she had indeed seen both on magazine covers and in TV commercials any number of times.

Josh was only a couple of tables away. Marta glanced toward him and saw that he was watching closely. She drew her attention back to Gerry, who was saying, "We were to meet another couple, a colleague of mine, but he got a last-minute call back to the hospital. Say, would you and your date consider joining us?"

Gerry sounded a shade too eager, and Marta decided he was a much better surgeon than he was an actor.

"That would be delightful," she enthused, and had to admit she overdid it a bit herself. "Let me get Josh."

She moved quickly to Josh's table to report, a little too breathlessly, "Josh, I just ran into a friend who's invited us to join him. Would that be okay?"

"If you like," Josh said indifferently. He stood, and Marta saw him reach for his cane. As they walked over to Gerry's table she was aware that Gerry Baskin, though still smiling broadly, was also evaluating Josh's progress with an experienced professional eye.

The head waiter bustled up and endorsed their altered arrangements after a brief explanation from Gerry. They ordered drinks; Marta introduced Josh, adding that he was the editor in chief of *Living, American Style*. Josh and Jeanne, it appeared, had already met. On several occasions she'd modeled for *Living* illustrations.

"And," Jeanne put in, "I know your work, of course, Marta. Which leave us to tell you what Gerry does, Josh. He's an internationally famous orthopedic surgeon."

"Oh, come on now," Gerry protested.

Marta saw Josh stiffen. She averted her face, afraid that her expression might give her away.

A selection of delectable appetizers arrived. Marta munched on a caviar-spread toast triangle. Gerry was asking Josh about the magazine, and she hoped that would focus attention away from Gerry's own career. But Jeanne, smiling her bright model's smile, piped in, "Marta, Gerry was telling me how you watched him operate yesterday and took pictures the whole time. Much as I love him," she said lightly, "there's no way I could do that. Just watch, I mean. I'm certain I'd pass out."

Marta could feel Josh's eyes boring into her, and had the horrible feeling that he already suspected the rendezvous was a setup. She said as calmly as she could, "It was fascinating, Jeanne. And I suppose I've become somewhat...hardened. I've seen enough in the course of my career that surgery in a well-ordered operating room isn't apt to faze me."

"Marta follows around in the wake of revolutions and a variety of other similarly shattering events," Josh told Jeanne, his voice ominously pleasant.

Damn it, he does know, Marta thought miserably.

The conversation went on, bland enough on the surface, but Marta could read hidden meanings into everything Josh said. It was a relief when Gerry asked, "Like to dance?"

"Yes, I'd love to," she said quickly, and couldn't wait to escape down the steps to the dance floor.

Gerry was an excellent dancer. He was the sort of dancer Marta loved to match steps with ordinarily...but right now her mind wasn't on the music.

Nevertheless she was startled when Gerry said softly, "Is it my fertile imagination, or are there really sparks going off under the surface up there?" He gestured toward their table with a slight toss of the head.

"I don't think it's your imagination." Marta admitted. "Josh is covering up pretty well—too well—but I think he's fuming. I'd bet he knows I arranged this with you, and I think I'm in for some well-directed fury. Josh is very cool and collected on the surface, but there's a volcano way down inside...."

"Why would he be so angry about your wanting him to meet me?"

"Because his handicap is his own damn private business," Marta snapped, "and he doesn't want anyone butting in." She sighed. "I'm sorry, Gerry. I didn't mean to take your head off."

A second later she asked, her voice ragged, "Gerry, do you have any opinion about him?"

"Josh Smith? He seems like a great guy, despite the undercurrents," Gerry told her.

"I mean . . . about Josh physically," Marta said.

"Marta, I only saw the man walk a few feet, then sit down," Gerry reminded her mildly. "I'm not that much of a genius at diagnosis."

"You were watching him very closely."

"So I was. Okay, from the little I saw I'd say he handles himself quite well. He's learned to compensate effectively with the cane. I would say he's had good instruction on that score, probably spent a fair bit of time in a rehab facility. I think that anyone—any professional, that is—would know that Josh's handicap is not a new one just by the way he does handle himself. Beyond that I can't go . . . without X rays, tests, examinations, the works."

They fell silent. For a few minutes they swirled to the tempo of the music. Then Gerry said softly, "Marta, I'm sorry my crystal ball isn't more efficient. . . ."

"Don't be silly, Gerry. I'm looking for miracles, I realize that, and you've told me a dozen times you're not a miracle worker. But maybe if I can persuade Josh to see you professionally, maybe . . ."

Marta's words trailed off, and she yielded herself to the music and the dancing.

Chapter Eleven

Josh tried to keep his eyes off the dance floor and attempted to concentrate on building a reasonably interesting conversation with Jeanne. She was as charming and witty as she was beautiful, but it still took a real effort to pay attention to her.

He'd wondered about this dinner date. Now he was sure he knew exactly why Marta had set it up, and the knowledge both infuriated and depressed him. Marta's action reaffirmed his conviction that she could never totally accept him as he was. Either that, or she'd become an intolerable do-gooder. Whichever, he'd never felt more like a human guinea pig.

Jeanne excused herself to go to the rest room. Josh sat and polished off his Scotch, then beckoned the waiter to bring him another. His self-control was snapping like a bunch of rubber bands stretched close to the breaking point, then released.

A few weeks ago he would have sworn he didn't have a jealous bone in his body. Now he was waging a silent battle with a second Green Monster. Regardless of Marta's reason for arranging this rendezvous tonight, she and Baskin made a terrific dancing team. With Jeanne gone temporarily, Josh couldn't keep his eyes off them. And it hurt, hurt too damned much, to watch them. He tried to force himself to focus on other things in the room. He surveyed the murals on the walls, which were quite striking. He watched the waiters doing their jobs with the quiet efficiency that was a mark of real expertise. Jeanne came back and favored him with a brilliant smile as she sat down alongside him. She *was* stunning. Coppery hair, big green eyes, superb figure, and a nice sense of humor thrown in for good measure. Josh asked himself why he couldn't simplify his life by falling in love with Jeanne or someone like her. He'd known quite a few women like Jeanne.

At last the music ended. Marta and Gerry came back to the table. The waiter brought dinner menus, which were consulted carefully. Orders were given. The music started up again. This time Gerry turned to Jeanne and asked her to dance. Which he should have done the first time around, Josh thought nastily. If he remembered his manners correctly, one always asked one's date for the first and last dances.

Ah, well, that wasn't about to be his problem ever again. Morosely he stared at the tablecloth, then gave himself a mental slap. If there was anything he truly despised it was self-pity.

"Josh?" Marta murmured tentatively.

"Yes?"

"Why don't you say what's on your mind?" she asked him.

"Okay." Josh decided upon the tack he was going to take. "I can't figure you out, that's what's on my mind."

"What do you mean?"

"I mean you're supposed to be marrying Tony Ashford less than three and a half months from now, and yet you're coming on like a searchlight to this doctor."

He saw Marta's eyes narrow. "I think I'm going to ask all over again, what do you mean?" she told him.

"Marta, I guess the old-fashioned word for it is flirting. Baskin is here with a date, yet you go out on the dance floor with him and . . ."

"You're working for the wrong kind of magazine, Josh," Marta interrupted.

"You think so?"

"Yes. You should switch over to a publication that features lurid tales. Your imagination's running away with you. I *danced* with Gerry, that's all."

"When did you meet him?"

"Last week," Marta said absently.

"That *is* fast work."

She glared at him. "Stop, will you? You're way out of line. For one thing, as you so succinctly pointed out, Gerry's here with a friend. For another thing, although I find him extremely likable, I don't even know him yet."

"I like the 'yet,'" Josh muttered.

"Oh, shut up!" Marta snapped. "If you must know, Gerry agreed to meet me here tonight because of you," she blurted.

"What?"

Josh kept his voice low, but it had the effect of thunder. Marta moaned, "Damn—oh, damn—oh, damn," and looked so miserable Josh almost felt sorry for her.

But not *that* sorry.

"I'd like to know precisely what you're talking about," he told her.

"Josh, I'm doing a feature on Gerry's work. I told you about it. I'm sure I told you about it . . ."

"It doesn't much matter whether you told me about it or not," Josh stated coldly. "You certainly didn't tell me you were planning to involve me. So explain, will you?"

"Josh . . . Gerry has helped so many people."

"Well, good for him," Josh huffed. "What does that have to do with me?"

"I thought . . ."

"Come on, Marta. Out with it!"

"I thought maybe he could . . . help you. I wanted the two of you to meet so you . . . could get to know him. I knew you'd never make an appointment with him just because I asked you to. I knew you'd need to be motivated to do it yourself, so I . . ."

Josh surveyed her dispassionately. "Quite the psychologist, aren't you?" he commented.

"I'm not trying to be a psychologist. Josh, I . . ."

"I suppose you want me to consult your friend with the hope he could make me whole again, is that it?" Josh demanded, each word falling like a crystal chip.

Marta flinched and said, "I've botched it. I've totally botched it."

"Yes," Josh agreed, "I'd say you have."

"Thanks for being so agreeable," she retaliated, but she looked so weary as she spoke that his heart twisted. At the same time he felt sharply divided. That was the only way he could think of it. Divided.

It hurt to have his suspicions about Marta's reason for wanting to come here tonight confirmed. It hurt to know anew that Marta liked men in her life who were tuned the way she was. The way he suspected Gerry Baskin would be. The way Tony Ashford certainly was. Active men, participants in active things. She had no room for someone on the sidelines.

He reminded himself that this was hardly news to him. After all, he'd concluded two years ago that a relationship between Marta and him could never last, despite the passion that flowed between them and the proof that their passion could attain the most exquisite culmination. Nevertheless logic and knowledge didn't ease the ache of now learning that Marta was so unaccepting of him as he was that she'd gone to great lengths to contrive this meeting with an orthopedic surgeon who, she obviously thought, would be able to work wonders with a magic scalpel.

On the other side of the coin... he had to admit he'd shared very little with Marta about the accident and the impact it had made on his life. He'd never told her about the way it had forced him into a new mode of thinking and being and behaving that had many pluses along with the minuses.

Intensely private, he'd never shared any of that with *anyone*... not even Jennifer, though he knew his sister read between the lines at moments and knew more about him than anyone else did. Even after twelve years he couldn't handle discussing his innermost feelings. Now he wished he hadn't been so reticent with Marta two years ago. He wished he'd been able to really tell her about himself.

Maybe, just maybe, there was more to that other side of the coin than he'd thought. For the first time, it occurred to Josh that he might have been wrong in his evaluations.

* * *

Marta and Gerry Baskin danced several more times that evening. And Marta found herself confessing to the surgeon that she'd made a mess of things.

"He caught on," she said abjectly. "I should have known I'd never be able to put anything over on Josh."

"I take it he's quite a charmer," Gerry told her. "Jeanne thinks he's terrific."

"Most women think he's terrific," Marta said glumly. "But he's totally unaware of that."

"Marta, I don't mean to pry...but he means a lot to you, doesn't he?"

"Everything," Marta said, without even pausing to think. And there...it was out. The truth, the whole truth.

"That's his ring you're wearing?" Gerry asked.

"Er...no," Marta said hesitantly. "I—I'm engaged to a friend in England."

"You're engaged to a 'friend' in England?" Gerry echoed, not bothering to try to hide his amusement. "Marta, do you have any idea how strange that sounds?"

"No—yes. Regardless, that's the way it happens to be. Gerry, don't ask me to try to explain it to you."

"I won't, though I admit you've certainly whetted my curiosity. Marta, listen..."

"Yes?"

"Try to persuade Josh to call and make an appointment with me. If I knew him just a little bit better, I'd suggest it myself. I'll be honest with you. As I said originally, the odds are against my being able to do much, if anything, for him. But if there's even the slightest chance..."

"I'll do my damnedest," Marta promised firmly. But inwardly she was convinced that her "damnedest" wasn't going to be nearly good enough.

The moment came for the party to break up. Gerry and Jeanne left first; Josh and Marta followed shortly thereafter. Outside Les Amis Josh hailed a cab. Marta expected him to say good-night and let her travel on alone, but he surprised her. He climbed in next to her and gave the cabbie the name of her hotel.

At the hotel he surprised her once again, by following her to the elevator bank and getting into the elevator with her. "What floor?" he asked.

Marta looked at him curiously. "Seven."

He punched the button and said, "I'm coming up with you. We need to talk."

Once in her room Josh asked, "Got anything to drink?"

She shook her head. "Nothing," she admitted. "Either alcoholic or nonalcoholic."

"What would you prefer?"

"Well, if you want to order up something I think I'll settle for ginger ale."

"Okay," Josh agreed, and ordered up two ginger ales.

The room service waiter brought the beverages and Josh poured them. Then, as if he'd come to a sudden, vital decision, he said tautly, "Okay...this is one time that I'm not going to allow the two of us to go our separate ways with a lot of misconceptions still hanging fire. We have to talk."

Marta didn't know how to answer that. Josh was usually the one who didn't want to talk things out.

Perched on the edge of the bed, she waited, wondering if he was about to accuse her again of flirting with Gerry Baskin, or something equally ridiculous. She watched with a mixture of curiosity, apprehension and a readiness to do verbal battle of her own as Josh sat down in the room's only armchair and said slowly, "Marta, I'm beginning to realize you meant well tonight."

"Well, thanks very much," Marta retorted, and wished she didn't feel the need to be so defensive with him.

"Marta, look...this is something I find difficult to talk about, something I never *do* talk about. But...in all fairness, I think I should tell you that everything that could have been done for me was done for me at the time of the accident. Okay?"

The words came out in a rush. Hearing them, Marta was speechless.

Josh stirred restlessly. "It was pretty bad going at first. They didn't know if they could save me, let alone the leg. I was in the hospital for...a long time. After that, in and out of hospitals and rehab centers for longer than I like to think about," he said.

He stared moodily at a point about a foot over Marta's head. "What I'm saying is, I had a lot of time to think. More consecutive time to do nothing *but* think than a lot of people would have in several lifetimes. Also, the doctors leveled with me all along the way. I knew early on that the damage was permanent.

"They did their best for me, Marta. The doctors, the nurses, the therapists. I did my best for myself. I followed every regimen they drummed up for me.... I gave it everything I could give it. Combined, we *all* did the best that could be done for me, and I've been told I'm lucky. The results could have been a lot worse."

Josh paused to take a deep draft of his drink. "All that time, and there was a great deal of it, I thought and I wondered. I wondered why this had happened to me, which is pretty much par for the course. I did my full share of railing against fate. Then...well, I'm not saying that all of a sudden I became quietly accepting of what had happened to me or that I stopped fighting, but I did begin to look beyond the purely physical. Am I making any sense to you?''

"Yes," Marta said, her voice just a notch above a whisper.

"I began to do a lot of things that for me were very different. I took correspondence courses on comparative religion, philosophy, psychology—you can take it from there. I read and studied all day, except when I was involved in therapy and exercise sessions, and half the night, as well. I began to write down what I felt . . ."

"What did you do with what you wrote?"

"Stuffed it in a box that's sitting way, way back on a very top closet shelf," Josh said with a faint smile. "I haven't looked at it in years. I have no desire at this point to look at it. Anyway . . ."

"Yes?"

"Well, in high school I'd fooled around with the school newspaper—in fact, I became editor of it when I was a senior. I began to take some correspondence courses in writing and editing—I knew that any career I chose would have to be a sedentary one," Josh said quietly. "Then, when I finally was able to hobble around a bit, I approached a friend of my father's who heads a publishing house here in New York. He agreed to try me out as a reader. Then they let me try my hand at editing, a lot of which I could do from my own home. After a time, after I'd edited a book on architecture, matter of fact, I got a bid from *Architecture, American Style* and went on the staff there. And you pretty much know the rest.

"By then I'd adjusted, Marta," Josh told her. "I think that's what I want you to know most of all. I *have* adjusted. I know where I stand . . . and how it's going to be for the rest of my life. I've accepted that, and I find mine a very good life. So, though I appreciate your efforts on my behalf, I want you to know that it's not out of stubbornness or whatever other names you might put to it that I'm saying thank you, but no thank you...."

Marta tried not to stare at him, but she was dumbfounded. This was the longest speech Josh had ever made to her...and the kind of speech she had never expected to hear from him.

Two years ago she might have considered it an opening wedge. Now she wasn't sure just what it was. Carefully she said, "Josh, I wasn't trying to tilt at windmills. I've seen evidence of some of the things Gerry's done for people, that's all. I thought it wouldn't do any harm for you to let him examine you."

Josh shook his head. "Thanks, but I've been examined more than enough."

"Josh, that was years ago."

"Regardless. Look, I go to a good doctor for routine checkups. I have a heart they tell me will last till I'm at least eight hundred. Everything else is in fine working order. That's good enough."

"How do you know what Gerry might be able to do for you if you won't consult him?" she demanded.

"Because I've been through the same thing...time and again," Josh told her.

"I just said, Josh, that was a long time ago. You know as well as anyone that terrific strides have been made in orthopedics in the past twelve years."

"I really don't keep up with orthopedics," Josh informed her coolly. "Matter of fact, I wouldn't mind never hearing the word again."

"Josh, must you be so stubborn?"

Josh frowned. "Marta, did Baskin tell you he thought he could enable me to throw away my cane?" he asked

her. "Did he take one look at me tonight and tell you that
with a couple of waves of his magic knife he'd have me
ready for the next Olympic ski trials?"

"Oh, God, can you ever frazzle a person!" Marta exploded. "Of course he didn't tell me anything like that.
He's willing to see you, that's all."

"Decent of him," Josh muttered.

"Look, Josh," she protested, "don't take it out on
Gerry. He was only agreeing to this because I asked him
to. What I'm saying is—"

"What you're saying is painfully self-evident," Josh
told her. "Believe me, I'm not about to take anything out
on Gerry. I know too well what it's like to be a victim of
your charms."

"You? A victim of my charms?" Marta laughed deri-
sively. "Aren't you getting mixed up, Josh? I'd say it's
been the other way around."

"Hardly," Josh observed dispassionately, adding, "I
don't fool that easily, Marta. Don't you think I know
you'd only be interested in me if I could walk straight and
dance with you and ski with you and run around all over
the place with you."

Marta froze. She was hearing what she'd always suspected was Josh's problem where she was concerned, but
the confirmation was traumatic for her. She thought of
the times they'd been together, times she'd thought were
the essence of love, as well as passion. She thought she'd
shown him, shown him so clearly, the depths of her feeling for him. Yet from what he was saying, he'd misread
her completely.

Josh met her eyes, and the rather sardonic smile that
had been curving his lips faded. "Don't," he murmured
huskily. "Don't look so stricken."

He stood, and his arms automatically reached out to her. Marta's face twisted, and she felt as if her heart were tilting dangerously, about to start off on a cardiac landslide. They met halfway, and with Josh's arms around her, Marta forgot about everything else in the world.

Josh kissed her forehead, her eyelids, the tip of her nose, and finally he claimed her lips. His tongue invaded and Marta, responding, wove her arms around him, clutching him closer and closer and closer to her. She felt as if her body were suddenly afire, her blood boiling. She writhed in Josh's embrace as his hands traveled to her breasts, her waist, her hips, her thighs....

Neither was conscious of moving toward the bed, but in another moment they were side by side, entangled in each other's arms. Josh tugged at the top of Marta's two-piece white wool dress, and she helped him finish the job. Her wisp of a bra followed the path of the dress top. Then Josh, his lips pressed first to one nipple then the other, began tantalizing her, starting her on the spiral route that could lead in only one direction.

After a time she began tugging at his clothes...divesting him of his shirt, then pausing to revel in his strong, beautifully formed chest and to cover it with her kisses. Finally, clothes discarded, they set off on small exploratory voyages, nuzzling and nibbling, feeling and caressing, invoking ecstasy with every caress.

Marta lost herself in Josh; she let him lead, willing to follow, wanting to follow. And he led skillfully, tenderly until, all at once, neither was the leader, neither the follower. They were equal partners in passion, ascending together, until all that could be wonderful between a man and a woman became theirs, and they in turn became one.

Relaxation came in the wake of passion, and contentment filled Marta even as Josh had filled her just minutes before. She lay with her head on his shoulder, his arm around her. She heard the steady rhythm of his breathing, felt the warm moisture of his skin against her skin, remembered how she loved him so utterly and completely. And then she fell asleep.

He was gone when she awakened. She knew it even before she opened her eyes. She felt the aloneness of a room without him, and was bereft.

For a moment she thought he might be in the bathroom. But he wasn't. Her eyes swept the furniture. There was not a vestige of his clothing in sight. She searched for a note, for a token of any kind. There was nothing. It was as if their hours together had never been.

Marta showered and ordered coffee sent up. She stared blankly at the walls as she sipped the coffee, hot, black and strong. She knew there were things she had to do today, but her mind was a blank—an unknown state to Marta's ordinarily active mind.

After a time, she took her appointment book out of her handbag and scanned it. She saw she had a late-morning meeting with the editor who'd commissioned her to do the coal-mining photo essay. And then she must call her father to tell him she would be coming home on the weekend.

Then she was to meet a friend for lunch. Gertrude Sanders, an artist she'd known back in the days when she'd lived in Soho. Thinking of Soho reminded her of Josh and Josh's resentment about her roommate, Stan, which she'd found so amusing at the time.

She forced her thoughts away from Josh and consulted the appointment book again. In the afternoon she was to meet Gerry Baskin at the hospital—the patient on whom he'd operated yesterday had agreed to further pictures and some conversation that Marta could record and pass on to the writer who'd be doing copy for the orthopedics story.

"You mean she'll be ready to talk to me tomorrow?" Marta recalled asking Gerry after the surgery.

"Sure." He'd grinned. "Why not? My patients recover fast."

Remembering that comment made her again think of Josh and his monologue last night, which in its way had been almost a confession. Now she wished she could have taped Josh's words, because she felt there would be volumes to read between the lines. As it was…much of what he'd said was imprinted in her memory; she could almost quote the sentences verbatim.

If he hadn't finished with that terrible comment "Don't you think I know you could never be interested in me unless I were able to walk straight?" she might have been able to talk to him about the things he'd just said to her. They might have opened up new doors.

Still, if he hadn't made that terrible comment they would never have made love last night. One thing had inevitably led to another.

And now?

Marta glanced at the clock and was glad she needed to hurry if she meant to be on time for her appointment with the editor who wanted the coal-mining story. The last thing she needed at the moment was more time to think.

Three times during the course of that day Marta called her hotel to ask if there were any messages for her. She felt sure Josh would call her. He had to call her. After last night, he couldn't walk out and close the door as if nothing had happened between them.

But Josh didn't call.

By the time she went to the hospital to meet Gerry and photograph his patient, Marta's nerves were again frazzled.

Talking with Gerry's patient was a welcome diversion. She was wearing a fluffy pink bed jacket, one of the nurses had combed her hair into soft curls, and she'd put on lipstick. Remembering this woman in the operating room only the day before, Marta marveled at the transformation.

This was a patient more than willing to talk about her doctor and to sing his praises. She was also able to chat easily about the car crash that had injured her so severely and the struggle, doubts and pain of the ensuing months.

In a way it was similar to hearing Josh talk, and yet it wasn't. Thanks to Gerry's skill, this woman's story was going to have a different ending from Josh's. She still had a road to travel, but before she reached the end of it she'd be "walking straight."

Gerry had left Marta alone with his patient while he checked up on a couple of other cases, but he rejoined her as she was leaving the room.

"Time for a cup of coffee?" he invited.

"Yes, I'd love one," Marta told him.

He took her to his office, where the coffeepot was always brewing. Pouring for both of them, he said, "I know I constantly exceed my caffeine quota, but I admit coffee gives me a lift . . . especially toward this time of day."

"Me, too," Marta agreed. "Though too much of it gives me the jitters."

"You looked like you were having the jitters last night each time Jeanne and I left you alone with Josh while we danced," Gerry observed. "I had the impression he wasn't too crazy about your dancing with me."

"He was being righteous," Marta said, and added, "it's a long story, Gerry."

"To do with that ring on your finger?"

"Yes."

"And the 'friend' you're engaged to?"

"Yes. I know it sounds insane. It is insane. Sometime I'll tell you about it," she temporized.

Gerry grinned. "I get the message, Marta, and I'll butt out."

"Thanks. Right now I'm not up to talking about much of anything."

"Up to answering a different kind of question, maybe?" he suggested. "Look, if your engagement isn't any more serious than you make it sound and if you're not committed to Josh Smith, how about our having dinner occasionally while you're in town?"

"What about Jeanne?"

"We're friends, that's all," Gerry said, and laughed. "That word does carry a lot of latitude, doesn't it?"

"Yes, I guess so. And I'd like to have dinner with you. If..."

"If we could keep it on a 'friendly' basis?" Gerry teased.

She smiled. "Exactly."

"You have my word. Saturday night?"

"That would be good. I'm going to Pennsylvania Sunday. I'll be away a few days."

"Another photo assignment?"

"That, yes, but I'll also be visiting my family. My father and my brothers, that is. My mother died a while back."

"Marta, Josh Smith said something to Jeanne last night about your returning to London before long. Do you live in London?"

"I have been for the past two years."

"He said you're getting married in London come summer. Would that be to the friendly fiancé?"

"Gerry!" Marta warned.

"I know, I know." He laughed. "But you stir up a man's curiosity, Marta."

"To tell you the truth," Marta said, "I do plan to go back to London in a few weeks, but I don't know for how long. Or where I'll be going next."

"The whole world's your oyster, I take it," Gerry commented rather enviously.

"I suppose you could say that," Marta agreed. But her tone was bleak.

Chapter Twelve

Esthertown, Pennsylvania, was almost directly in the center of the four-hundred-eighty-square-mile strip in the eastern section of the state that contained the world's highest ranking anthracite coal bed.

The town literally had been built on coal, prospered on coal...and suffered because of coal. Marta remembered her father's saying that when he was growing up, there wasn't a family in town that hadn't lost at least one of its men in the mines.

Mining was safer now than it had been when Jeremy Brennan had gone to work in the Belden mines at the age of seventeen. But there was still danger, there were still disasters, despite the advances in technology. The Brennans had lost one of their six men fifteen years earlier in a cave-in. Marta's eldest brother, Joe, was twenty-three when he died; she'd been seventeen. She had adored him, and even now she couldn't think about him without grief welling up inside and pressing against her chest like a dark bird trying to escape its cage.

When she thought about Joe and his death, she thought, too, of her mother. Mary Brennan had never been the same after Joe had died. It was as though all the color had been drained out of her. Marta remembered her mother, in earlier years, as a pink-cheeked, pretty woman. After Joe's death she was ghost pale, probably because she rarely left the house then. Once, she confided to Marta that she couldn't face the sight of the mine shafts on the edge of town.

The last time Marta had been home the weather had been as bleak as it was today, the sky oyster white, the denuded tree branches stark and black against that sky, the rivers and streams a dull pewter.

The last time, she'd flown in from London and her brothers Jim and Hank had met her at the Philadelphia airport and had driven her the rest of the way. This time she'd opted to rent a car and drive by herself. Though it was icy cold, the highways were clear, and no snow was forecast.

The last few miles were the hardest. Though she'd been brought to this town as a baby, and lived in it through all her growing-up years, Marta couldn't wait to get away, and she'd gotten away right out of high school.

It had dismayed her terribly when Jim, Hank and her brother Tom, as well, had followed in their father's—and in Joe's—footsteps and had gone to work in the mines right out of high school. Only her brother Bert had turned his back on what had become a Brennan tradition. The day after his graduation from high school he'd enlisted in the army, and only after he'd signed up did he come home to tell his parents what he'd done. That was eight years ago, if Marta remembered correctly, and none of them had seen Bert since. He communicated, but he hadn't come home for their mother's funeral. The last Marta heard he was stationed in Germany.

As she drove into the town, she interpreted the familiar scenes from a new viewpoint—a professional viewpoint, which had become so sharpened these past few years that it came as no great surprise to discover that she was seeing things differently.

She preferred working in black and white. Like many photographers, she considered black and white a medium capable of far more artistry than color. Now she determined that although she and her editor had discussed her doing the Esthertown photos in color, she would convince him that she had to go with black and white. She supposed the sunless day was partly responsible for her decision. It emphasized the chiaroscuro contrasts of the freight yards with the empty hoppers waiting to receive the lustrous black anthracite. The gray houses. The dingy mine shafts.

Viewing the scene professionally helped her get through the last few minutes of the drive. But then she pulled up in front of the old frame house that had been home for as long as she remembered, and all she could think of was her mother. This would be the first time in her life she would be coming home without her mother there on the doorstep to greet her.

Hank Brennan was married with a baby daughter and had a house of his own a couple of blocks away from Marta's father's house. But Jim and Tom still lived in the old family place with their father.

Jeremy, after forty-five years of working in the Belden mines, had been retired six months earlier at age sixty-two. The retirement had been at the insistence of the mine physician, who, during the course of giving Jeremy a physical, had discovered his heart wasn't as strong as it might be.

Her father, Marta soon saw, still hadn't adjusted to what he considered "idleness," even though he did most of the housecleaning and a major share of the cooking for himself and his two sons.

"I could have gone on another three years at the least," Jeremy had insisted to her as they lingered at the kitchen table the morning after her arrival. "It would have meant more money, for one thing, both pension and social security...."

Marta had tried to take a light touch with him. "What would you do with more money, Dad?"

"What would anyone do with more money?" her father had demanded. "It costs a mint today just to eke by."

Marta knew that the house had been paid for years earlier and that both brothers who lived there were contributing to its upkeep and paying board. Her father had never been one to spend money frivolously. In earlier times he'd never had any money to spend frivolously, and now the habits of a lifetime were ingrained. She guessed, correctly, that he missed working in the mines, and wondered if maybe there might be a part-time job he could handle, perhaps in the mine offices. That would make him feel in closer touch with the work arena that was in some ways more like home to him than home itself.

She decided that when she went to see Fred Belden at the mines this afternoon she would ask him. She'd gone to high school with Fred. There'd been a time when they'd been considered a couple locally. Then Fred had gone off to college, and Marta had gone off to New York, clutching the camera the whole family had pitched in to buy her as a graduation present. She'd been in love with picture taking ever since her brother Joe had given her a Brownie camera when she was ten. Leaving home, she'd been determined to make her mark in photography, and that determination had seen her through some lean times to the first rungs of the ladder to her tremendous success.

Her appointment with Fred Belden was at two. By then Jeremy Brennan had pretty well filled his daughter in on the status quo at Belden Mines. Fred had taken over the management three years earlier, after his father had suffered a stroke that had left him partially paralyzed.

"Right away Fred had the offices redone," Jeremy Brennan reported. "Pretty posh. But, then, Fred's one of your Yuppies."

Marta was thinking of her father's description as she walked into Fred's office, which was indeed "posh," with thick, cinnamon-colored carpeting, sleek, blond wood furniture and a series of vivid, abstract prints lining the walls.

Fred himself also conformed to the Yuppie image in his charcoal-gray suit, white shirt and red-and-silver striped tie. The years had not been too kind to him. His hairline had receded, and he'd lost his boyish good looks. But, then, living in Esthertown and running the family coal mines would be enough to make anyone lose his looks, Marta thought, not without sympathy.

When the pleasantries were over—both of them trying to recall high-school classmates they'd lost track of and Fred updating Marta on some of their mutual acquaintances who still lived in town—Marta got down to the basic reason she'd made this appointment.

"For my story, Fred, I need to go down in the mines," she told him.

"No can do," Fred said, smiling apologetically.

"Why not?"

He laughed. "You never were one to beat around a bush, were you, Marta? Well...in this case, you should know the answer. Despite the technological improvements—and let me tell you, Belden Mines are state of the art, in that respect—it's too dangerous to take outsiders down where the actual operations are going on."

Marta bristled. "I wouldn't say I'm an outsider, Fred. The men in my family have been working in your family's mines for years. My brother Joe *died* in one of your mines...."

Fred flinched slightly, but said only, "I'm aware of that. It doesn't alter my position."

"And I presume the decision is all yours?"

"I make all the decisions concerning Belden Mines, Marta," Fred informed her smoothly.

"Well, I'd like to speak to your father about that," Marta stated. "Doesn't he have any say at all in the mine operations these days?"

"Dad hasn't been able to speak since he suffered his stroke," Fred told her.

"I'm sorry," Marta said quickly and sincerely. She'd always liked Fred's father.

"He's in a wheelchair, Marta. It's a miracle he's hung on as long as he has. So you can understand the one thing I don't want is anyone bothering him about matters concerning the mine."

"I'm not about to invade your father's privacy, Fred," Marta said. She spoke calmly, but the fire in her dark eyes gave her away.

Fred chuckled. "You haven't changed. And...that makes me happy. Sometimes it seems to me that most of the people I've known as long as I've known you have not only changed, profoundly in a lot of cases, but seldom for the better."

"That's cynical, Fred."

"Maybe. Regardless, you're even prettier than you were when I took you to our junior prom."

"And sent me a gardenia wrist corsage," she recalled.

"Right."

"What about you, Fred? Do you feel you've changed so much?"

"What do you think?"

"Maybe you look a wee bit older," she said tactfully. "But, then, we all do. And obviously you have a lot of responsibility on your shoulders. Are you married, Fred?"

"Divorced," he said briefly. "I met her at college. When I brought her home, she wasn't too taken with life in Esthertown. When I had to take over for Dad at the mines, it was the crowning touch. We divorced three years ago."

Fred added slowly, "I was sorry about your mother, Marta. I was away on business when she died. Later I heard you'd come home for the funeral..."

"Yes."

"I was sorry to miss you."

The sympathetic look in Fred's eyes was beginning to make her uncomfortable. She turned the conversation back to the reason for her visit. "Fred, look, about my going down in the mines..." she said.

He shook his head. "You always were tenacious."

"Okay, then, I'm more tenacious than ever. Being a professional photographer tends to suppress the timidity in one's nature. And the fact is...I want to do something real and good about Esthertown. I want to show this community, and the mining operations that gives it its pulse, exactly as it is."

Fred frowned slightly. "What do you mean by that?"

"I want to bring out what the town is like, what the mines are like, what coal mining is like... here in one of the world's major hard-coal belts. I want to do the very best photos I've ever done, Fred," Marta went on, becoming more and more enthusiastic about the project.

"I've seen your work, Marta," Fred acknowledged. "And I've been as impressed with it as everyone else is. But I admit, I'm a little apprehensive about your turning all that talent and attention on Esthertown and the Belden mines."

"Because you think the result will be negative?"

"I guess so, yes," Fred admitted.

"That's not my intention, Fred. My intention is to focus on the importance of the mines, and yes, on the sacrifices the men who work in them make. We're so computer and technologically oriented these days, I think we—I'm talking about the whole public—tend to forget about many things that have been around a long time... like coal mines. True, your operation, as you say, employs all the state-of-the-art mechanization available. But... they're still coal mines."

Fred nodded. "You're right about that. And..."

Fred seemed about to say something more, but Marta got the impression he thought better of it. Instead, smiling slightly, he told her, "I'm aware that any minute you're going to ask me again about going down in the mines... and knowing you as I do, I'm sure you're not going to let me off the hook easily."

Marta returned his smile. "Yes, that's so," she admitted.

"Marta, I can see what you're aiming for, and while initially I was afraid that kind of exposure would do us more harm than good, you've made your point with me. It could do no harm to focus on mining. In fact, it could do a lot of good—provided you're not excessively negative."

"Truthful, not negative," Marta promised him.

"Okay."

"Does that mean you're giving me carte blanche to go down into the mines?"

"No, but I'm going to clear your way as much as possible so you can have carte blanche about everything other than actually riding in one of the trains that take the men down. I think you're going to find so much to photograph that you won't need to go down to the working level."

"Can we put that thought on hold?" Marta asked.

"For the moment, yes," Fred said.

Marta left his office shortly before three o'clock with the promise that she could start photographing the following morning.

"Come to the office first," Fred instructed. "I'll introduce you around. Meantime I'll alert people to what you'll be doing. I think I can assure you you'll get max cooperation from everyone," Fred said, walking her to the door.

They exchanged friendly good-byes, but Marta's mind was focused on the work she'd be starting in the morning...and on her conviction that as that work progressed, Fred would become more and more lenient, so that before she finished she'd get exactly where she wanted to go in Belden Mines.

She'd insisted that she was going to fix dinner that night, and dinner was going to be a Greek stew she'd learned to make while on a photo assignment in the Greek islands early the previous spring.

She stopped at a supermarket on her way back to her father's house and was carrying her purchases up the front steps half an hour or so later, at about the same time there was a major cave-in at Belden Mines.

It was weird. It was like an echo of Africa's famous tribal drum system, Marta thought. But for as long as she could remember, whenever there was trouble at the mines word spread through town like a wind whispering along the streets and filtering through the cracks in the windows of the tired old frame houses.

The feeling of disaster became a part of the air people breathed, so that when Marta met her father at the kitchen door it was not even such a shock to hear him say, "There's been an accident at the mine." But when he'd continued, "And I think both Hank and Tom are down there today," Marta stared at him speechlessly, riveted by fear. Though she'd had an eerie premonition about the mine even before he'd spoken, she'd not thought about her brothers being there on the site . . . possibly trapped.

Within minutes Marta and her father were driving toward the mines, and in slightly less than an hour since she'd left Fred she was standing at his side, ready to help and willing to do anything she had to do to convince him to let her.

Things had not gone well for Josh that day. A staff writer he'd always had a lot of faith in had turned in a story that was completely botched up, and Josh had summoned the man to his office, ready to do battle.

One long look had shown him that the writer was in the throes of a problem Josh diagnosed privately as a severe hangover. Subsequent conversation revealed that the man's wife had left him three weeks earlier and was now in the Virgin Islands with a musician she'd evidently been seeing for quite some time.

"Can you believe it?" the writer asked, his pale, red-rimmed eyes mirroring his misery. "After twelve years she walks out cold. Can you wonder," he finished, "that I could count on the fingers of one hand the sober breaths I've been drawing lately? Especially since I got a notice from her lawyer ten days ago telling me she's filing for divorce in St. Thomas."

Josh couldn't help but be sympathetic. There'd been enough moments lately when he'd felt like drowning in Scotch himself. On the other hand, he was faced with a huge hole in his next issue, because there was no way this man's story could be rescued in time. Much of the rest of the day was spent unearthing suitable material to plug the hole. He paused only long enough to have a brief lunch with Trina Cataldo, in from London to appear as a guest on the *Today* show, and he knew he miffed Trina when he told her frankly there was just no way he could meet her for dinner that night.

It was after six when he escaped the office, took a taxi home and poured himself a liberal jot of whiskey as soon as he got inside his apartment. For just a moment he surveyed the amber liquid distrustfully. He had no wish to follow in the steps of the writer he'd dealt with that morning. Then he downed the Scotch, because right now a drink seemed the right prescription.

All day, despite the pressure of other work, he'd been unable to thrust Marta out of his mind. He knew she was going to Pennsylvania to do her coal-mining photos, but he wasn't sure exactly when she was leaving. He also knew he should have called her long before now. His behavior was inexcusable. But his problem was that he was in as much of a funk in his way as the writer who'd turned to alcohol to keep himself going.

Josh headed for his living room and dropped grate-fully into his favorite armchair next to the picture win-dow. He'd been making all kinds of excuses to himself for not calling Marta, and he was only too aware he'd been rationalizing every step of the way. The real reason he hadn't called her was that he felt so damned guilt-ridden about what had happened between them in her hotel room. What made things considerably worse was he knew in all honesty that, were history to repeat itself, he'd do exactly the same thing all over again.

The telephone rang. For convenience's sake, Josh had several phones in his apartment and he reached for the one immediately at hand, on a side table.

"Josh Smith?" a crisp British voice asked. "Tony Ashford here."

Surprised and feeling that familiar twinge of guilt, Josh said, "Well, hello. You're in New York again?"

"No, I'm calling from London."

Josh glanced at the clock by the phone. He calculated that it was approaching midnight in London. Late for a casual call. "What is it, Tony?" he asked, suddenly on the alert, as Marta's name began to thud silently in his head.

"Have you seen the telly?" Tony asked.

"No. I just got home from the office, and I haven't turned it on."

"Marta's in Pennsylvania," Tony said, "as you prob-ably know. Esthertown's the name of the place, and she's there to do a story about coal miners and coal mining. Specifically, the Belden Company's mines, an enterprise where her father worked for a major part of his life and where two of her four living brothers now work..."

"Yes?" The thudding was getting louder.

"There was a cave-in in one of the mines at midafter-noon today your time," Tony said. "I don't know if

Marta was at the mine then, but she's there now. As I understand it, at least one of her brothers was among the men trapped ... and as you must know she lost her eldest brother in that same manner many years ago.''

Shocked, Josh couldn't even speak. He was appalled to think he hadn't even known about Marta's loss.

"Josh?" Tony queried.

"Yes."

"I'm at the studio. Needless to say, I'm monitoring every scrap of news coming through from the States, but right now we're getting very little from Esthertown. It occurred to me there might be more on your television. I'd be appreciative if you'd watch and get back to me if there's anything ... definitive.''

"Of course," Josh said quickly. "I'll get back to you in any event within the next half hour or so.''

For a moment after he'd hung up Josh sat very still. He was stunned. Stunned to think that Marta had lost a brother and had never told him about it. Shocked to think that the terrible loss might be repeated again. And *terrified* to think that Marta herself was at the disaster scene.

God knows what she might do under pressure.

That thought rang in Josh's ears as he reached for the TV remote control and switched on the set. Almost at once, as if it had been predestined, he saw a reporter with a microphone in hand standing in front of the mine entrance. In a daze, he heard the man saying, "Rescue workers are on the way to the underground chamber in which five men have been trapped since approximately three o'clock this afternoon. With them, accompanying mine owner Frederick Belden, is Marta Brennan, the internationally famous photographer. Brennan has been in Esthertown, where several members of her family live, on assignment to do a photo essay on modern coal mining and its impact on people and places. Two of her brothers, Thomas Brennan and Henry Brennan, are among the five miners trapped in a sudden roof fall. As of this hour, fears have been expressed that there may be further falls from the roof of the working face. That's to say, further cave-ins in or near the affected area . . ."

The words burned themselves into Josh's mind, and he felt numb all over. Then suddenly, savagely, he went into action, calling sources at NBC, CBS and ABC, as well as the Cable News Network. Men and women who were all good friends of his—and now the most valuable sources of information he could hope for.

It was close to an hour before he had the chance to call Tony Ashford, and he immediately apologized. "I had to wait for several people to get back to me," he told Tony.

"You have some word?"

"Not very good word. You know Marta. Evidently she insisted on going down with the mine owner, a guy named Fred Belden, with whom she apparently went to high school. I can't imagine what Belden must have been thinking of. I also know Marta's powers of persuasion, however. . . ."

"So do I," and Tony chuckled wryly.

"They're afraid of more cave-ins. I don't know what the devil to do," Josh said distractedly. And then he tugged in his reins and said, "I can imagine how you must feel. After all . . ."

"Yes."

"Well, she's *your* fiancée."

There was silence across the Atlantic. Then Tony said heavily, "It's a rotten time to get into anything like this, but under the circumstances I can't let you think that."

"What are you saying?"

"Marta's not my fiancée. When she came to London last month, not long after meeting you again in Washington, it was to break our engagement."

"She still has your ring on her finger."

"I know that, but it's only because I asked her to keep wearing it. I had the hope that maybe, if she had enough time, she might reconsider. I didn't know where *you* stood in all of this."

"I see."

"No, I don't think you do see, Smith. Nor can I expect you to, when I'm sure neither of us can think straight at the moment. I can only visualize Marta in that mine..."

"That makes two of us," Josh said soberly.

The men were alive. That much had been learned during the rescuers' first exploratory ride down into the earth. They had traveled in the streamlined steel train ordinarily used to transport miners.

In this subterranean world, there was a veritable city that even Marta, who'd heard about mines all her life, had never fully envisioned. The huge machines used in modern mining operations were contained in vast underground facilities. There were miles of roads—used mainly for haulage—railway tracks, and complete telephone and radio systems, as well as electric lighting within the main passageways.

But regardless of the latest in technology, there still was danger. Marta knew it, and knew Fred was even more aware of it because of her presence.

Despite her fear for her brothers, she photographed feverishly, knowing that a moment was going to come, and soon, when Fred was going to insist they return to the surface. But it was while she was down there in a strange and alien world that she heard that the advance rescue team had received signals from the men. So up to now, anyway, they—at least some of them—were alive. Marta plunged into her work and didn't let herself think beyond that.

The moment came when Fred said, "Marta, we're going back up," and she knew that this time he was not about to brook any interference from her. It had taken everything she had in her to persuade him to let her make the ride down with him, and she knew he was acting against his better judgment. But two of her brothers were down there... and she'd lost one brother to the mines already.

On the surface, friends and family members had converged, and Marta plunged into work again, talking to people, photographing, trying to keep her terrible fears at bay.

Finally the rescue team broke through, and the men who'd been trapped were brought to the surface. Through her tears, Marta kept on photographing and photographing and photographing, stopping only when she saw her brother Tom and, just behind him, her brother Hank. Then she put aside her camera and ran to join the others who were welcoming the men back into the world of living. Things could so easily have gone the other way....

By that time there were television cameras on the scene, and another photographer took Marta's picture as she and her two brothers clutched one another in a fervent embrace.

There was a television close-up of Marta, her dark hair tumbling wildly about her shoulders, tears of joy streaming down her face.

Josh saw her on the midnight news... and had never before loved her quite so much.

Chapter Thirteen

Marta, there's a guy named Josh Smith who wants to speak to you,'' Tom Brennan reported.

Tom had gone to answer the phone. The rest of the family was in the kitchen, sitting around the old round oak table. It was two o'clock in the morning. Jeremy had just fried sausages and scrambled eggs for all of them, and Marta had been marveling at the fact that Hank and Tom and Jim were devouring the food as ravenously as if they'd just finished a normal working day.

One man had suffered a broken leg in the mine accident. The other four had emerged unscathed—which in itself was a kind of miracle.

The past eleven hours had been so traumatic that Marta felt a total sense of unreality, made greater by what Tom had just told her. How could Josh possibly be on the phone? She doubted he even knew the name of the Pennsylvania town she came from.

It occurred to her that they both had left big personal gaps in their discussions about so many other things.

"Marta, are you going to speak to this guy?" Tom prodded.

"Yes," Marta said, but she made her way slowly down the front hall, still disbelieving.

At her tentative hello, Josh demanded, "Marta, are you all right?"

"I'm fine," Marta said automatically. "Why? What I mean is, how did you—"

"Why?" he cut her off. "I've been *frantic*, that's why. That's to say, we've been frantic."

We? She frowned. "Josh, how did you know where to find me?"

"Tony Ashford told me."

"Tony?"

"He called from London several hours ago. I just talked to him, and I said I was going to call you. Needless to say, he hasn't had a wink of sleep, and he was going to try to catch a couple of hours before he has to do a morning telecast."

"I don't understand," Marta said weakly.

"Tony got news of the cave-in in London. He knew you were in Esthertown. He called me, hoping I could get some further word. I learned that you...oh, God, I still can't believe you did that...that you actually went down in that mine."

"My brothers were down there, Josh."

"Yes, I know. And it's true they're safe, isn't it?"

"Yes."

"And you...Marta, are you sure you're all right?"

Josh wasn't attempting to conceal his anxiety, which was unusual. Marta tried to imagine how she would feel if she'd heard Josh had gone into a mine where there'd just been a cave-in, and she was sure she would have torn her hair out. But she and Josh were so different. Anyway, Josh didn't feel about her the way she did about him. She was so mixed up. And exhausted. And right now she wanted Josh's arms around her more than she wanted anything else in the world.

"Marta..." Josh began.

"Honestly, I'm fine," Marta said, her voice softer.

"When are you coming back to New York?"

"In a couple of days," Marta said. "Why? Do you need more on the Grants?"

"Yes, I may, but that's not what I was thinking of. I..."

"Yes?"

Marta knew Josh so well she could picture exactly how he looked right now, thinking about something he didn't know whether he should say or not. Contemplative. Deciding finally to be casual. Sounding very casual as he said, "Call me when you get into town, will you? We need to get together."

"Sure," Marta said wearily. "Yes. Of course." And on that note she rang off.

Hanging up the receiver a second after Marta did, Josh swore silently. Everything in him had urged him to spill out some of his feelings for her, but he'd suppressed the urge. He was so damned used to suppressing urges it had become second nature, he thought savagely. And he wasn't particularly fond of that aspect of his character.

The phone rang. It was his sister Jennifer, up in Rhode Island.

"Josh, I've been trying to get you for hours," Jennifer said. "Your line has been consistently busy. You saw the TV news?"

"I've seen hours of TV news," Josh told her.

"Then you know Marta is safe?"

"Yes."

"I saw her when she ran to her brothers and the three of them hugged and kissed one another. I cried buckets," Jennifer said.

Josh had wanted to cry buckets. As usual, he had resisted the impulse.

"Look," Jennifer said, "do you know when Marta's coming back to New York?"

"In a couple of days, I think."

"You have more magazine business with her?"

"Well—er—yes."

"Josh, please bring her up here to Watch Hill with you for a couple of days. Kerry says it doesn't matter whether it's on a weekend or not—he'll take time off. We both want to see the two of you. I especially want to talk to Marta before she heads back to London. Do you know when she's getting married?"

"She said June 10," Josh told his sister, which, after all, was what Marta had told him. He still couldn't figure out the charade Tony Ashford had told him about. It didn't make sense. Maybe if Marta came back from Pennsylvania without that ring on her finger it would begin to make sense. But until then...

They met for lunch at L'Auberge. Josh, casting discretion to the wind, had again reserved a table in the upstairs room with the fireplace.

Marta was pale; there were dark smudges under her eyes; Josh thought she was thinner than ever. Though maybe that was his imagination, he admitted, because she also appeared more beautiful than ever. Just looking at her made him yearn to take her home with him, fatten her up and make love to her—not necessarily in that order.

She started to talk about the mining accident, and he let her talk. He had the feeling she'd been holding all this in while still in Pennsylvania and she needed to let it out. Unlike himself, Marta wasn't very good at suppressing things. Which, he thought wryly, made her the more fortunate of the two of them.

"What galls me is that you'd think mining, with all the advances in technology, all the machinery they use now, would finally have become safe," she told Josh. "But it isn't. I checked out everything I could, and I discovered that mechanization has actually increased the risk of accidents."

"Why?" Josh asked her.

"Well, in simple terms, it seems that faster progress, understandably, is made with the machines than when mining was totally, or even relatively, a man-powered operation. But that means there's more chance of roof falls at the working site, which is what happened the other day.

"What really gets me, though," Marta went on, ignoring the glass of Dubonnet Josh had ordered for her, "is that comparisons have been done of mine accidents in Europe and the United States, and the results show that there are fewer site accidents in Europe."

"Why, do you know?"

"Yes. They have safer methods, stricter regulations, even though that means higher production costs. Still, even the average coal miner in America is a lot safer today than he was back in the days when my father went to work for Belden Mines."

"That doesn't make sense," Josh protested.

"Well, it does, actually, because despite a higher risk of cave-ins, the daily wear and tear on workers is milder today. Men don't have to work as many hours today to make a living as they did back when Dad went into the mines. Also, because of the machines, more tonnage can be mined using less manpower." Marta paused, looked closely at Josh. "I must be boring you to death," she said.

"No, not at all," he denied. "Matter of fact, you make my mental wheels turn. If you hadn't already contracted to work on this for a competitor, I think I might have asked you to do something for *Living*."

"I rather wish I were doing the story for *Living*, Josh," Marta said rather wistfully. "Because I think the pictures I took in Esthertown are probably the best photographs I've ever done."

Before Josh could analyze that remark, Marta progressed quickly to something else. "What about the Grants?" she asked him. "Do you have everything you need?"

"Insofar as their house is concerned, yes, I think so," Josh said. "But something else has come up. And anyway, the 'Transitions' series is one of the reasons I wanted to meet with you today. I've decided to scrap it, Marta."

Marta sat back, her dark eyes narrowing as she stared at him. "Would you mind telling me why?" she demanded.

"No. That's why I asked you to meet me for lunch. I intend to tell you why."

"Well, then?"

"I intend to go with the Grant story...in fact, I've written more than half of it. That's the first thing I wanted to tell you. But I'm going to bag the other five episodes. I think it would drag, Marta. Too much on the subject. The concept can be gotten across with just the Grant story."

"I don't see how you can say that," she protested. "The other couples you planned to use are entirely different people. Different ages, different backgrounds, different rationales...."

"I know. And maybe later on we'll pick up on them, do vignettes with a single photo, or maybe before and after pictures if they've made a move. That would cover the spectrum adequately. By then we can gauge by reader response how interested people are in the topic."

"It doesn't sound as if you're very much interested in it yourself, Josh."

"I was, or I never would have instigated the project," Josh told her quietly.

And that was true enough. But Josh had reason to feel slightly guilty, knowing that he hadn't told her the whole truth about why he was ending the project. In part, his reason was that he couldn't face up to the multiple conferences with her if the original concept was adhered to.

He would be assigning the other five articles to staff writers, true. He'd still have to coordinate the whole effort, though, deal with the writers and photographers— photographer, in this case, he amended. Which would mean more meetings with Marta than he felt he could handle under their present circumstances.

The first thing he'd noted as he and Marta had sat down opposite each other at the choice table that had been reserved for him was that Marta was still wearing her sparkling diamond on the proper finger.

Marta, insofar as visible evidence was concerned, was still engaged to Tony Ashford. Which meant that someone was lying. Both Marta, with her announcement of a June 10 wedding date, and Tony, with his insistence that he and Marta hadn't been "really" engaged for weeks, couldn't be telling the truth.

If she'd gone to London to break her engagement to Tony, why on earth hadn't she told him so when she'd come back to New York and they'd met for lunch in this very same place?

On the other hand, why had Tony said what he had? Was he trying to get out of his engagement to Marta, and so his statement on the phone had been preliminary to taking some more definitive action?

Tony was certainly anything but indifferent to Marta. That much had been proven to Josh by the sound of the Englishman's voice on the phone, by the man's intense worry about her. Tony had been pretty distraught. Then, when Josh had called to tell him Marta was safe, his relief had been profound, his expression of it heartfelt.

Well, maybe Tony cared about her...but maybe he didn't love her, Josh mused. At least not as a man needed to love the woman he was going to marry. Tony *was* a fair bit older...though not that much older. Also, he'd had two marital failures. Could it be that as the calendar edged toward the day when wedding bells would ring for him for the third time he was getting cold feet?

"Would you mind telling me what it is you're thinking about?" Marta said impatiently. "You have the oddest expression on your face."

"I was thinking about you," Josh said. And that certainly was the truth.

"Thinking that you wish you'd never gotten me involved in the 'Transitions' articles in the first place, is that it?"

"No," Josh said hastily, "that's not it at all. Which brings us back to the Grants."

"Does it? Look, Josh, although we did have an oral agreement about my doing the photography for you on *six* different pieces, not one, I'm not about to sue you for breach of contract or anything."

"Marta..."

"I'm serious. Not that I wouldn't have grounds."

"Come on..."

"I'm serious."

"So . . . you're serious."

"I'm not asking for anything from you," Marta stated, her cheeks suddenly flushed. "So if you're going to try to embellish the Grant story just as a panacea for me . . ."

Josh had to smile. "I'd be the last ever to offer you a panacea, Marta," he told her. "A panacea, correctly defined, is a remedy or cure-all. What you mean is a sop, isn't it?"

The flush deepened. "I hate it when you pick on the words I use and define them properly and make me feel like an unschooled idiot," Marta flared. "It's an insult to my intelligence."

It was all Josh could do not to circumvent the table between them and kiss her. He said mildly but nonetheless sincerely, "I'd be the last person ever to try to, or want to, insult your intelligence, Marta. Look, why don't you let me tell you what I have in mind about the Grant story, and you decide for yourself?"

"If you must."

"Well, the Grants plan to spend a couple of days next week going condo shopping. Then they're going to make their decision. I think they're having second thoughts about selling the house and uprooting totally. To tell you the truth, I think some of your preliminary photos of the house, which I've shown them, have had the effect of making them realize what a beautiful place they have there. Mrs. Grant had tears in her eyes when she looked at your pictures.

"So," Josh went on when Marta didn't respond, "my thought is for you to follow the Grants around when they condo shop, photographing all the way. You can catch their reactions, their pleasure or displeasure. If they decide on one of the condos, you can go back with them with the thought of our doing a larger spread on it. If they turn thumbs down on moving, you'll be able to show, photographically, why they opted to stay with the old rather than to go with the new. Does that make sense to you?''

"Yes," Marta admitted grudgingly.

"Then you'll do it?"

"Yes, I'll do it."

"I wonder if maybe you'll consider doing something else."

"What?"

"Jennifer called. She saw the cave-in stories on TV and was as frantic as the rest of us until we knew you were safe. She and Kerry are begging me to bring you up to Watch Hill for a couple of days. The sooner the better, but definitely before—"

"Yes?" Marta probed when Josh broke off.

"Well, before you go back to England," Josh said, and, unable to wrest his eyes away, stared down at the sparkling ring on her finger.

Marta's assignments—including following the Grants around and taking pictures of the various condos they looked at—kept her so busy that March came in like a lamb and was on it's way out like a lion before she could take time off to go to Watch Hill with Josh.

It was a gold-washed day, the sun reigning in a clear blue sky. As they drove up the Connecticut Turnpike, Marta opened the car window on impulse and sniffed.

Josh slanted a glance at her. "Too warm for you?" he asked.

"No," Marta said, closing the window again. "It's not too warm. I wanted to smell spring, that's all."

"Seems to me the trees are pretty bare."

"The willows are green-gold," Marta pointed out. "And I think I saw some forsythia beginning to bloom in the side yard of a little house back a ways."

"You're imagining things," Josh teased. He took his eyes off the road just long enough to glance at her again, and smiled. Marta was wearing a bright yellow coat, and she looked like a harbinger of spring. She looked tired still, but . . . gorgeous. And . . . much too desirable.

"Well," Josh asked her gently, "*did* you smell spring?"

"Yup," she said, nodding.

"How does spring smell?"

"Don't you know?" She sounded honestly surprised.

"Well," Josh admitted, "I don't think I've ever gotten out and tried to actually smell it. I guess I wait for the feeling in the air."

"That comes later. Spring's smell is first, and it's earthy. That's it! Spring smells like earth. New earth."

"Is there such a thing as new earth?"

"Must you be so literal?"

He laughed. He loved sparring with her like this over foolish little things. And he was pretty sure she enjoyed their verbal fencing as much as he did, when it wasn't over anything important.

Maybe he was the literal one and she was the imaginative one—though, actually, he wasn't nearly as literal as she seemed to think, and there'd been times when he'd seen a definitely practical side to Marta's nature. All in all, they balanced each other. In so many ways . . .

Marta was watching Josh's face, and she saw a play of emotions on it that was rare for Josh. She would have given a great deal to know what he was thinking, wished that if she asked him, she might hope for even half an answer. Also, she was just recovering from that smile he'd bestowed on her. Josh didn't smile like that nearly often enough. But when he did, it rocked her from head to toes. Josh had a dazzling smile. He was handsome enough anyway, but when he smiled, he was . . . irresistible.

The sun, slanting across his hair, brought out burnished lights in it . . . dark copper, antique bronze. Marta feasted her eyes on his hair, his profile, on Josh, and her love for him welled up in her.

As if he felt her watching him so closely, Josh said, "A penny."

"What?"

"A penny for your thoughts."

Marta felt absurdly flustered, but she managed to say, "A penny doesn't buy much these days, Josh."

"Ouch," Josh retorted, but he didn't pursue the matter.

They stopped along the turnpike for coffee. Josh had a hamburger and eyed disapprovingly at the peanut-butter-filled crackers Marta munched.

"When are you ever going to learn to eat properly?" he asked her.

"Oh, maybe when I settle down," Marta said flippantly.

It was merely a remark she tossed out casually, but she saw the expression on Josh's face change. "Well, that should be pretty soon, I'd think," he told her stonily.

"Josh . . ." Marta began, then stopped. She'd been on the verge of confessing that her engagement to Tony wasn't real. But this wasn't the place for the kind of explanations she'd need to make before she could hope to satisfy Josh. He was not only a good editor, he was a good reporter. She knew she could expect an in-depth interview once she told him why she was wearing Tony's ring.

"We'd better be getting on," Josh said abruptly.

And Marta preceded him out to his car, aware that once again what had been a precious mood between the two of them had been shattered.

Thanks to Kerry's architectural skills and Jennifer's talents as an interior designer, the Gundersen home at Watch Hill was a showplace.

A couple of years back, when restoration of the old mansion was newly completed, the Gundersens had had their privacy invaded by swarms of sightseers. Now curiosity had ebbed, and most of the time they were able to live exactly as they wanted to.

They were both there to welcome Josh and Marta when they arrived, and Jennifer led Marta upstairs to the exquisitely furnished guest room she'd chosen for her.

"You know," she observed, perching on a boudoir chair covered in apricot tapestry, "I very nearly didn't work a downstairs bedroom into my plans when I was redoing this place for Kerry. There are five upstairs bedrooms, after all, plus the master suite, and that seemed more than enough. But then I decided that having a small downstairs suite with a bedroom and an adjacent study and bath might be useful. Now for Josh's sake, I'm so glad we have the first-floor suite. Our front staircase is magnificent, but there are a lot of steps to climb."

"You already knew you'd be marrying Kerry and Josh would be visiting you," Marta teased.

"I most certainly did not," Jennifer protested with mock indignation. Then she asked suddenly, "Marta, are you really going to marry Tony Ashford on the tenth of June?"

The question, coming like the proverbial bolt of lightning, took Marta totally by surprise. Especially when she realized that the matter of her marriage must be so at the forefront of Jennifer's mind that Jennifer couldn't keep from asking her about it at the earliest opportunity.

She faced her friend and said honestly, "I'm not going to marry Tony at all, Jen."

Jennifer sagged briefly, and her "Whew!" was heartfelt. Then she asked, "Does Josh know that?"

"No."

"Why haven't you told him? And why are you still wearing Tony's ring?"

"It's a long, complicated story, Jen. Don't ask me to go into it right now," Marta pleaded. "Okay, let's just say that initially I agreed to do Tony a . . . well, a sort of favor. Actually, at the time it seemed a move that would be beneficial to both of us."

"Are you saying that's the way you originally felt about accepting his proposal?" Jennifer asked incredulously.

"No, no . . . I accepted his proposal, Jen, because I'm very fond of Tony. I love him . . . in a way. I thought we could make a good life together. And I . . . I never expected to see Josh again. Not for years, anyway. Until we were both old and . . . and the fire had died." Marta ran her hands through her thick black hair. "Oh, damn," she said. "You see . . . just getting into it unnerves me, Jen."

To Marta's surprise, Jennifer smiled, then said gently, "Okay, we won't get into it. I know you have good reasons for anything you do, Marta. You may seem like an impulsive extrovert to the rest of the world, but I know you better. I got to know you very well when we were both working on this house together. And I don't in the least blame my brother for being so hopelessly in love with you. Now," Jennifer concluded brightly, "shall we go back downstairs and join our men?"

I don't in the least blame my brother for being so hopelessly in love with you. That statement of Jennifer's kept ringing in Marta's ears through the rest of the afternoon and on into the evening.

Was Josh really hopelessly in love with her? More important, would he ever really love her even half as much as she loved him?

There was nothing new about those questions, Marta reminded herself wryly. Since she'd met Josh again, she'd silently posed them a hundred times...without ever coming to any satisfactory answers. She knew that the chemistry, the potent sexual attraction, was as powerful for Josh as it was for her. What concerned her went beyond the physical into the deep, deep feelings between a man and a woman that linger after passion.

She stole a glance at Josh. He was sitting near the blazing fireplace, talking to Kerry. The two men were close friends and had much in common. Kerry was now an internationally famous architect. Josh, until moving over to assume the top position at *Living, American Style*, had been as involved in *Architecture, American Style* as in the sister magazine. That's when he'd met Kerry, and it had been the start of a friendship that had been flourishing ever since. Now their mutual interests went way beyond careers. At the moment they were animatedly discussing whether the Boston Celtics were going to win the NBA play-offs. Kerry, a New Englander by adoption, was an avid Celtics fan. Josh, a New Yorker by adoption, was making it plain that he was rooting for the Knickerbockers, and he appeared to be just as much a basketball fan as Kerry.

Something else she didn't know about Josh, Marta thought ruefully. Why hadn't he ever told her he was a basketball addict? She'd played basketball in high school back in Esthertown, but she loved the game a lot more as a spectator sport. Why, the two of them could have gone to Madison Square Garden one night!

What else did Josh like to do that she didn't know about? Marta wondered.

Although Kerry and Jennifer had household help, they both liked to cook, and that night Kerry prepared dinner while Jennifer—with Marta's willing help—got the twins fed and ready for bed.

Again the boy baby named after Josh tugged at her heartstrings. "He's growing by leaps and bounds," she said to Jennifer.

"So's Caroline," Jennifer pointed out, "though I have to admit that Josh is already the bigger of the two."

"Well, he *is* a boy," Marta said, and knew that although Caroline was equally adorable, Josh was the one who would always charm her the most. Impulsively she asked, "Jen, do you have any pictures of Josh when he was little?"

Surprised, Jennifer said, "Funny you should ask. I was going through some family stuff just the other day and I came across a photo album full of pictures of Josh and me and our parents. We traveled a lot, with our father in the army, and I was a real shutterbug. But it's pretty obvious that unlike you my talents didn't lie in that direction. Nevertheless . . . there are some good shots of Josh growing up, and some baby pictures of both of us that I caged from Mother." Jennifer smiled. "I don't think I have to ask you if you want to see them."

"I'd love to see them," Marta confessed readily.

"All right. Why don't you go on back downstairs and I'll ferret out the album and put it in your room," Jennifer suggested. "Then you can browse through it later to your heart's content. And if you want to snitch a photo or two . . . I won't hold it against you."

Jennifer laughed conspiratorially. "Just don't tell Josh," she cautioned, then sobered. "He'd have a fit," she said seriously. "He doesn't like to look at what he considers his 'before' pictures, and I don't think he'd relish the idea of your seeing them, either."

Chapter Fourteen

It was late when Jennifer and Kerry, Josh, and Marta went to their rooms. As Marta walked up the curving staircase she paused to glance back and saw Josh moving down a short corridor to his small, private suite. The urge to follow him, to be with him, became so powerful it was all she could do to continue mounting the rest of the steps. He stood straight when he walked, his shoulders squared, but his progress was of necessity halting, and he looked so damned *lonely*....

Well, she reflected bitterly, he was no lonelier than she was.

She saw the album Jennifer had left for her the minute she entered her bedroom. She hardly could have missed it. Jennifer had placed it atop the fluffy, pale-orange satin quilt folded at the foot of the bed.

Marta was sorely tempted to sit down immediately and start thumbing through it, but for the moment resisted the temptation, forcing herself to try to relax by soaking in gardenia-scented bubbles in the circular, turquoise tub in the adjoining bathroom. Wickedly it occurred to her that it was a tub plenty big enough for two . . . and the thought of Josh sharing it with her was so tantalizing she suddenly got out of the water, grabbed an oversize bath towel and vigorously began to rub herself dry.

Thoughts wafted as she rubbed. It had been a good evening. They'd played a new edition of Trivial Pursuit, which was fun, and Josh had won three games in a row. The range of his knowledge never failed to astonish Marta. Thinking of that reminded her of the wonderful evenings they'd shared in front of the big picture window in his river-view living room. They'd talked and talked and talked as they sipped wine. And then in the wee hours they'd gone to bed together. . . .

Marta tried to turn her wandering thoughts away from the past, but it wasn't easy. Ironically, it was only the reminder of the album waiting to be perused that lured her back to the present. And finally she curled up in bed, propped pillows behind her head and started to turn the pages.

Before she finished, she was crying. She got up and pattered to the bathroom for some tissues, and angrily daubed her cheeks. Then she kept daubing them as she scanned the pictures all over again, page by page.

Yes, she could see why Josh didn't want to look at pictures like these. The earlier ones might not be so hard for him to take, but the later ones, especially from the time he entered the air force academy, were bound to be pretty painful.

Marta went back to the early pictures again and, remembering Jennifer's invitation, filched two of them. The first showed Josh when he was just a few months old, about the age his namesake was now. And she would have sworn that there was a decided resemblance between Josh I and Josh II.

Lucky Josh II, she thought, if he grew up to look like his uncle.

The second picture she chose dated from when Josh was about five. He was a sturdy, handsome child, and the grin on his face totally captivated Marta. He looked like a cherub, but she could see the mischief lurking behind that wide smile.

At moments she'd seen that same glint of mischief in the adult Josh. And she'd wished so much that she had the power to encourage the fun side of his nature. So much of the time he was far too serious.

She moved on. And came to the pictures of Josh in high school when he'd been a star athlete. He, too, had played basketball. And he'd been on the track team. And there was a picture of him water-skiing on a mountain lake in Switzerland. Marta remembered Jennifer talking about their taking Swiss vacations when her father was stationed in Germany.

Then there was a picture of Josh as an air force cadet, and she caught her breath, he was so handsome in uniform. There were quite a few pictures of him taken during the cadet years, usually snapped by Jennifer when he came to visit the family on his leaves from the academy. And finally there was a picture of him in flying garb. Under it Jennifer had written, "This was taken just a week before Josh crashed."

After that, the pages in the album were blank.

Marta riffled the pages back to a shot taken during the air force academy years, when Josh had been home on a visit and the quarters General Smith and his family had at that time boasted a swimming pool.

Josh, wearing snug swimming trunks, was standing on the diving board. Every detail of his terrific physique was revealed, and he looked young and tanned and healthy. Impulsively Marta slipped the picture out and put it with the other two.

Finally she turned out her bedside light. Yet she couldn't get to sleep. Her thoughts about Josh were all mixed up. But as they whirled together she came to the conclusion that she would do anything, absolutely anything, if she could persuade Josh to make an appointment with Gerry Baskin. And she would do anything, anything, if Gerry Baskin could make the same kind of miracle happen for Josh he'd made happen for other people.

If only, if only. Sometimes life was made up of if onlys, and conjecturing about that brought on such a restlessness that Marta could no longer lie in bed and pretend that sleep would come at any instant.

She yielded to her instincts. Slipping on a robe that matched her coffee-colored satin-and-lace nightgown, she silently slipped down the curving staircase and headed for Josh's room.

Josh was wide-awake. Leaving Marta at the bottom of that staircase had been incredibly hard. Then he'd told himself that maybe it was just as well as he would find it difficult to handle that number of steps. Otherwise he could have predicted the consequences.

He wanted her so damned much.

The yearning tore at him. His need for her threatened to drive him slightly crazy. For a while he tried to focus on a book Kerry had loaned him. It was a clever mystery, but he couldn't concentrate on the story, much as it ordinarily would have intrigued him. He put the book aside and turned off the light, because he knew if he kept on reading, he would never remember what he'd read, anyway.

It was very still in the house. Not even any wind tonight to whisper against the windowpanes. He heard the doorknob turn, and a sharp instinct warned him who it was quietly entering his room.

He wasn't ready for her.

His guard was down, Josh knew, the symbolic pieces of armor strewed all over the place. He tried to reassemble them as he also tried to pretend he was asleep. And he heard Marta say softly, "Josh?"

When he didn't respond, she said a bit louder, "Josh."

When he still didn't respond she reached out and touched his forehead, and it was like receiving an electric shock. Josh sat bolt upright, and Marta said, "Oh, I didn't mean to startle you."

He reached for the switch on the bedside light. A soft, pale white glow spread around him . . . and bathed Marta in gentle radiance. And her beauty swept Josh away.

Marta sat down on the edge of his bed. "Look, I had to see you," she said in a low voice.

Josh grasped desperately for a touch of humor. "Well," he managed rather hoarsely, "you're seeing me."

"What I meant to say was, I have to talk to you." Marta tried again. "What I *mean* to say is there's something I have to tell you."

"Something so important it can't wait till morning?" Josh queried, trying not to look at the way her satin robed molded the soft thrust of her breasts.

"Something that shouldn't have waited at all," Marta said, glancing down at her hands.

Josh looked, too, and saw that her ring finger was bare.

"I know," he said. "You've lost your diamond, and you're afraid to tell Ashford."

She shook her head. "No, the diamond's upstairs on the dresser."

"Oh. You take it off at night, then."

"I've taken it off for good."

"What are you trying to say, Marta?"

"I'm not *trying* to say anything. I'm saying it."

Josh's usually firm grip on his self-control was weakening. He clutched at it, tried mentally to pump some strength into it. The attempt wasn't too successful, but he somehow managed to keep his voice reasonably level as he said, "Are you suggesting you've broken your engagement?"

"I broke my engagement two months ago, Josh."

Josh sank back against the pillows and closed his eyes. He was hearing what she was saying, all right, but he was having vision problems at the same time. His eyes were all filled up with the sight of her, and the sight of her was arousing him to a point where it was becoming a genuine physical problem.

The whole situation was becoming too much to handle. Josh tried to blacken out the image that was tormenting him and to think of the right thing to say to her all at the same time. That didn't work, either. He found himself stating, "I know. Ashford told me."

The silence roared. The pressure of the roar beat against Josh's eardrums, and he opened his eyes. Marta was rigid, her dark eyes enormous as she stared at him. "Tony *told* you?" she echoed disbelievingly.

Josh had to try to be snide in self-defence. "Your incredulity's showing, Marta," he said. "Yes, Ashford told me."

"When?"

"When we were both afraid you were trapped in that mine cave-in."

"Then when I got back to New York, why didn't *you* tell *me*?" Marta demanded.

Josh sat up straight. "Why didn't I tell you?" he echoed. "Come on! That was your move, wouldn't you say? It was your engagement. Regardless of what either you and Ashford are saying now, you were still wearing his ring. Maybe you just like big flashy diamonds and you couldn't bear to give it up. On the other hand, you did happen to mention that you and Ashford were going to be married on the tenth of June."

"That was just to get you off my back," Marta snapped.

"That does have a funny ring to it, Marta."

"Don't be lewd, Josh,"

"Well," Josh said, "that's a new one. At least, I don't think you've ever accused me of *that* before."

Marta got up and paced across the room to the window, then paced back. She reminded him of a trapped tiger, or maybe a leopard. Graceful, taut, but moving sinuously, energy contained. God, Marta had so damn much energy to be unleashed....

"I'm not sure I can forgive you for this," she said.

Josh was honestly astonished. "Forgive me for *what*?"

"For not telling me Tony told you about the engagement. Tony didn't tell me he told you about the engagement, either."

"Well, good for Tony," Josh approved. "Maybe he thought you deserved to stew a little."

To his surprise, Marta's beautiful eyes suddenly filled with tears. Until recently Josh had never seen tears in Marta's eyes. As it had before, the sight again bothered him ... profoundly.

"Look," he began, chastised.

"Look, nothing," Marta shot back. "There were reasons for the arrangement Tony and I made..."

Marta broke off, and Josh said encouragingly, "Yes?"

But she only stood and crossed the room to the window.

She looked out upon a black night. There was not even a moon to give her an excuse for staring into the darkness. No magical, silver-accented scenery. The waters of Block Island Sound that bordered the beach at the edge of the Gundersens' property could have been a thousand miles away.

Marta kept her gaze riveted on the blackness, though, because she couldn't turn around and face Josh again.

Was there ever truth to Walter Scott's phrase "O, what a tangled web we weave, when first we practice to deceive!"

Marta felt as if she were caught up in a web, and the fact that it was largely one of her own making was no help at all. Still averting her face, she said to Josh, "I guess I can't expect you to understand this, but for a time both Tony and I felt it best that I keep wearing his ring, even though the engagement was off."

"Oh?" Josh queried politely. "Why was it best?"

"There's really no need to go into that."

"Isn't there?" Josh drawled. "Personally, I find the subject fascinating. And I have this strange feeling that you pretended to be engaged to Ashford so that you could keep other men from...annoying you, shall we say? Were you so sure that I'd make a nuisance of myself pursuing you, Marta?" Josh finished sharply.

"No," Marta retorted quickly. "You've never pursued me."

"Haven't I? Who was doing what to whom then, until you took off for London a couple of years ago?"

Marta crossed the room slowly, but she didn't sit down on the side of his bed again. She chose a small armchair at a relatively safe distance, and surveyed him.

"I'd like to think that neither of us was *pursuing* the other, Josh," she said finally. "To me, pursuit connotes thunderous chasing and a lot of heavy breathing...."

"Well, that's a definition I might or might not agree with," Josh told her. "You certainly must know I was very much interested in you back then."

"It seems to me we were very much interested in each other," Marta managed feebly.

"Okay, I'll buy that. Certainly we *were* very much interested in each other. Certainly there's still a very strong something between us. Call it chemistry, a sexual current...."

"Do we really need to put a name to it, Josh?"

"Maybe not." He laughed shortly. "I think we both feel it sufficiently so we don't have to define it. But..."

Marta's smile was wry. "Don't stop now," she advised. "Even though I think I know what you're going to say. You're going to repeat what you said two years ago, aren't you? In other words, you're going to say *that* kind of attraction isn't enough for a real and lasting relationship."

"Yes," Josh agreed, staring at a spot on the curtain a foot or so above Marta's head, "I guess that's essentially what I was going to say."

"Well," she advised him, "I don't want to repeat the scene we had two years ago."

"Neither do I," he told her. "Nor do I think we're about to. Two years ago we weren't able to discuss things as calmly as this."

She could agree with that. They hadn't been able to discuss much of anything calmly. After Josh had said his piece, she'd spiraled into a flaming temper display. They'd been flinging recriminations at each other by the time she'd stormed out of his apartment. It had been bad. Very bad.

"Marta, because we're good in bed together doesn't mean we'd necessarily be good in life together," Josh said, and she nearly flared into a flaming temper again. "Basically, we're too different."

Marta bathed her rapidly heating emotions with mental ice water. "I don't think we're very different at all," she announced.

"Our life-styles are completely opposite. I could never adjust to yours. You could never adjust to mine. You'd become very bored with the kind of life I lead," Josh reproved.

"That's what you've always been afraid of, isn't it?" Marta demanded, suddenly finding the courage to frame the question she'd wanted to ask him two years earlier.

"It's not a question of being afraid of your becoming bored," Josh said quietly. "I know you'd become bored. I know you'd have an incredibly difficult time adjusting to living with me on a day-to-day basis. Believe me," he finished wearily, "I thought this all through a long time ago, and the circumstances haven't changed."

With foolish courage Marta released her next thought before she fully considered what she was saying. "Will you please, will you *please*, make an appointment with Gerry Baskin?" she urged.

She saw Josh's jaw tighten, saw the steel come into his eyes, and knew she'd said the wrong thing.

He nodded sagely, as if she'd just proved an important point. "That's the bottom line, isn't it," he said. "If Gerry Baskin could wave a magic scalpel, you think everything would be resolved between us. Then I could ski with you and dance with you and cavort with you all over the globe.''

The steel edged its way into his voice. "You're wrong, Marta," he advised her. "I'm not saying I wouldn't enjoy doing any of those things again. I'm sure I would. But I don't waste my time brooding about what can't be. I learned a long time ago to live with reality, and doing that has taught me a lot I'd never have known under other circumstances. I've learned more about people and places and art and music and philosophy..."

"You still like basketball."

"Sure I like basketball," Josh agreed. "Why wouldn't I?"

"You used to play basketball...when you were in high school."

His eyes narrowed. "How did you know that?"

"It doesn't matter."

"The hell it doesn't matter. What else has Jennifer been telling you about me, Marta? I thought my sister, at least, had accepted how my life changed after the accident. I didn't think she'd be one to go into maudlin reminiscences."

"She didn't and she doesn't," Marta said sharply. "Please don't involve Jen in this. She adores you, you know that. It just happens that she's also pretty fond of me..."

"So?"

"Oh, Josh, Josh." Marta could feel the damnable tears welling again. "Please! Don't be so didactic."

"Didactic, huh?" Josh mused. "You say that as if it's a synonym for *stubborn*. But it isn't."

"All right, all right," Marta snapped. "So I've used the wrong word again. I wish you didn't always feel the need to be such a dictionary."

"I wish you'd learn to say what you mean," Josh countered. "And I'm not talking about correct definitions. I wish you'd stop hedging with me and come out and say what's on your mind. You never have, not all the way."

"That's not true."

"It damn well is," Josh contradicted. "Right now, for example, I'd like you to level with me and tell me what kind of garbage Jennifer has been feeding you."

"Ugh," Marta retorted. "For someone who has such a way with words that statement leaves a rather nasty image."

"All right. You know exactly what I mean, Marta. Stop hedging."

"I'm not hedging. Jennifer hasn't said anything to me about you for... for a long time."

Marta had stumbled over her tongue by the time she finished that statement, because she had suddenly remembered something Jennifer had indeed said about her brother recently.

He's so hopelessly in love with you.

Thinking about that, Marta could feel her cheeks beginning to burn.

"You look guilty as hell," Josh observed. "But if you don't want to betray my loving sister it's okay. I suppose I should admire your loyalty."

"You're getting an entirely wrong impression," Marta managed after spending an intense moment trying to gather her thoughts and feelings. "But, then, you often do."

"Do I really now?"

"Don't be coy, Josh. Yes, you do. That day last February when you walked in on Jennifer and me at your apartment you got an entirely wrong impression."

"Oh, you mean when you were talking about all the things Ashford can do that I can't?"

So he remembered. "Yes," Marta said nodding. "What actually was said..." She reconsidered. "It doesn't matter," she finished evasively. "Let's move on to today. What happened today is that I was helping Jennifer with the twins, and I was giving Josh his bottle, and...and I wondered if he looks the way you did when you were a baby."

Josh's eyebrows rose. "Are you serious?"

"Of course I'm serious. I...I was really curious."

"Babies look like babies," Josh announced flatly.

"You know better than that. I've seen you looking at your niece and nephew, and you certainly don't look at them as if they're just...any old babies. Anyway...I asked Jen if she had any baby pictures of you."

"Oh?" It was a very quiet question.

"She said she had a picture album and I could see it if I liked. So she put it in my room, and after I got into bed I looked at it and..."

"And?"

"That's all that happened, Josh."

Josh gave her a long level look. Marta felt as if he were seeing right through her, and she actually squirmed. "Good," he said then, and added, "Look, Marta, I don't know about you, but I'm bushed. I need to get some sleep. So if you don't mind..."

It was a clear dismissal. Marta went back to her room, fighting those unfamiliar tears every step of the way.

Chapter Fifteen

Although Jennifer and Kerry played their roles as gracious hosts to the hilt, Marta was sure they were fully aware something had gone very wrong between their two houseguests.

For the balance of her stay with Josh at Watch Hill, the Gundersens saw to it that there were few idle moments. They did everything as a foursome, from watching old black-and-white movies on the VCR, to playing four-handed Scrabble, to sitting around in front of the fire, talking. When that happened, Kerry rather determinedly led the conversation, and Jennifer filled in any gaps in the stream of dialogue. Josh rather tended to speak when spoken to. Marta said as little as possible.

The night before she and Josh were to drive back to New York, the four of them watched the late news together on the TV in Kerry's study. The lead story dealt with a powerful earthquake that had left a terrible wake of destruction on one of the Greek islands. Towns were in ruins, hundreds were dead; thousands were homeless. Watching, Marta quietly made up her mind about her next course of action.

Two days later she was at the earthquake site. Getting there had taken a lot of doing...she'd used all the contacts she could think of and had touched base with influential Greeks she'd met on her previous trip to their country. Her path was made smooth for her as it never could have been under the present circumstances if she hadn't "known people." Reservations were made at a hotel in Athens, and transportation to the ravaged island was arranged.

For the next four days, Marta nearly forgot about Josh as she photographed an epic in human suffering. By the time she returned to Athens, she was exhausted physically and drained emotionally.

The message light was blinking on her room phone.

The assistant manager informed her that a gentleman from the States had been calling every few hours for the past three days. A Mr. Joshua Smith.

Marta glanced at her watch. It was nearly five in the afternoon Athens time, which meant that it was around midnight in New York. Chances were Josh might already be in bed. Nevertheless she put through a call to his apartment.

There was no answer.

Marta tried twice more during the evening before giving up and going to bed. Josh was still out...and her imagination began to run around in circles.

She was busy throughout the next day and then went out to dinner with Greek friends that night. The Greeks, she'd discovered, tended to eat late and long. It was after midnight when she walked in the door of her hotel room, and saw the red light on her telephone winking again.

She was tired and totally wrung out. Her friends had asked her a thousand questions about the earthquake site. Telling them what they wanted to know had meant practically reliving the whole experience—something she really didn't need to do. The horror and tragedy of the things she'd seen were so deeply imprinted she could imagine she'd be dreaming about them for a long time to come.

She flung herself down on the bed, picked up the phone and spoke to the assistant manager again. Mr. Smith, it appeared, had called twice that evening. Marta calculated the time difference between Athens and New York, knew it was too early for him to have left for his office, and so again put through a call to the apartment. This time he answered on the first ring.

She heard his sharply indrawn breath as she said, "Josh?"

But then Josh sounded as calm as if this were any ordinary call as he said, "Well, I gather you finally made it back to Athens."

"Yes, I got back yesterday."

"You might have returned my calls."

"I tried to. I guess you made a pretty late night of it last night."

"I went to a dinner meeting of the magazine editors' group I belong to," Josh said rather grouchily. "Marta...are you all right?" There was a strangely hollow sound to his voice as he posed the question.

"Yes."

"You don't sound too all right, Marta."

"Josh . . . it's been a pretty heavy experience."

"I can imagine."

"Not as bad as it could have been, I guess. Not as bad as the earthquake on Zante back in 1953."

"Zante?"

"Another of the Greek islands. That same quake also did a tremendous job on both Ithaca and Cephalonia, two of the other islands."

"I see." Josh's laugh was short and mirthless. "I guess I'm not as well traveled as you are."

"Josh, please," she said, "I don't want to spar."

"Frankly, neither do I. You . . . you must be worn out, Marta."

"I've felt better," she admitted. "It was . . . terrible to see the way the people had suffered, were suffering." She sought for a change of emphasis. "I learned a lot about earthquakes, though."

"Oh?"

"We think of this earth, and I'm speaking of our planet, as being so solid and secure, but actually it's pretty unstable," Marta said. "There's a constant mobility to the earth's surface. Forces are at work all the time molding the face of the globe as well as distorting it and fracturing it. Earthquakes are caused by a sudden break in rocks that have been distorted beyond the limit of their strength. The earth's shaking all the time. They say that if every little quake were recorded, there'd probably be over a million of them a year. Yet . . . a single major quake can release more energy than all the little earthquakes in a year put together, all over the globe. Each year there's about one really big quake and about ten major ones. I guess the one I've just dealt with would be called major. After that come destructive quakes—there are about a hundred of those every year—then damaging ones—there are about a thousand of those each year."

Marta's words were coming faster and faster, something she wasn't aware of until Josh commanded, "Slow down, will you? When are you coming home?"

Home? Where was home? Marta wondered somewhat incoherently. Was New York home? Or London? Or Esthertown, Pennsylvania? When she started to think about it, she really didn't have any home.

"I plan to fly back to New York in three or four days," she said. "I have friends here with excellent photo lab facilities, which they're going to let me use. So I'd like to do the initial work right here."

"I hope if you're not totally satisfied you won't be rushing back to that island again. Sometimes there are subsequent quakes after a big one."

"I know. No, I don't think I'll be coming back. I took so many pictures I don't see how I could have failed to cover everything. But we'll see...."

Josh hung up the phone and seriously contemplated flying to Athens himself the next day. The problem was that Marta might suddenly decide to rush off somewhere else, despite her plan to process her photos while in the Greek capital. Or if there were a follow-up quake on the island, she might very well go back, regardless of the number of pictures she'd already taken.

He didn't think he could handle it if he flew to Greece and then missed her.

He reached for the phone again and dialed Tony Ashford. Tony had called when he'd first picked up on the BBC the fact that Marta was in Greece at the earthquake scene. Her fame made her newsworthy. He'd called Josh, extracting the promise that Josh would call him back, regardless of time differences, as soon as he made contact with Marta.

"Well," Josh said resignedly once he had Tony on the phone, "she's okay. Exhausted, I guess, but okay."

Tony opted for some American slang. "So what's new?" he asked with a sigh.

Marta arrived back in New York on an April day when a tributary of the Mississippi overflowed its banks and a widespread area in southern Louisiana was flooded.

She paused only to take a bath, change her clothes, pack her small traveling suitcase with a few clean things and make sure she had an adequate supply of film. Then she headed for the airport and New Orleans.

Josh left his office shortly after five that day, went home, made himself a drink and tried to settle down in the chair by the window. But he couldn't sit still. Restlessness was rare for him, but that afternoon he felt as if he were possessed by demons intent on continuously scratching his nerves.

It was a week since he'd spoken to Marta in Athens. She should be home by now, he told himself, as he'd already told himself at least a hundred times. And he wished to God she'd call him. He'd tried the hotel she'd stayed at previously in New York, but she wasn't registered there.

He wasn't a mind reader, damn it. He had no way of knowing where she was or what she was doing.

The phone at his elbow rang. Josh picked it up, to hear Tony Ashford's smooth British tones. "Sorry to bother you, old man," Tony said, "but...have you seen the telly news recently?"

"No," Josh said rather shortly. "I just got in from the office."

"I had an evening broadcast on, and it seems there's some serious flooding in your southeastern United States."

"So I read in the morning paper," Josh said.

"Well, with the spring thaws and all that sort of thing in the North, I gather the danger of more flooding is increasing. As it is, according to the report there have been a number of deaths. Many homes have been lost. It sounds like a rather major disaster."

"I don't mean to sound callous," Josh said, "but spring floods appear to be a way of life. In the United States, at least. Every year, certain sections of the country suffer from floods."

"Yes, I know," Tony said. "But I don't think you know that Marta's down there in Louisiana, snapping that shutter."

It was too much to take in. "Are you serious?" Josh asked wearily.

"They did a short interview with her on the news that was broadcast over here," Tony reported. "She was with some rescue workers. I'd say she looked as though she'd been helping in the rescue operations herself. It was pouring rain, and she appeared to be drenched through, even though she was wearing one of those bright-yellow macs that are supposed to be waterproof."

Tony paused. "She didn't tell you she was going to Louisiana?"

"No, she didn't tell me," Josh answered bleakly. "The last I heard she was in Athens, planning to come back to New York."

"Sometimes," Tony said, "I wonder why she keeps running."

That statement of Tony's kept echoing in Josh's mind long after they'd ended their phone conversation. And he began to wonder why it had never occurred to him that Marta had been running consistently for these past two years.

Before that she'd traveled on assignments, of course. But sporadically, compared to the course she was following now.

Even when she was talking, Josh mused, she often gave the impression that she was running. Especially when she talked about her work. He was beginning to think that her work was an express escape route.

Why did Marta need an escape route so badly? Why had Marta started running this way only two years ago? She had always worked hard, but this was different.

Was he mixed up in this compulsive need of hers to escape?

This time Josh acted without pausing to reflect on possible consequences. He called an airline ticket office and booked a flight to New Orleans.

Marta walked into the small, charming hotel in New Orleans's French Quarter where a friend who was a native of the city had booked a room for her. She felt wet all the way through as she approached the registration desk. Her hair was damp; her clothes were damp; her feet were damp . . . and her spirits were *very* damp.

The registration clerk smiled and said, "Ah, yes, Ms. Brennan. A two-bedroom suite. Everything is ready for you and—"

"A two-bedroom suite?" Marta interrupted, puzzled. "I think a mistake's been made. All I need is a single room, any kind of a single room..."

"We had reserved a single room for you," the clerk explained, "but when the gentleman arrived, he altered the arrangements. In fact, he insisted upon having our—"

"Thanks, but I'll take it from there," a familiar voice informed the room clerk, and Marta swerved around disbelievingly.

Josh stood there, surveying her as calmly as if rendezvousing with her in a New Orleans hotel lobby was an everyday event. "Come along, Marta," he urged, and propelled her toward the elevator.

Puzzled, Marta noted that the several members of the hotel staff in evidence were smiling benevolently. The bellman who carried her small suitcase was obviously of Gallic extraction, and his face was wreathed in a downright euphoric expression as he threw open the door to a large corner suite and proclaimed, "Voilà!"

Marta stepped into a living room exquisitely furnished in a gold-and-white Louis Quinze decor. Through an open door she glimpsed a bedroom similarly furnished but the second bedroom wasn't visible.

What was visible, though, was the silver bucket on the coffee table, in which a bottle of champagne was nestled in a bed of ice. And there were flowers everywhere. Yellow roses. How did these people know yellow roses were her favorite?

In a daze, she watched Josh tip the bellman and heard the man say, "My very best wishes for your happiness, monsieur." With a bow to Marta he added, "And to you, madame."

The bellman exited. The door thudded closed behind him. Marta frowned and asked, "What was all that about?"

Josh shrugged. "French chivalry," he said.

"Sort of excessive, wasn't it?" she asked. "You'd think we were newlyweds."

The words rolled on her tongue. She looked at the flowers, the champagne, then at Josh. "I think they think we are newlyweds," she decided. "Josh, you should straighten them out. We shouldn't have this suite, and I feel as if I'm taking the flowers and champagne under false pretenses."

Marta's words were again coming out in a rush.

By way of answer, Josh moved over to the coffee table, and before she knew what he was about to do, he'd opened the champagne and was pouring the sparkling golden liquid into two tulip-shaped glasses.

"Here," he said, holding her glass out to her.

She knew it was difficult for Josh to carry things, especially brimming liquids. His gait wasn't that steady. Almost automatically, therefore, she went to him—and was astonished to find that his fingers were trembling slightly as he handed her the glass.

"Suppose," he said, "we just propose a silent toast for right now. Okay?"

"Yes, I suppose so."

He clinked his glass to hers, and she was both fascinated and puzzled by the expression in his eyes. Those gray eyes that could be so icy looked as if they'd melted. At the same time, Josh seemed anything but sure of himself. She could remember few times when Josh hadn't appeared totally in command. Except, maybe, right after they'd made love....

She perished those thoughts, but they brought other thoughts in their wake. "Where are you staying?" she asked Josh.

"Why, here," he said with a feigned air of innocence that was not at all like Josh. "You said yourself you don't need a two-bedroom suite all to yourself."

"Josh, you know perfectly well..."

Josh smiled. And Marta's heart stood still, the way it always did when Josh smiled.

"Look," he said, "you look sort of...dank."

"Thanks a lot," she managed. "You always do know how to make a person feel great."

"You look great," Josh said, and she glanced at him suspiciously, to see that he actually seemed to mean it. "But you do look...on the damp side. Maybe it's just an illusion because I know you've been wading around in flood-swollen waters with the rain beating down on you."

"Sometimes I wish they'd never invented television," Marta said bitterly.

"If they'd never invented television, I could certainly never hope to keep tabs on you," Josh commented. "Look, Marta...what I was going to say is, do you want to take a bath and get into something dry first, or do you want to talk first?"

"Talk about what?"

"Don't sound so apprehensive. Talk about a lot of things. I'd say we have a lot of things to talk about. Which doesn't mean it'll take us that long to cover them. At least...I hope not. Not what's important, anyway. We can cover the details later—" Josh stopped, realizing he was rambling.

"Okay, then," Marta said, "maybe we'd better talk now."

"Yes . . . maybe we'd better," Josh said nervously.

As she watched, Josh drained his glass of champagne and poured another. Then he glanced at her glass and observed, "You've taken only one sip."

"I haven't had much to eat," Marta confessed. "I don't want to get . . . rocky."

"When *did* you last have a square meal, Marta? Before you went to Greece, I suppose."

"No. I ate a lot in Athens. Greek food is terrific. I love it." Glass in hand, Marta sat down on the nearest chair, her legs suddenly feeling wobbly. But that wasn't because of lack of food. It was because of Josh. He was surveying her so . . . intently. And the smile was gone from his face. She'd never seen him look more serious, and all at once that frightened her.

Josh regarded her levelly. "So," he began, "tell me about this latest episode in your life. You didn't even have time between treks to phone and tell me you were back in the U.S., did you?"

"Honestly, I didn't, Josh," she said. "I heard about the floods as soon as I got to the airport—got in from Greece, that is. And . . . well, I felt I had to get down here."

"Do you always feel you have to be wherever calamity strikes, Marta? I mean, have you appointed yourself the guardian of chronicling the world's woes?" Josh challenged.

"No, of course not," she retorted swiftly. "But . . . you know what I do best. People . . . what's happening to them."

"Right. I presume you took any number of fantastic photos of flood victims, homeless people—"

"I don't like the way you're saying that," Marta interrupted. "You make me sound . . . sadistic."

"No," he said gravely. "Not that. And I know you respond to drama. I also know you ... empathize with people who've been under fire, so to speak. I know you'll always be that way. But I do think that for about twenty-six months now you've been overdoing it."

Striving for self-control, Marta said, "I don't know what you're getting at. Anyway ... I did learn a lot about floods and flood control. The control steps can't always keep rivers and streams from overflowing and causing terrible damage. Still, without modern flood-control technology, we'd be in dire straits. The damage would be overwhelming, both in dollar costs and in human suffering. Obviously, as I've said, not all of the damage can be prevented, for a variety of reasons. Engineering factors. Economic reasons."

Marta paused, then went on, "I admit the flood aftermath didn't get to me the way the earthquake aftermath got to me. I don't know why. Maybe earthquakes just terrify me more. There's something so basically frightening about the concept of the earth moving. But floods are just as devastating, perhaps even more so. Do you know, the first recorded flood—at least I think it was the first recorded one—was back in China around 2400 B.C. The vast plains were flooded with billions of tons of water ... completely covered. There'd been incessant rain, and the rainwaters were swollen by melting snow, and rivers flooded their banks. And ..."

Again Marta was speaking faster and faster. She paused briefly, then finished, "They say that flood lasted for over a century and a half."

"Mmm," Josh said.

"Josh ... you're not even listening to me," she protested.

"Oh, I'm listening to you all right," he assured her. "I'm just trying to evaluate what I'm hearing, that's all. It rather proves the validity of something Tony said when he called to tell me he'd seen you on British TV with a bunch of rescue workers in Louisiana."

"Tony?"

"Yes. The two of us seem to feel obligated to keep each other informed about whatever particular danger you've placed yourself in the middle of."

"And what did Tony say?" she asked suspiciously.

"Tony said he wondered why you feel so impelled to run. That's what he called it. Running. That's what I call it. But I might add another word. Running away. Right now, you're running away from a conversation with me by going on about earthquakes and floods."

"I think maybe I'll go take a bath and get into something dry," Marta said unsteadily.

"I think that can wait a few more minutes," Josh informed her. "It won't take that long really to say what I have to say."

She looked at him uncertainly and suddenly asked, "How did you find me here? I mean, how did you know I'd be in New Orleans."

"I tried to use a little logic," Josh told her. "It seemed logical to me that you'd stop off in New Orleans to rest up a little—or maybe not rest at all, come to think of it. Maybe the stop in New Orleans would be to borrow the photo lab facilities of one of your legions of friends so you could process your film. I don't know. Whichever, it seemed logical you'd stop off in New Orleans.

"Oh, the hotel where you'd be staying? Elementary, my dear," Josh said with a faint smile. "I commandeered my whole staff to get on the phone and check every lodging in the entire area till they found where you were registered. One of them hit pay dirt on the eleventh try, fortunately. They said here that you hadn't arrived yet but were expected just about when you did walk in. Which gave me time to get here myself, thanks to the jet age.

"So," Josh said, pausing first to drink his champagne, "I phoned and asked if they had a suite available. They told me they had the honeymoon suite."

"So," Marta said, "everyone here did think we're newlyweds."

"I don't know what everyone thought, Marta. All I know is that I wanted to be here with you and straighten out a few things."

"You ordered the champagne and the yellow roses."

"Yes."

"But why, Josh, why?" she demanded. "I don't understand any of this."

"Maybe because I had visions of making the honeymoon suite a honeymoon suite," Josh told her.

"What?"

"That's right."

"Do you realize what you're saying?"

"Oh, yes," Josh assured her. "I know exactly what I'm saying. But before I actually ask *the* question, there's something I need to know."

"I don't understand any of this," Marta repeated, shaking her head. "What do you need to know?"

"After Tony made that comment about your running and I began thinking about it, really thinking about it, it occurred to me that maybe what you've been running away from is me. The running started about the time we broke up...."

"The time you broke us up," Marta put in, her bitterness showing.

"All right. Anyway...it occurred to me that maybe the reason you've felt you had to run and run and run was that...maybe...you love me. People do strange things in the name of love. God knows I love you, and I've done some pretty strange things. It occurred to me it could work both ways. But—" Josh raised a cautioning finger as Marta was about to speak "—before you say anything at all, you need to know that I'm talking about *love*. Not the chemistry that flows between us, fantastic though that may be. I'm talking about something much, much deeper. Something that gets better and deeper with the years and...and goes on forever."

Josh's voice faded slightly on the last words, and Marta, watching him, wanted to ask him to repeat the speech he'd just made all over again. Not because she hadn't heard it the first time, but because she couldn't believe what she'd heard.

"Something else," Josh said, staring down at the now empty glass in his hand. "I made an appointment with Gerry Baskin while you were in Greece, and...I've seen him."

Marta found that she was holding her breath as she leaned forward, her eyes anxiously scanning Josh's face.

"I could have told you that it would be a futile exercise," Josh said, still concentrating on the champagne glass. "In fact, I did try to tell you, but you wouldn't hear me. Everything that could possibly be done for me was done a long time ago. Gerry concurs in that. He told me, regretfully, what a few orthopedic specialists have told me over the years when, out of misguided hope, I've consulted them. This...is it. Which means..."

Josh paused, still not looking at her. "Which means," he said, not quite able to control his voice as he might have wished, "that...if you want me...you'll have to take me as I am and accept the fact that this is the way I'm always going to be."

Marta stared at him, and anger's flame shot through her with a searing heat. She sprang to her feet and glared at him. "Can you possibly think that the reason I wanted you to see Gerry Baskin was on *my* account?" she demanded.

Finally Josh looked up, his gray eyes opaque. "Well, wasn't it?" he asked her.

"No, damn it!" she sputtered. "It was for *your* sake, because I've felt in my bones all along that it was *your* hang-up that was causing all our problems. And I was right, wasn't I?"

When Josh didn't answer her, Marta seethed. "Do you seriously believe that I give a damn about your gimpy leg?"

For a moment Josh stared at her, expressionless. Then he said with mock thoughtfulness, "Well, there's a word I think I like." He grinned. "Maybe there's a chance you and I will be able to communicate, after all," he teased.

Marta flew toward him. She flew into his arms, her heart fluttering like a wild bird as she pillowed her head against his chest. Josh pushed her away slightly, to tilt her head up and survey her with eyes that didn't quite conceal his anxiety. "Just one more time," he said thickly. "Are you *sure*?"

"Would you like to find out?" Marta asked him.

The sunset bathed New Orleans in glowing colors. With night, the sky turned to black velvet, embroidered with glittery stars. Toward midnight, Josh ordered up more champagne and some food. The obliging person who took their order didn't tell him that room service normally closed at ten o'clock. For honeymoon couples the hotel was prepared to go all the way.

They sipped champagne as they stared at each other with moonstruck eyes. They made love again, and only when they were lying quietly, arms entwined, did Josh say, "How about getting married tomorrow?"

"Can we? That fast? In Louisiana?"

"I haven't checked the law yet," he admitted, "but where there's this much will, there's always a way. Incidentally..."

"Yes."

"Did you give Tony back his ring?"

"No," Marta said.

Josh raised himself on one elbow and peered down at her. "Can't you bear to part with it?"

"Of course I can bear to part with it. But I don't want to send it through the mail."

"Maybe we should hit London on our honeymoon," Josh said. "You know...I have a funny feeling Tony's going to be pleased about us."

"Well...he's a very generous man," Marta murmured.

"Just don't elaborate on that," Josh cautioned. "Though I've sent my green monsters back to the swamp, there's always a chance one of them could resurface."

"What are you saying?"

"Doesn't matter. One thing, though."

"And what's that?"

Josh smiled the smile that turned her heart upside down. "Next time you're in a diamond mood...please let me be the first to know," he told her.

*   *   *   *   *

FOUR UNIQUE SERIES FOR EVERY WOMAN YOU ARE..

Silhouette Romance

Love, at its most tender, provocative, emotional... in stories that will make you laugh and cry while bringing you the magic of falling in love.

6 titles per month

Silhouette Special Edition

Sophisticated, substantial and packed with emotion, these powerful novels of life and love will capture your imagination and steal your heart.

6 titles per month

Silhouette Desire

Open the door to romance and passion. Humorous, emotional, compelling—yet always a believable and sensuous story—Silhouette Desire never fails to deliver on the promise of love.

6 titles per month

Silhouette Intimate Moments

Enter a world of excitement, of romance heightened by suspense, adventure and the passions every woman dreams of. Let us sweep you away.

4 titles per month

Silhouette Special Edition

COMING NEXT MONTH

#499 LOVING JACK—Nora Roberts
Steady Nathan Powell was jolted upon finding impulsive
Jackie MacNamera ensconced in his home. Living with her would
be impossible! But *loving* Jack soon proved all too easy....

#500 COMPROMISING POSITIONS—Carole Halston
Laid-back cabinetmaker Jim Mann definitely wasn't ambitious
Susan Casey's type. So why were his warm brown eyes lulling her
into such a compromising position?

#501 LABOR OF LOVE—Madelyn Dohrn
Alone and pregnant, delicate Kara Reynolds temporarily leaned
on solid John Brickner. But Kara's innocent deception—and
Bric's buried secrets—gave new meaning to "labor of love."

#502 SHADES AND SHADOWS—Victoria Pade
Talented Tyler Welles lived in the shadow of a well-publicized
scandal. Eric Mathias was determined to expose her...until he
discovered the precious secret behind her shady reputation.

#503 A FINE SPRING RAIN—Celeste Hamilton
Haunted by the miraculous and tragic night they'd shared years
ago, Dr. Merry Conrad reappeared in farmer Sam Bartholomew's
life. But could she convince him she belonged there forever?

#504 LIKE STRANGERS—Lynda Trent
Five years ago Lani's husband left on a cargo flying mission—
and never returned. Suddenly Brian was back...but like a
stranger. Could they ever be man and wife once more?

AVAILABLE THIS MONTH:

#493 PROOF POSITIVE
Tracy Sinclair

#494 NAVY WIFE
Debbie Macomber

#495 IN HONOR'S SHADOW
Lisa Jackson

#496 HEALING SYMPATHY
Gina Ferris

#497 DIAMOND MOODS
Maggi Charles

#498 A CHARMED LIFE
Anne Lacey

ATTRACTIVE, SPACE SAVING BOOK RACK

Display your most prized novels on this handsome and sturdy book rack. The hand-rubbed walnut finish will blend into your library decor with quiet elegance, providing a practical organizer for your favorite hard-or soft-covered books.

Only $9.95

Approximately 16" x 8" when assembled

Assembles in seconds!

To order, rush your name, address and zip code, along with a check or money order for $10.70* ($9.95 plus 75¢ postage and handling) payable to *Silhouette Books.*

Silhouette Books
Book Rack Offer
901 Fuhrmann Blvd.
P.O. Box 1396
Buffalo, NY 14269-1396

Offer not available in Canada.

BKR-2A

*New York and Iowa residents add appropriate sales tax.

Silhouette Desire®

1989
IS THE YEAR OF THE MAN!

What makes a romance? A special man, of course, and Silhouette Desire celebrates that fact with *twelve* of them! From Mr. January to Mr. December, every month spotlights the Silhouette Desire hero—our **MAN OF THE MONTH.**

Sexy, macho, charming, irritating…irresistible! Nothing can stop these men from sweeping you away. Created by some of your favorite authors, each man is custom-made for pleasure—*reading* pleasure—so don't miss a single one.

Diana Palmer kicks off the new year, and you can look forward to magnificent men from **Joan Hohl**, **Jennifer Greene** and many, many more. So get out there and find your man!

Silhouette Desire's
MAN OF THE MONTH …